FREE

FALL

A NOVEL

Cliff:
In gratitude for our many
years' association & friendship!
Nina Atwood

NINA ATWOOD

Free Fall: A Novel

Published by Nina Atwood Enterprises, LLC

Dallas, Texas

[E-book] ISBN-13: 978-0-9702809-4-7

[E-book] ISBN-10: 0-9702809-4-7

[Print] ISBN-13: 978-1-7363470-0-3

[Print] ISBN-10: 1-7363470-0-3

Other Titles by Nina Atwood

Unlikely Return, Nina's previous full-length novel, is available on Amazon and through these retailers: Nook, Apple Books, and Kobo.

Nina's next full-length novel, **What About Roxanne?** is scheduled for release in mid-2021. (See excerpt.)

Get Nina's FREE Novella, *Unlikely Beginning*, when you join her **VIP Reader Club**:

www.ninaatwoodauthor.com/freenovella

CHAPTER ONE

Hannah Lee Winn breathed in once, twice, and felt excruciating pain. It began in her lower back and extended to her abdomen. It was dark, but that was only because her eyes were closed, or so she thought. *Don't bother opening your eyes; you won't like what you see.* She lay still for a while, drifting in and out.

Later, she swam out of the darkness behind her eyes and into real darkness. Her brain couldn't register her location, only the biting cold. She focused, concentrated as hard as she could through the waves of pain. First, she wiggled her fingertips, felt dirt, tiny pebbles, and some type of plant matter. *I'm outside, lying down, on the ground.*

What happened to me? How did I get here?

But before she could answer those questions, she needed to figure out the condition of her body.

She focused on her body, trying to assess the extent of her injuries. Something was terribly wrong in her lower back and abdomen. She moved her feet slightly, and that gave her a tiny ray of hope. *Not a spinal injury.* That was a good sign. She raised her right arm in the air, but that seemed to generate another wave of pain in her abdomen. She raised the left, gritting her teeth with the pain.

◦❧◦

Hannah Lee lay still for a while, letting her mind drift to the possibilities. She struggled to remember. *Was I thrown from a car?* She listened but couldn't hear any vehicles passing nearby. She might be in a ravine beside a highway, the road too far above for her to hear the traffic. Maybe someone would notice the place where her car left the road.

Wait. She slowly rotated her head, looking around. There was no sign of a vehicle. There was, however, some kind of large, tent-like piece of blue fabric or canvass lying nearby. That brought a faint glimmer of memory, but not enough to formulate a chain of events, not enough to understand how she'd gotten there.

If she lay somewhere with no roads, the likelihood of another driver noticing her was remote. It was up to her to get herself out of there. A shiver of anxiety traveled from her scalp down her spine. *Time to try.*

She tried to roll over on her side, hoping to get into position to sit up, maybe stand. That tiny bit of movement set off another wave of unbearable pain. She felt herself slipping away from consciousness. This time, she fought the darkness, sensing that she needed to stay awake, stay alert.

It was cold, and she felt the temperature plunging. She began shivering, couldn't stop. She had to do something to avoid hypothermia. She looked again at the tentlike fabric. It seemed so far away. But she had to get to it, had to cover herself.

She began pulling herself along the ground. It was agonizing. You don't realize the purpose of core muscles until you lose them, and with her abdomen in so much pain, she could barely move.

It seemed to take forever, but she finally got close enough to touch the fabric with her fingertips, then to grasp the edge of it. She pulled with all her might and, at last, succeeded in covering most of her body. Gradually, she stopped shivering.

She looked around at the deep velvet night. The moon rode high and shed light over the landscape. Her view encompassed rocks, scree, hillside, and scrub. But, where was she? And how did she get here?

She noticed a sense of altitude. Even though she couldn't see beyond her immediate surroundings, she sensed she was at the top of a ridge or on the side of a mountain.

Hannah Lee lay silently, watching the stars slowly wheel overhead, glowing brilliantly. Every movement brought heightened pain, so she lay still. She heard night birds calling, their whispery ululations echoing in the canyon below. Insects chirped and buzzed nearby. She wondered absently if there might be snakes, poisonous snakes.

An owl hooted as it swooped overhead. Owls were such beautiful night creatures—swift, silent, and deadly. She felt so small, so feeble, so vulnerable.

"Hello!" she called out for the umpteenth time. Her voice cracked, a whisper in the wilderness. She didn't believe anyone could hear her, but she tried at least every hour anyway. She swallowed dryly, wishing she had water.

The rocks and scree under her body made it impossible to lie completely still. It was just too uncomfortable. She moved her head slightly to try to get off of the small rock that punched a hole in her scalp. Like a pebble in a shoe that won't move, this one stayed firmly underneath the back of her head. Slowly, she reached with one hand and brushed away the pebble under her head. That brought scalp relief but increased her other pain.

She wondered how many bones were broken. A terrible thought occurred to her—what if her initial assessment was wrong? What if she had internal injuries? Dread filled her mind, and her pulse skittered in fear. What if she was bleeding internally? Panic rose.

Stop it!

She made herself take deep, cleansing breaths. She began to pray. *Please God, bring help. Bring it fast. I don't ask for much, but this time, I'm asking.*

Her thoughts drifted, searching for answers. *What is the last thing I remember? Basics—start with basics. Breakfast? What do I normally eat? Granola, yogurt, and fresh coffee with just a trace of real half-n-half. Yes, that's it. Where is my favorite place for breakfast?*

She visualized her spacious wood deck, cantilevered on the side of a hill, hummingbirds darting around potted geraniums and impatiens, the morning sun hovering just below the horizon. A cushy deck chair with a light throw, a small, round table topped with multi-colored glass, her coffee mug sitting within reach. And the view—Carmel Valley, filled with lush, rolling green hills.

A memory surfaced. Breakfast on the deck, interrupted by her husband, Ryan, asking her something. What was it? She couldn't pull up the entire memory. It was as if she saw a brief clip of a movie that suddenly faded away. Desperate, she tried to remember the rest of it, but couldn't. Even more disturbing, she had no idea if that was this morning, yesterday morning, or a month ago.

Ryan! He must be so worried. She never went anywhere without letting him know. She had no sense of the passage of time, but at a minimum, she'd been on the side of this mountain for several hours. Her hands and lower arms were cold, and she couldn't feel her feet.

How long can someone lie in the cold darkness, injured, and survive? She vaguely recalled stories she'd read in the media of people lost in the wilderness, who survived on water they found and food they scrounged.

But that wasn't her. She'd never find water if she couldn't move, couldn't stand, couldn't even crawl. Forget food.

The pain in her lower back and abdomen began to spread. It was unbearable, and after a couple of minutes, she felt herself slipping away. This time she didn't fight it. Darkness descended, and she welcomed the escape.

∞

Hannah Lee swam out of the darkness. She heard a loud *whump, whump, whump* overhead. It grew louder, then faded away. It sounded familiar, but she couldn't place it.

Her mind swirling, she tried again to recall where she was, recent events. *What day is it?* Impressions emerged—the clear blue sky, the wind, followed by utter quiet, and, suddenly, the sensation of falling. Then, the impressions quickly receded behind a curtain.

Fingers of crimson spread gradually in the sky—dawn's early light. She peered around, saw that she was on a ridge, on the side of a small mountain, as she'd theorized. But where? The horizon lay far away, shrouded in low clouds. Nothing looked familiar.

Fear gripped her. How could she not know where she was or how she got there? It was far too difficult to stay focused, so she began fading. Faintly, in the distance, she heard voices calling out. She fought the blackness but it didn't matter. Darkness descended.

∞

Light penetrated the darkness, and voices swelled. *Why don't they turn out the lights, be quiet, and let me sleep?* She wanted to fade away, to go back into the darkness where there was less pain.

"Hannah Lee! Hannah Lee, can you hear me?" Someone was calling her name. The voice was soothing and calm, and somewhat melodious, but distinctly male.

"Hannah Lee!" There it was again. She moaned, unable to call out.

"Over here!" shouted a deeper male voice nearby.

"She's semi-conscious, possibly in shock," said the first voice.

"She's hypothermic. Let's get her warmed up," said the other voice.

Someone wrapped something around her. She shivered uncontrollably.

"Let's stabilize her neck with a brace."

Something was wrapped firmly around her neck. Then something hard slid underneath her body. It was even more uncomfortable than the ground had been.

"Hang in there, Ms. Winn. We're getting you onboard. In just a short time, we'll get you to the hospital, where you will be in great hands. They know you're coming because we've radioed ahead. You're going to be fine," said the first voice again.

She felt movement, the hard platform on which she lay in motion. *They're taking me somewhere.* She could hear the sounds of breathing nearby. There was jostling for a moment, awkward movements, the hard surface tilted, all of which elicited another moan.

"Sorry, Ms. Winn. We need to get you up this hill, and then it will be less uncomfortable."

The shivering decreased. She was still, could hear voices around her, and then the loud rotor she'd heard in the distance, now right next to her. *Whomp! Whomp! Whomp!* The noise and vibrations increased in intensity, and she could feel the entire vehicle take off and move rapidly upward.

I must be in a helicopter, she thought just before consciousness began slipping away. She heard someone say, "Check her blood pressure—it's dropping like a rock," and then, "She's bleeding internally!"

After that, the darkness was complete.

CHAPTER TWO

Hannah Lee heard soft laughter in the distance and some kind of machinery nearby. An odd, rhythmic pumping sound whirred away on a regular beat. Several beeping noises alternated with the pumping sound. At first, it was nothing more than white noise. Then her brain registered the source of the sound, and she began to stir.

Then she felt it—a tube inserted in her mouth, snaking impossibly down her throat. She began to squirm. She reached up with her hand and tugged at the tube. Her heart rate zoomed—she was choking. Panic struck swiftly.

"Oh, my God—she's waking up. Nurse! She's trying to pull out her breathing tube. Hurry!" shouted a familiar male voice.

There were sounds of rapid footsteps, then gentle hands pulled her fumbling fingers away from the tubes. Suddenly Hannah Lee felt a dropping sensation as drugs were pumped into the IV line connected through a port in her hand. She tried to fight it, but it did no good. Darkness descended.

❦

The next time Hannah Lee's eyes opened, she looked into a man's concerned gray eyes. She remembered the tube and swiftly put her hand to her face, but it was gone.

"It's okay, there's no tube this time," he reassured her. He sat close to the bed, which was surrounded by a curtain, holding her left hand. His sandy hair fell over his forehead, giving him a slightly disheveled look.

Ryan, her husband. She immediately recognized him, and that gave her a sense of assurance. She hadn't lost *all* of her memory.

She lay in a narrow bed with side rails. Tubes snaked into her arms and her chest. Machines measured every bodily function. The hospital—*why was she in the hospital?*

"What happened? What's going on?" she pleaded, squirming again with anxiety. She struggled to move, to sit up, but her body refused to cooperate. "Why can't I move?"

Her heart thudded, and her chest tightened. She managed to push herself up with her left arm, but not far before pain shot through her lower back and abdomen.

"You have to calm down, Hannah Lee," Ryan said, as he gently pushed her back against the bed. "You've been injured, but you're going to be okay. It was an accident."

"I don't want to be here," she said, throat tightening.

Ryan stroked her arm and spoke soothingly. "It's okay, I'm here. Calm down."

But it wasn't okay. Nothing was.

"Let's go home, please, Ryan," she pleaded. She'd never felt so trapped, so helpless.

"You can't go home yet. You have some broken bones, and you need time for things to set before you can move around. Please, baby, settle down." He sounded almost panicky.

Hannah Lee forced herself to lie back down. She focused on her husband's eyes, took a deep breath. His fear transferred itself to her, so she closed her eyes, took another deep breath.

She opened her eyes again. Ryan looked concerned but no longer panicked.

"What happened?" she asked him.

"What do you remember?" he asked slowly, studying her closely.

At his question, she was bombarded with a cascade of images in her mind: deep blue sky punctuated by clouds, white on top, dark on the bottom; the ocean; mountain tops. "I don't remember anything. Just images," she said, eyes cutting rapidly to the left.

She shivered with the memory of the chill wind. Then, the memory of sheer terror, of a far-too-rapid descent, overshadowed everything. Her chest constricted, and her breath caught in her throat. She reached out and gripped Ryan's arm.

"What is it? What do you remember?" he asked, looking stricken. Near hysteria, Hannah Lee could do nothing but shake her head as tears streamed down her cheeks, her mouth open in silent horror.

Then, she found her voice as she squirmed, trying again to get out of the bed. "I have to get out of here!" She cried out, though she felt weak, unbelievably tired.

"Nurse!" yelled Ryan. "We need help in here!"

Footsteps approached, the curtain around the bed slid back, and a nurse appeared—young, with long dark hair tied back, and calm features. She reached out and touched Hannah Lee's arm soothingly.

"It's okay, Ms. Winn," she said as she injected something into the I.V. "I'm Becca, your nurse. This is a mild sedative, just to help you relax. We don't want you pulling out your lines or re-breaking any fractures."

Hannah Lee felt the panic loosen its grip and a floating sensation. She felt a deep sense that all was well. Then she thought about the memories, and a flutter of fear emerged. A tiny alarm bell tried to sound in her brain, but it was too far away. Not important. Her eyes closed, and she gradually drifted into a deep sleep.

❦

Hannah Lee's eyelids felt heavy, so she kept them closed. She was conscious, but barely. She breathed softly, not stirring. Gradually, she noticed low voices nearby. One of them was her husband, and that brought a tiny smile to her lips.

"You shouldn't be here! What were you thinking? Are you crazy?" whispered Ryan urgently.

"Why not? It's not like I had anything to do with it," said a female whisperer.

Hannah Lee's breath hitched. *Who was that?* She didn't recognize the voice. *Was it the nurse?*

Urgent, indistinct whispers followed. Hannah Lee heard a slight huff and then, "You know what, you're being a jerk!"

"Wait! Don't leave. No, let's step outside—we have to talk, figure this out. I'll go first, so it doesn't look so weird."

Was that her husband? Who was he talking to? What were they talking about?

Hannah Lee felt distant, fuzzy, sleepy. It was so difficult to concentrate, to make rational sense out of what her ears detected. Who would be here, with Ryan? Someone she didn't know, but that made no sense. She knew all of Ryan's business acquaintances, and he didn't really have friends.

She heard the curtain swish. Then silence for a heartbeat or two.

Someone stepped closer to the bed. Hannah Lee lay still, keeping her breathing steady and long. Something told her it was vital to give the appearance of deep sleep. Someone stopped at the side of the bed. Straining to listen, Hannah Lee could just barely hear soft breathing. She caught the faint scent of perfume.

Fingers brushed her hair. Hannah Lee froze, made herself continue breathing, steady, long breaths.

"Why?" Big sigh. "Why didn't you just die on the mountain?"

Who was that? Who wanted her to die? Her mind swirled in confusion, foggy in the narcotic soup.

The curtain swished again, and Hannah Lee heard the nurse, Becca, ask, "What are you doing here?"

"Oh, I'm so sorry. I thought this was my mother's bed. I got lost," said the sheepish, apologetic voice. "I'll go ask for the information again."

The nurse bustled around the bed. She did something to the I.V. line and smoothed the blanket over Hannah Lee, who now felt drowsiness rapidly descend. She tried to speak before she drifted off but wasn't sure she actually spoke aloud.

She tried to say, "Wait," feeling the urgency to tell the nurse, or someone, something. *What was it?* She knew it was important. But she couldn't remember. Her breathing slowed, and she slept.

CHAPTER THREE

Hannah Lee slowly swam into consciousness. Light pressed against her eyelids. She cracked her eyes and saw that she was alone, in a private room—still in the hospital. She drew in a deep breath, willing the oxygen to clear her head. She gazed around.

The room was small but pleasant. To her left sat a long sofa covered in blue fabric, and above that a small window allowed soft light into the room. Behind her a wood-paneled wall frame featured a number of medical devices, some of which were connected to her body.

Straight ahead on the wall was a flat-screen TV, currently off. Multiple flower arrangements filled the two end tables on either side of the sofa.

She felt thirsty, but as soon as she reached for the water beside her bed, pain shot into her lower back and abdomen.

What was wrong? What had she broken?

She fumbled around until she found the controls on the side of the bed. She pushed buttons randomly, causing the top half of her bed to move upward swiftly (bad), so she lowered it. One of the buttons was labeled with a red circle, so she pushed that, hoping to alert a nurse.

"Ms. Winn, do you need something?" a voice magically emerged from a speaker, hidden somewhere nearby.

"Yes, I'm thirsty, and it hurts to try to pick up the cup," said Hannah Lee, hoping she didn't sound too weak.

"Of course. I'll be right there."

The door swished open, and an attractive nurse entered. With brunette hair pulled into a high ponytail, purple scrubs, and a bright smile, she brought a wave of positive energy into the room.

"Good morning, sleeping beauty," she chirped. "Thirsty? Here, let me help with that." She placed the plastic water container with the straw into Hannah Lee's hand, who gratefully brought the straw to her lips, sucking greedily.

"Let's get the table in the right spot so you can reach it better," said the nurse. "Do you remember me? I'm Becca," she continued, pulling the rolling tray table snug to the side of the hospital bed.

Hannah Lee finished slurping and placed the water bottle on the table. "No, I don't. I'm sorry."

"That's okay. The drugs tend to affect short term memory," said Nurse Becca. "That and the trauma of the accident."

"How long have I been here?" asked Hannah Lee. "Has my husband been here?"

"You don't remember? He has—in fact, he's been here almost nonstop since you came in. I think he's—"

"When was that?" Hannah Lee interrupted.

"When? Let's see, I had just come on shift when you arrived, uh, on Tuesday, early morning. They brought you in with a Care Flight helicopter—it was quite exciting! Media everywhere, and— "

"What day is it today?" asked Hannah Lee, interrupting again.

"It's Friday," said Becca. "They took you immediately to surgery and kept you in ICU for two days after that. But you're doing really well, considering," she finished.

Hannah Lee's mind swirled with confusion. *Three days in the hospital?* She didn't remember any of it, except for something vague about a woman she didn't know. The image was foggy and indistinct. She couldn't recall what had happened, only that it left her feeling terribly uneasy.

"What do you mean, considering," she asked Becca, feeling anxious and wondering why her husband wasn't here. "What's wrong with me? I can't move without pain."

"I have to let the doctor talk to you. He's doing rounds in about an hour, so if you can wait until then, he'll explain everything."

Subject matter closed, she bustled around the bed, adjusting lines, and checking monitors.

"Please, can't you tell me something? I can't wait another hour to hear about my condition. I promise not to let the doctor know you were talking to me," pleaded Hannah Lee.

Nurse Becca shook her head gently no. "I can't, honestly, because I'm not qualified to tell you anything about your medical care. But," she paused, glancing at the door to the room as if she expected the hospital police to show up and nab her in the act of...talking.

"I can speak in generalities. Once a patient is moved from ICU to a private room, that means you are no longer at serious risk. It means you're recovering, and in fact, that usually means you will be going home soon. Of course, with fractures such as yours, there's still a long rehabilitation process."

She held up her hands as Hannah Lee began formulating another question.

"I've said too much already! I can't say any more. But I will watch out for your doctor and see if I can get him to make your room a priority on his rounds. Now, how about some breakfast?"

Though she protested she wasn't hungry, Nurse Becca insisted. "You haven't eaten anything solid in three days, and your digestive system needs something so it can begin working normally again. That's one of the things you have to get underway before you can be discharged. I'll have someone bring in a tray, but I'll be back later to check on you."

She left the room, and soon a male orderly in blue scrubs entered the room bearing a food tray. He raised the table, swung it over Hannah Lee, and helped her adjust the top half of the bed so that she could sit up enough to eat.

She eyed her breakfast—scrambled eggs, toast, and a small fruit bowl covered in cellophane. She picked up the fork and took a cautious bite of the eggs. Not bad. She took another bite. She nibbled on the toast.

After a few more bites, she felt full, and pushed away the tray. She looked around and located a television remote attached to one of the bed rails. She surfed for a news channel and found a local station. But there was nothing other than regular programming.

She looked around the room, hoping to find a clock, but no dice. Frustrated, she threw down the remote and buzzed the nurse's station.

"Yes, Ms. Winn?" said a strange voice, not Becca.

"Um, could you have someone find my cell phone?"

"It should be in your locker in the room," said the voice, matter of fact. "Let me know if you need anything else."

"Wait! I can't get to the locker. I can't stand up or walk yet," said Hannah Lee.

No answer. She buzzed the nurse's station again.

"Yes?" impatient now.

"I can't get up yet to get my phone," she told the disembodied nurse.

"I'll send someone in," she replied.

Hannah Lee lay back again, frustrated. She willed herself to be patient, surfing the television.

After what seemed like an hour, Nurse Becca sashayed into the room, beaming. "Let's see if we can get that phone for you," she said. She opened the locker and fished around, finally holding it up.

"It's okay to use it," advised Nurse Becca, "but tuck it away when the docs are in the room. It's antiquated advice, but the 'old school' docs think it interferes with the medical equipment." She rolled her eyes with a smile.

"Of course," said Hannah Lee, pushing the button to turn it on. It did, but with only a couple of bars of service and little remaining battery life. Quickly, she tapped a text message.

Where are you? Just woke up in a private room.

Nurse Becca turned to go, but Hannah Lee stopped her.

"Wait. I was wondering. Uh, did you see someone in my—I guess it was a cubicle in the ICU? Someone other than my husband?"

"As a matter of fact, I did. It was two nights ago. I walked in on a woman standing by your bed, but when I asked who she was, she said she was looking for her mother. I thought it was rather odd. Typically, no one gets into ICU without an escort."

Hannah Lee digested that, then shrugged. It was probably just a lost family member. She felt her eyelids droop. She was tired, so tired.

"What's wrong with me?" she asked Nurse Becca, barely able to keep her eyes open. "I feel so tired." She glanced at the screen on her phone. No reply.

Becca told her not to worry, that the doctor would explain everything.

Hannah Lee drifted off.

CHAPTER FOUR

Hannah Lee woke abruptly when the door to the room swung open. Her eyes popped open, but it wasn't Ryan.

"Ms. Winn, I'm Doctor Hudson," said a tall guy wearing hospital scrubs. He wore wire-rimmed glasses and appeared to be in his 40s. Behind him stood Nurse Becca, smiling as usual.

"Let's see," he said, consulting the tablet at the foot of the bed. "You are one lucky lady," he said, as though her situation was a stroke of good fortune.

"You broke your pelvis, which caused internal bleeding and other injuries. They found you in time, got you to the trauma center here, and we were able to get you immediately into surgery. Your situation was dire, but luckily, the surgical team quickly repaired the source of the bleeding. It could have been arterial, and given how long you were on that mountain, if that had been the case, you wouldn't have made it. But you were lucky—the bleeding was venous."

She listened intently.

"The pelvic bones have been surgically set with a few pins and a plate, and you'll notice you have a binder on the outside. You'll need to wear that for some time while the bones are still healing. Later, we'll see if it makes sense to surgically remove the pins."

He wrote something on her chart. "You will be in physical therapy for some time because with these kinds of traumas..."

He continued talking, but she felt herself drift away from the conversation. She'd never had a serious injury in her life, never even been seriously ill. It was surreal to lie in this bed, barely able to move, not knowing when she might resume normal activity.

"Ms. Winn?" the doctor asked, "What questions do you have right now?"

He looked impatient and ready to leave, so she shook her head. "Nothing right now."

He nodded and turned to continue his rounds.

"Wait!" Hannah Lee called out. He stopped, waited.

"I—I don't remember much before the accident. In fact, I don't remember anything that entire day—where I was, how I got on that mountain, nothing. I don't remember the day before that or the one before that. It's fuzzy, like a dark curtain that I can't see through. Please, is there something terribly wrong with my brain?"

"It's not unusual for people to have memory loss from a traumatic event," the doctor said thoughtfully. "The accident, spending the night in the dark on the mountain—your brain may have blocked those memories to protect you. I'll order a neurological workup to rule out other factors, but when you were brought in, the trauma team quickly determined that you did not have a head injury."

He turned and was gone before she could ask the next question. The room door swished shut behind him, leaving her stunned. *What kind of accident did she have? How did she end up on a mountain severely injured?*

She didn't have a head injury—that she was fairly confident of given that she had no headache, no dressing on her head. She could understand, rationally, that the accident itself was traumatic enough to...to what? She didn't *feel* emotionally traumatized. She felt extremely weak and tired, and the pain came in waves.

Maybe she didn't know how to handle this situation—maybe she wasn't that resilient. But her strong self-awareness said otherwise. She'd been through a lot emotionally, and how was this any worse?

Nurse Becca arrived, bustled around, refilled her water, and gave her pain medication. As she turned to leave, Hannah Lee stopped her.

"Wait. Please, tell me. What kind of accident did I have?"

Becca hesitated only briefly. "You were paragliding. You don't remember that?"

Hannah Lee was stunned. "No, I don't remember anything from that day."

"I'm sure you will. It's the trauma and the drugs," she said before leaving.

Hannah Lee's mind swirled. *Paragliding?* She knew what that was, but she couldn't imagine herself doing it. Confusion marred her thoughts again. For once, she was grateful for the drugs. Since she couldn't solve the puzzle that had become her life, she could at least temporarily escape her wildly swirling, anxious thoughts.

Before drifting off, she wondered again. *Where was Ryan?* She hadn't seen him since the oddly surreal night in ICU. What had happened that night? He was here, then, wasn't he? No, he was with her two days ago when she first woke up from surgery, when she'd fought the breathing tube. Then, later? Or maybe not. She couldn't be sure her vague memories weren't just dreams.

One thing was certain. As soon as she could tolerate it, Hannah Lee would stop taking the pain medication. The fuzzy headedness, the difficulty with memory—that had to stop.

⌘

"Good morning."

Hannah Lee cracked open her eyes. A well-muscled guy in scrubs stood at the end of her bed. His features were sharp, chiseled, and his neck was large. But his smile was warm. He introduced himself as Seth, her physical therapist.

"I know you're anxious to get out of that bed, but before you can do that, we need to start with a few basics to rebuild some of your strength."

He asked her first to try to lift her right leg. She strained and managed about an inch before her leg flopped back onto the bed. She frowned, then tried again.

"What's wrong with my leg?" she asked, worried.

"You're having a reaction to the trauma and the pelvic break. It's normal to lose strength in your legs after these kinds of injuries. That's what we have to work on."

Seth took her through a series of small movements that involved flexing her feet, pulling them up, stretching them out. She managed to lift both legs, one at a time, for short periods of time, but only a couple of inches off the bed.

After about fifteen minutes of the tiny exercises, she was exhausted.

"I think that's enough for today, Ms. Winn," Seth told her. "You did really well."

"You can call me Hannah Lee."

"Okay. I'll be back again tomorrow, Hannah Lee. Meanwhile, about once every couple of hours, I want you to practice the exercises we just did."

After Seth left the room, Hannah Lee picked up her cell phone and checked for text messages. Well, for one particular text message. Nothing.

She felt terribly alone. She could barely move and found her only companionship in the trail of nurses, doctors, and physical therapists periodically entering her room.

Where was Ryan?

If he didn't answer a text message, it was unlikely he would answer a call. Still, she had to try. Selecting the only person listed in 'favorites,' she waited while it rang. And rang. His recorded voice message spoke to her.

This is Ryan. Do the thing.

She left a message: *Where are you, Ryan? I've texted you. I'm in a private room now...I don't understand why you're not here...I'm in room 408. Please come. I need to see you. [sigh] I love you...Okay, bye.*

Her phone went officially dead at that point.

She wondered how she had come to this—sitting alone in a hospital room, her husband gone, completely out of communication. Oddly, it wasn't inconsistent with what she expected. She never quite believed she had actually pulled off the fairy tale ending. And now...well, it was simply a return to something that felt familiar.

CHAPTER FIVE

EIGHTEEN MONTHS EARLIER

"Excuse me. Are you waiting for someone?"

Hannah Lee looked up from her book and into the gray eyes of a stranger.

She glanced around the coffee shop, alive with the buzz of early morning on Saturday. There wasn't a single vacant seat except the empty place on the other side of the leather sofa she occupied.

"Um, no. Feel free to sit here," she said, gesturing to the open spot.

"Thanks," he said, smiling. He set his coffee on the low table in front of them, along with a laptop, and settled in. Rubbing the bridge of his nose while peering at the screen, he began tapping the keys swiftly.

Hannah Lee stared at her e-book while sneaking a peek at the guy from the corner of her eye. Late 30s. Dark blond hair, short on the sides, a little longer on the top, and sticking up in various directions. Wide forehead, face narrowing a bit toward the chin, which was strong and stubbled. He was slender, his body well-toned, and he wore a tee-shirt and cargo shorts. He had a serious look on his face as he worked.

In short, he was a guy who would catch the eye of most women. He wasn't for her, though she'd felt a small tingle when he looked at her. It wouldn't do to get caught staring at him, but she risked one more peek. His lips curled at the corners, and he said, without looking at her, "What are you reading?"

She blushed and glued her eyes on her e-book, hoping desperately that he hadn't seen her watching him. She looked up innocently and said, "Just a novel."

He turned to her, smiling. She felt flutters in her chest.

"What novel?" he asked.

"Um, *Love in the Time of Cholera*," she said, feeling embarrassed for some reason. *Was he really interested or just being polite?*

He looked up for a moment. "Ah, let's see. Latin America, early 20th century, a man who finally wins his sweetheart after decades of waiting for her husband to die." He swung his eyes back to her.

Astonished, she said, "Yes, that's the one."

He looked chagrined. "I'm sorry—I forgot to say, 'spoiler alert.'"

"It's okay," she said. "It's not my first time reading it."

"Good books are like old friends, aren't they? You don't just visit them once," he said, lips curling upward at the corners.

"Um, yes, I guess they are," she said lamely. Not knowing how to follow that, she sat awkwardly, looking down.

"Hey, listen, I didn't mean to interrupt you," he said apologetically.

"No! It's okay, I mean," said Hannah Lee. "I was ready for a break. Plus, I am waiting for someone..." and as he began to rise, "not to sit here. I have to leave when my...friend shows up."

On cue, a short, curvy woman with dark hair opened the door of the coffee shop, searched the room, spotted Hannah Lee, and rushed over breathlessly.

"I'm so sorry, Hannah Lee! I just finished going over the final inspection with my clients, and of course, there were problems. Turns out he didn't tell her that he changed several items that pertained to the overall design palette. She doesn't like subway tile; he does. She doesn't like gray, he had both bathrooms done in shades of gray and white, and I'm afraid they're going to get a divorce over this! I knew I should have consulted her, but he kept telling me he had it covered, that she knew about all the changes."

Danielle stopped, brushed dark bangs out of her large brown eyes, and blew out a breath. She had a heart-shaped face and wore lots of make-up, uncharacteristic for northern California, and tended to draw the attention of people in whatever space she occupied. Her heart was huge, and she directed her energies solidly toward the care of everyone she loved. Hannah Lee had felt blessed by her friendship since college.

"It's really my fault, of course. I know not to do that, to change anything the woman wants without her express approval. I've known that for years! Why didn't I follow my gut? But she was always out of town, so..." She stopped, realizing they weren't alone. She looked at the guy, then back at Hannah Lee, raising one eyebrow.

Hannah Lee just stared open-mouthed at her friend, not knowing what to say.

Danielle smiled. "Sorry about that, sweetie. I'm just so frazzled about it. Are you ready?"

Hannah Lee nodded and stood abruptly. Her e-reader flew out of her lap, crashing into the coffee cup on the table. *His* coffee cup, knocking it over. She watched in horror as the mocha liquid splashed all over his laptop.

"Oh, God, what have I done? I'm so sorry!" she said, frantically grabbing the two small napkins on the table and trying vainly to sop up the mess.

He gently took the napkins from her, swiped his keyboard a couple of times, and said, "It's okay, don't worry. It was just a few drops. Most of it is on the table and the floor."

She looked at the floor and felt herself turn red. She ran to the half-n-half station, grabbed huge handfuls of napkins, and ran back, getting on her hands and knees to clean up the mess. Once again, the guy took the napkins gently, pulling her to her feet.

"Please, let me clean that. Go, go with your friend. I've got it," he said, smiling calmly.

How could he be so calm? "It's okay, really," he said, nudging her.

"I'm so sorry," she said again, backing away in complete embarrassment.

"Come on," said Danielle. "I think he's got it covered." She flashed a brilliant smile at the guy, then pulled Hannah Lee's arm, and the two of them left the coffee shop.

"What a cutie!" gushed Danielle as they rolled away in her dark gray Range Rover. "Didn't you think he was cute?" she asked, cutting her eyes over to Hannah Lee.

"Sure, he was," she said noncommittally.

"So underwhelming is your answer," said Danielle, smiling impishly.

Hannah Lee said nothing.

"So, maybe you noticed how he couldn't take his eyes off of you," said Danielle.

"I don't think so," Hannah Lee answered doubtfully. No way he couldn't take his eyes off of her.

Who was she kidding? Danielle was a good friend as well as a great home remodeler, but she might have been a little too enthusiastic in her observations about would-be suitors for Hannah Lee.

Danielle rolled her eyes. "Once again, refusing to see the truth. Honestly, sweetie, I've seen you pass up three great guys in the past six months, each time, the same story."

She made air quotes, "'*He's just not that into me*'—same old, same old. Which you somehow know without even agreeing to so much as a coffee date. Why do you have so much difficulty picking up on the clues that a guy is interested?"

Hannah Lee was silent, staring out the window. It was true. She'd never been able to pick up on clues about men, certainly not the ones that might have saved her a load of heartache.

It was far too late for that now. Besides, she had something wonderful to focus on today. She smiled to herself.

※

They rolled onto the property, located on a ridge overlooking a valley. In front of them sat a modest, fifty-year-old rancher, now meticulously updated. Hannah Lee had to restrain herself from running to the front door. She waited for Danielle, and together they walked into the spacious main entrance, which opened immediately into the great room.

A large, open space with a beamed ceiling and medium ash wide-planked hardwood floors, it featured floor-to-ceiling sliding glass doors that opened to an expansive wood deck. Part of the deck was covered, another area featured a large fire pit, and the rest was open to the sky and unobstructed view. Beyond the deck rolled the hills of Carmel Valley.

The great room included a small but well-appointed gourmet kitchen, dining area, and living space with a large fireplace, all designed to reflect the beauty of the area. Natural stone, wood, and understated design elements complemented the breathtaking setting.

Hannah Lee's heart swelled with the beauty and sense of peace, quiet, and reflection that awaited her in her new home. "It's beautiful," she breathed, turning in slow circles. "Oh, Danielle, it's stunning! I thought it would be, but nothing could have prepared me for this!"

She'd deliberately stayed away in the final stages of renovation, trusting that Danielle would oversee all of it in minute detail. Her designer friend had a driving commitment to excellence, so she knew her project was in good hands. She'd wanted this moment—to be stunned, awed.

They made their way to the master bedroom, complete with floor-to-ceiling sliding doors opening onto the deck, with a fireplace in the corner. The master en-suite was done in soft beiges, white, and gray, with natural stone countertops. There was space for a reading nook between the fireplace and windows and for a king-sized bed with two end tables. She visualized the furniture she'd selected for the space, sighing with joy.

"So, I guess you're pleased," said Danielle, smiling.

Hannah Lee beamed. "Yes, I am." She turned in slow circles again, touching the walls, the stone on the fireplace. She pulled open the sliding doors, gasping when they disappeared from view into the walls. "You did it! I love this design," she declared, grinning at Danielle. "The great room has sliders as well?"

"Yep, and that was really tricky," she said. "You definitely owe me a nice bottle of wine for that one. It was extra work for the subs, and even though they're getting paid, they don't particularly like that kind of installation. But I used my powers of persuasion, not to mention my magic wand, and got it done." Danielle swished an imaginary wand in the air with a flourish.

She brought out a form, and they began the process of going through the house, room by room, every nook and cranny, checking off completed punch list items, and writing down new ones. An hour later, they drove away, both satisfied that move in would take place within two weeks.

CHAPTER SIX

A FEW WEEKS LATER

Hannah Lee carefully balanced a plastic plate filled with barbecue, potato salad, baked beans, and a roll, with a wine glass in her other hand. She made her way to a deck chair and sat down gratefully. She took a sip first, carefully placing her wine glass on the low table nearby, then nibbled on the roll.

She sighed and looked around cautiously, surveying the large outdoor area, filled with tables and chairs, overlooking the valley. It was a Chamber of Commerce event at a local winery, and she'd forced herself to attend, mainly at the urging of Danielle, who, of course, was nowhere to be found.

People of all ages stood in small groups, talking, and laughing, taking bites of food. They looked so comfortable, so at ease in sharp contrast to Hannah Lee's discomfort. Familiar feelings of insecurity surged. The ones that had dogged her most of her life—feeling different, apart, a stranger to others, no matter the setting.

Even at this beautiful venue, she struggled to feel at ease. Where was Danielle? She wanted one friend to whom she could turn and converse, at least put on the appearance of 'networking'—something she was supposed to want to do in her new hometown, at least, according to Danielle.

"You need to meet people, sweetie. You need a social life. You live in that gorgeous home now, and who are you going to invite over for dinner?"

Nobody thought Hannah Lee, *and that's fine with me.* She enjoyed solitude. She never got tired of sitting on her deck and looking out at the valley, slowly following the path of the birds of prey soaring overhead. She never had enough of the sunrise each morning—sitting still, waiting until the hummingbirds buzzed and floated impossibly close, just as curious about her as she was of them.

She installed a hammock on the deck and spent long afternoons lazily pushing herself into a gentle swing with one foot on the ground, alternately following the words on her e-reader and simply staring at the sky. She often allowed her eyes to close, falling into a light slumber.

Evenings were sometimes the best. She'd prepare a small tray with nuts, a couple of slices of a fresh baguette, cheese, hummus, and cut veggies. With the addition of a chilled glass of chardonnay or pinot grigio, she'd light the fire pit, sit on the deck, and watch the sunset while nibbling and sipping.

Because she lived far from neighbors on a bit of acreage, the only sounds were the wind soughing through the hills, the occasional cry of a bird of prey, and as dusk descended, the chirrup and soft buzz of night insects. It was, quite simply, heaven.

Hannah Lee's reverie broke with a voice. "Excuse me, are you waiting for someone?" Startled, she looked up and into the eyes of Coffee Shop Guy, who carried a loaded plate and glass of wine. He smiled, and she felt that flutter.

He grinned. "Sorry, I couldn't resist that. But I would like to sit here if it's okay with you." He nodded to the chair next to her.

"Of course," she stammered, looking down quickly. Her stomach clenched. As cute as he was, she would now be socially obligated to make conversation. Where was Danielle? If she'd only appear, she could make a run for it, leave the scene on the pretense of needing to greet her friend.

He sat but thankfully didn't stare at her, instead looking out at the crowd of people with a friendly expression. Because his chair was slightly forward of hers and turned a bit away, she could watch him surreptitiously.

He took a bite of barbecue, chewed thoughtfully, swallowed. She couldn't help noticing the skin on his neck—lightly tanned, Adam's apple bobbing slightly with the swallow, that small hollow at the base of his neck.

He picked up his glass of wine, and she noticed his hands—long, tapered fingers, neatly clipped nails. He tipped the wine glass to his lips—full, slightly rosy—with the kind of grace that indicated he used his hands frequently, perhaps in his work.

"This is my first Chamber of Commerce event," he said, still looking away. "I've lived here for a while but never been to one. Everyone says you've got to do it, that it's good to 'network' and meet people." He smiled as he said it, and Hannah Lee felt herself relax a bit, feeling more comfortable.

"But until I spotted you, I almost left early. In fact, I wasn't even going to eat. I don't really know anyone, and getting to know a bunch of strangers isn't exactly my thing."

He turned slightly in her direction. "Does that sound rude and obnoxious? I don't mean it that way."

"No, it doesn't," she said. "I, um, I find it hard to meet people as well. My friend, Danielle—"

"The lady from the coffee shop?"

"Yes. Anyway, she insisted I come, but it's not really my thing either."

"Oh, jeez, I'm showing you just how lame I am with people," he said suddenly, wiping his hand on his jeans, then extending it to her. "My name's Ryan."

She took his hand, shook it quickly, and withdrew hers, though she wanted to continue holding it. His hand felt dry—not hot, not cold—skin smooth. His handshake was firm but light, not the finger-crusher she'd been given so many times in business over the years by alpha males who couldn't resist showing who was on top, even with female colleagues.

In short, his touch was ideal. She felt the tingle long after the handshake ended. "I'm Hannah Lee," she offered, feeling her cheeks warm.

"Hannah Lee," he repeated softly, making it sound almost musical. "Are you named after anyone?"

"Well, it's Biblical," she said, embarrassed. "Which is typically just 'Hannah,' but my father's name was Lee, and my mother wanted me to have both names."

"What did your father want?" he asked.

"I guess he was okay with it." She looked down, not sure how to continue.

"Well, it's beautiful," he said.

They both sat, eating, for a few minutes. Oddly, Hannah Lee felt comfortable sitting with this man she barely knew, quietly eating. She didn't feel the usual urge to create casual conversation, to fill the silence with something, anything so that she wouldn't appear socially lost. She relaxed further.

Danielle approached in the company of a man, talking animatedly. She halted in front of Hannah Lee, took one look at Ryan, and smiled broadly. "Hannah Lee! I see you have company." She stared pointedly at Ryan.

"Um, this is Ryan. We just met. I mean, again. Um," Hannah Lee stammered, feeling awkward.

"Nice to meet you, Ryan," Danielle said, reaching out to shake his hand. "Wait, aren't you the guy from the coffee shop?" she asked, smiling.

"Yes," said Ryan, smiling back.

"And this is Mike, who I just met at the bar. Mike, this is my good friend, Hannah Lee, who I was telling you all about."

Mike looked at Hannah Lee like she was dessert. He was middle-aged, had collar length dull hair, and dark eyes set close together in a chubby face that matched his body.

He held out his hand, and Hannah Lee cringed as she shook it—sweaty and warm, and just a bit too clingy. She had to pull her hand away by yanking slightly to escape his grip. She resisted the urge to wipe her hand on her pants leg.

"Let's sit here," said Danielle, despite the warning look Hannah Lee shot her friend. Mike pulled over two chairs, placing his as close as possible to Hannah Lee without actually touching her.

He sat and launched into a one-way conversation about himself—all of his connections on the city council, his business (restaurant owner), how long he'd been divorced (three months), his son's admission to Stanford, the size of his home, which he'd won in the divorce (4,500 square feet on prime Carmel Valley real estate), and when he was available to cook dinner for Hannah Lee (Monday night, his night off because the restaurant was closed on Monday nights).

Hannah Lee nodded helplessly, trying to avoid too much eye contact. She attempted to join the conversation between Danielle and Ryan but finally gave up. Her mind wandered since she wasn't needed for a response.

"Well?" Mike's voice snapped her out of her reverie.

"What?"

"Dinner," said Mike. "My house?"

"Um, I would have to check my calendar," she said lamely. She tried to come up with a quick excuse but wasn't fast enough.

"Great! Let's plan on it then," Mike said, grinning. He took a huge bite of barbecue, chewed, swallowed, and issued a critique of the chef. "Not bad, but it would be a lot better with a slower cooking method and less sauce." That didn't stop him from taking another huge bite, sauce dribbling on his chin as he chewed.

35

Hannah Lee shuddered inwardly. "Well, I guess—"

"Hannah Lee—remember, we have plans," said Ryan, leaning her way, touching her hand. "I know we just met for the second time, but still—" he smiled.

"Oh! Of course. I'm so lame—yes, we did just decide that didn't we?" she said quickly, thankful for the lifeline. "Monday night, yes, for, uh—"

"Drinks and dinner in Carmel," Ryan finished for her.

"Yes, drinks and dinner—" she said.

"I'll pick you up at 6:00," he filled in. "And that book I promised you—it's in my car. Is this a good time?" he asked.

"Good time? Oh, yes, it's perfect," she said, standing abruptly, knocking over Mike's wine glass. He picked it up and glared first at her and then at Ryan.

Danielle rolled her eyes. "Well, bye, sweetie. Let's catch up tomorrow, huh?" She wiggled her eyebrows suggestively. Hannah Lee nodded quickly, turned, and stepped out of the tangle of chairs.

Ryan said goodbye to Danielle and Mike, then made his way out of the winery and into the parking lot, walking by Hannah Lee's side.

As soon as they were out of earshot, Hannah Lee stopped. "Thank you for the quick rescue." She smiled at him and turned to go to her car.

"Wait! Where are you going? I don't know where you live. How am I going to know where to pick you up?" he asked, touching her arm lightly.

"What? No, you don't have to do that—it was a nice rescue, but, um, really, no obligation," she said, somewhat confused, turning away again.

"Hannah Lee. The *timing* of it was a rescue, but the intent was not. I would really enjoy dinner with you. Unless you're not interested..." he trailed off. But he gazed at her with his open, expressive eyes, and her heart melted.

"I—of course, I'm interested. In dinner," she said, still hesitant. Her heart thumped so loudly she wouldn't have been surprised to hear Ryan say, "What is that?"

"Good. It's a date then," he said. "All I need is your cell phone number."

She gave him her number but was too shocked to ask for his.

"Six o'clock Monday," he said, grinning happily. "Oh—plan on dressing up a bit."

"Okay," she said. He bowed slightly at the waist, turned, and walked away, still smiling.

Hannah Lee stood there for a moment, stunned.

CHAPTER SEVEN

PRESENT DAY

Hannah Lee's eyes slowly opened, and she took a deep breath. Soft daylight illuminated the hospital room, though the blinds were mostly closed. She felt peaceful for a moment, until she remembered.

Ryan. He wasn't here, again. How long had she been asleep? She reached for her cell phone, but then remembered it was dead. She placed it back on the table and sighed, wishing she could call Danielle—too late for that.

She shifted a bit, and that was when she felt the fullness of her bladder. Suddenly, it was urgent. She pressed the call button, gratified to hear Nurse Becca quickly respond to her request.

"Of course. I'll be right there," she said.

Almost immediately, the door swished open. "Let's get you into the restroom," she said, lowering the bed's side rail. "Now, we'll have to go slowly," she said, raising the head of the bed. That set off a mild wave of pain, and Hannah Lee let out a grunt.

"Are you okay?" Becca asked.

"Yes," lied Hannah Lee. "Let's do this a little faster," she said, slightly breathless.

"Of course."

Nurse Becca helped Hannah Lee with every step to the restroom and back. It seemed to take hours, and it set off waves of pain. Finally, she lay back and took deep breaths, trying to will away the pain.

"Time for your pain medication," said Becca, offering two pills from a tiny paper cup. Hannah Lee swallowed them gratefully with a large sip of water.

"We've had you on intravenous morphine, but it's time to wean you off of that and onto pills," said Becca. She turned to go, but Hannah Lee stopped her.

"Wait. Can you, um, spare a couple of minutes?" Hannah Lee asked, feeling weak and desperate.

"Of course, just a few," said Becca.

"You said this morning that my husband was here non-stop since I came in, but I haven't seen him all day. My cell phone battery died, so I don't know if he's trying to reach me. Did he come by while I was sleeping?"

"Oh," said Becca, her forehead wrinkling slightly. "I just assumed you'd been talking, that you'd heard from him. I've been working with lots of patients, and I thought—"

"No. I haven't seen or heard from him all day. So, you don't know if he came by? Maybe, he was here, in my room, while I was asleep? Is that possible?"

"Yes, of course, it is, but—"

"But what?"

"Well, normally, I can tell if someone visits a patient."

"How? How would you know?" Hannah Lee pressed.

"Well, usually family members hang out for a long time, you know, talk with their loved one, sit watching television while they sleep. And of course, I'd see them since they're here for such a long time."

"Yes, I see," said Hannah Lee, embarrassed and resigned.

Nurse Becca gazed at her compassionately. "I'm sure something held him up, right?" she said brightly.

"Yes, I'm sure," said Hannah Lee, turning her face away, hiding tears on her cheeks. "Um, I'm really tired. But thanks...for talking, and all that," she said, pushing down a sob.

"Of course," said Nurse Becca. "Just push the call button if you need anything."

After her departure, the room felt empty. She tried not to, but she couldn't help it—the tears she couldn't stop soaked the pillow. A couple of small sobs escaped into the air and lingered for a moment.

How she wished for her home, for *their* home, for the comfort of their bed and Ryan's arms around her. She longed to hear his voice whispering in her ear, telling her everything would be okay. She wanted to press her lips to his, to feel his hands touching her, and to fall asleep in his arms afterward.

She sobbed harder because it was a dream, a delightful fantasy. The truth was, she couldn't remember the last time she and Ryan had made love. And was it an actual memory that he'd ever been that tender and passionate? Or was it something she'd made up, to convince herself, so she could continue to cling to their marriage?

Was her marriage to Ryan just as broken as her body? *How did it get that way?* Her thoughts drifted back to their first date.

∞

Hannah Lee pulled on the skirt and slipped on a matching tank top. Sliding her feet into sandals, she ran her hands through her thick, wavy hair. She gazed in the mirror, wondering what she was doing. Clothing lay tossed around her bedroom and closet. She could never make up her mind about what to wear. Each outfit seemed worse than the last. *Wardrobe anxiety.*

It stemmed from her overall social anxiety. Uncomfortable in general with people, she was convinced she was deficient in social graces, out of touch with fashion, and therefore, unattractive.

Her skin was too pale. Her hazel eyes, not her worst feature, gazed back at her as she scanned her body in the mirror. She wasn't good with make-up, so she wore little. Thankfully, that was the culture in Northern California, unlike her hometown in Texas, where women wore false eyelashes and red lipstick to the grocery store. She chronically carried a few extra pounds, so she never felt as slender as she wanted. Her hair wouldn't lie down.

At least she had nice jewelry. She pulled out a matching necklace and bracelet—both sterling silver with a deep blue-green gemstone—that sparkled and complemented her eyes. She put them on, smoothed her hair again, and sighed.

The doorbell rang, a soft chime. Her pulse jumped. *What am I doing? This is going to be a disaster*, she thought. *Maybe it's not too late to say I don't feel well. But I can't answer the door looking well and say that I'm not.* She sighed.

The doorbell rang again. She quickly made her way to the great room, stood in front of the door, took a deep breath, and opened it.

Ryan stood there, smiling. The evening sun reflected in his eyes, giving them a sparkle. His white teeth contrasted with the light tan of his skin. He wore a turquoise golf shirt with short sleeves, open at the neck, with just a hint of chest hair showing, untucked over nice jeans. Black, casual jacket—California dressy.

His arms and legs were lean and taut, evidence of regular workouts. He sported a light beard stubble, which made him look slightly rugged. Without it, he might have been a bit too...*pretty*, she thought.

She felt her face flush and quickly averted her eyes.

"Hey," he said. Both stood awkwardly. "Um, are you ready to go?" he asked, gesturing towards his vehicle.

"Yes! I mean, of course," she said lamely, grabbing her bag from the entryway table. On the street, he opened the passenger door of a pickup truck, holding it open for her. The cab was surprisingly nice.

Like a southern gentleman, she thought. It wasn't very modern of her, but she appreciated it, nevertheless.

The drive into Carmel-by-the-Sea was quiet. He turned on the sound system, played soft jazz. She felt tense, her stomach in a knot.

"I hope you like this place," he said, keeping his eyes on the road. "It's quiet, and the food is really good."

"As long as it's not Mike's restaurant," she said, prompting a chuckle from Ryan.

"Nope! I wouldn't do that," he said, smiling. He tapped a forefinger on the wheel in time to the music. She began to relax a bit.

A short time later, they sat on wooden deck chairs gazing at a breathtaking view of Point Lobos and the Pacific Ocean in the distance. A few people shared the space at nearby tables, sitting in groups of three and four, chatting quietly.

Hannah Lee took a large gulp from the glass of chardonnay she clutched in her hand. Ryan gazed into the distance, smiling faintly, wine glass dangling casually from three fingers.

"Here you go!" said the bubbly waiter, setting down an appetizer platter—baked goat cheese with sundried tomatoes and flatbread crackers. Hannah Lee reached over and served herself a generous portion. She couldn't seem to stop herself as she stuffed her mouth. Ryan gazed up, amusement in his clear gray eyes. "Good?"

"Un-hunh," she said, trying desperately to swallow. She gulped, felt a large lump passing down her throat, and took a huge swig of wine. She coughed, feeling herself turn pink.

Ryan's amusement quickly turned to concern. "Are you okay?"

"Yes!" she gasped helplessly. He reached out with his slender, graceful fingers, picked up a glass of chilled water, and handed it to her. She sipped gratefully until the coughing stopped.

Searching desperately for a conversation starter, she blurted, "Where did you grow up?"

His smile faded a bit but then returned. "Here and there. My father was military, so we moved a lot."

"Oh." *Now what?*

"He served for twenty-five years, finally retired with my mom. But they were both killed in a car accident a couple of years later." He spoke with no emotion, his face flat.

CHAPTER EIGHT

Hannah Lee was stunned. If she'd lost even one of her parents, let alone both, she'd be devastated. Seeming to sense her consternation, he turned toward her with a sad smile.

"I know it sounds cold, but I had to put that event away emotionally a long time ago. It's painful to re-live it, so instead, I just recite the headline, like something you'd see in a newspaper. It makes it easier."

He searched her face, his expression soft.

"I understand," she said, though she really didn't.

He seemed relieved. She relaxed a bit.

"What about you, your family?" he asked.

"Well, my parents live in Texas, in a small town. My mom is a retired schoolteacher, and my dad's retired also. He ran a small manufacturing plant. I worked there during summer breaks in college and he taught me the basics, which really helped later."

He peppered her lightly with more questions: where she went to high school and college (University of Texas), what she studied (Business Administration), did she have siblings (one, a younger sister she rarely heard from or saw), and finally, had she ever been married?

That question triggered embarrassment, and she hesitated.

"It's okay," he said. "If you're not ready to talk about your past relationships. Takes time to get to know someone. After all, it's only our first date."

Hannah Lee was floored. *Their first date?* As if there would be more. Her mindset was that this was date one-of-only-one. That he was here solely to rescue her from Creepy Mike, and that he felt sorry for her.

Maybe she was reading too much into it. *First date* could mean a lot of things. It didn't necessarily mean he was envisioning a future. Her mind returned to his unanswered question, hanging in the air between them.

People ask about past relationships on dates, she thought. It was perfectly natural. How to answer? It was a sore subject, not one she'd anticipated having to address tonight.

It had been many years since she'd had a romantic relationship, at least not one that lasted past a few dates. She figured there was no point in discussing the past, no need to reveal the intimate details of her life.

But since this was going to be date one-of-only-one, she had nothing to lose. "I was married once, a long time ago," she blurted, surprised at herself.

He waited, one eyebrow slightly raised.

"It was one of those marriages early in life, the kind you have when you don't yet know yourself."

He nodded thoughtfully. "How old are we talking?"

"I was not long out of graduate school." She didn't tell him she'd completed her MBA by age 21.

"He lived in my apartment complex, and we began running into each other."

TWELVE YEARS EARLIER

Hannah Lee stopped in front of a guy who stopped in front of her. They were both trying to access their mailboxes in the common room. She stepped left at the same moment he stepped right. She stepped right, and he did the same.

He giggled and said, "Want to dance?" That was when she looked into his face for the first time.

He was slender, her height, and meticulously dressed. His eyes held more than a hint of humor, and his face was open and friendly. She'd seen him around the complex, probably a handful of times. He stuck out his hand.

"Kenny."

She returned the handshake.

"I'm Hannah Lee."

"How long have you lived here?" he asked, and that started the typical conversation between apartment-dwelling neighbors. They briefly exchanged hometowns, colleges, and timelines since graduation.

She checked her cellphone for the time and made her excuses. She really did have to run because she was meeting someone for dinner. They both headed out of the common room, mail forgotten and turned in different directions.

"Hey, Hannah Lee," he said. She stopped.

"You know you have a first name and a middle name that is actually a last name. That means you have two last names." He grinned and walked away.

After their first meeting, they stopped and chatted whenever they ran into each other. He waved and called out to Hannah Lee, "Girl with two last names!" But he beamed when he said it, so it never felt offensive.

He talked with his hands at times, waving them slightly in the air as if erasing what he'd just said. The more they ran into each other, the more they opened up about their lives.

Kenny lived with a roommate he didn't particularly like, but he was clean, and that was important. He worked at the most expensive retail store in town, sold shoes to women with buckets of money. One of them, he told her one day, glancing around as if paparazzi were listening, was the widow of a famous musician who'd tragically died in an airplane crash many years before.

"She invited me over with a few of her friends one night, and the phone rang," he said, eyes wide. "It was Paul McCartney! *Paul McCartney*, who apparently was one of her husband's close friends and who still occasionally checked on his friend's widow."

Although Hannah Lee wasn't impressed with name-dropping, she found Kenny attractive and charming, if not as overtly masculine as the men she typically found interesting. He was kind, a natural giver. He offered to take care of her cat while she was out of town. He once brought soup and left it on her doorstep when he found out she was down with the flu.

One day, after weeks of friendly banter, she invited him over for dinner. Although Hannah Lee had never asked a guy out, she'd grown tired of waiting for Kenny to make the first move. She knew he was single because he'd told her so, and she sensed his attraction to her strongly enough that she felt confidant he'd say yes. He did.

The day of their first date turned out to be a hellish day at work. She worked as the operations leader for a small manufacturing company—medical devices—and that day's surprise was a visit from two representatives of the FDA.

That meant long hours of inspecting the manufacturing lines, answering scores of questions, opening files, and assembling her team in one meeting after the other. The real work of getting products out the door was suspended, which meant she could anticipate overtime for everyone the next couple of days.

Exhausted, she arrived home at 8:00 p.m., dragged herself out of the car, and trudged down the sidewalk to her apartment. As she drew near, she spotted Kenny and suddenly remembered. Their date! She was supposed to cook dinner! And she had nothing on hand. She'd forgotten to go to the store on the way home.

"Kenny! Oh, my God—I'm so sorry! I had a, uh, I had an emergency situation at work, and I lost track of time. I'm sorry I'm so late, I..." she trailed off. "I guess this isn't going to work out," she finished lamely.

"Are you going to invite me in, or what?" Kenny asked.

"Huh?"

"Usually, when you invite someone over, you let them in the door," he said with a totally straight face. Was he angry, or was he kidding?

"I just figured...um," she said.

"Figured what?"

"Nothing," she said, turning the key in the lock and swinging open the door. Her cat, Mr. Whiskers, sauntered over, let out a loud meow, and rubbed furiously around her legs.

"Mr. Whiskers!" said Kenny, picking up the cat and stroking him. "I bet you're hungry, right, little guy?" he crooned.

"Let me feed—" she began, but Kenny interrupted, "Why don't you go get into more comfortable clothes? I'll feed Mr. Whiskers and start dinner."

That's when she noticed that he'd brought a large, stuffed grocery bag, now sitting by the front door. A wine bottle poked out of the top next to some kind of leafy greens.

By the time she emerged from the bedroom, Kenny had chilled wine poured for them both and a wedge of cheese with crackers sitting on the countertop. He handed her a glass, they clinked, and he said, "cheers," with a smile. A large salad sat already tossed, the oven was on, and the savory scent of baking chicken wafted in the air.

Had she died and gone to heaven?

Dinner was delicious, the wine worked its magic, and her tension melted away. Their conversation flowed easily. After dinner, they sat on the sofa, and Kenny removed her shoes and gave her an amazing foot rub. Of course, that was after he cleaned the kitchen more thoroughly than she'd ever seen it before.

Later, she squirmed as she lay back on the sofa, feeling aroused and frustrated. She sat up, leaned in, and Kenny leaned in with a warm hug.

She moved her face slightly so that their cheeks aligned more closely, praying he'd turn further and give her the kiss she anticipated. He pulled a strand of her wavy hair through his fingers and breathed, "You have the most amazing hair."

She closed her eyes most of the way, lips slightly parted with desire. Finally, she reached with her hands, gently put them on either side of his face, and brought her lips to his. They kissed, and she moved her lips, parting them, touching his tongue with hers. He gasped slightly, and their kiss deepened.

Finally! She scooted closer, running her hands down his toned arms. Their first kiss led to a heavy make-out session, but before it could progress to the bedroom, he pulled away. He yawned, said they both needed rest, and made his way out. Hannah Lee sat back by herself on the sofa.

Oh, well, she thought. *Maybe he's just not that into me.*

But he called minutes later, as she pulled the covers up to her chin in bed, and said, "Hi, it's me."

"Hi," she said softly.

"I had a wonderful time with you, Hannah Lee," he said softly. "That was some make-out session."

"Yes," she said, smiling.

"You are an incredible kisser," he said.

"So are you."

"Can I see you again tomorrow night?" he asked, and her heart leaped.

"Yes!"

"Okay, I'll pick you up at 6:30. Good night, and sweet dreams," he said before ringing off.

She hit 'end' on her phone and lay smiling in the dark.

CHAPTER NINE

After that, Hannah Lee and Kenny saw each other almost daily. They dined in, dined out, went to plays and concerts, laughed, and talked endlessly. They never tired of their conversation, never seemed to tire of each other. Occasionally, their dates ended with make-out sessions.

Hannah Lee felt herself falling in love, and he seemed to feel the same. But after weeks of intense contact, they hadn't yet made love.

That frustrating situation boiled up one night as they lay on his sofa holding each other, kissing furiously. Hannah Lee came up for air and blurted out, "So, when are we going to do it? I mean, if you're waiting for me to say yes, this is me saying yes. To sex."

Kenny pulled away, disentangled himself from her, and sat away on the sofa. He fidgeted, looking down.

"What?" she asked, panicked, wondering again if she'd misread him, if maybe he really wasn't that into her. Or was he dating someone else?

"I have to tell you something," he said.

Dread put a lump in her throat.

"It's just that I—I don't have a lot of experience," he said, clearly embarrassed.

Stunned, Hannah Lee waited for more, but he was quiet. She thought about his age. He seemed roughly the same age, but she'd never asked. Could he be a lot younger? No, that didn't make sense. He'd been working at his job for at least two years, according to his stories, and that was after college, so he was at least 23 or 24.

"Are you a virgin?" she asked softly.

"Yes," he whispered.

"Huh," she said, relieved. She scooted close to him, ran her fingers through his hair, pulled up his chin, looked him in the eyes, and declared, "I really don't care about that."

"You don't?"

"No, I don't. I love you. It's not a big deal. Everyone starts with someone, right? Why not with me? I'm not a virgin, but it's not like I've had a string of lovers. I'm just a girl who's crazy about a guy."

He smiled sadly but leaned in for the kiss she offered.

She stood up and took his hand, pulled him into the bedroom. They made love that night, and it was good. It wasn't great, but she figured that was from lack of experience.

❧

The rest of the story of her first marriage was an old one. Boy meets girl. Girl takes charge of the relationship; doesn't realize she's dragging boy into something about which he is unsure. They marry after knowing each other for about a minute, both colluding in the setup of denial and frustration that will haunt them.

She found Kenny irresistibly sweet and sexy. She wanted him badly, but he was perpetually distant. He was tired, he was uncomfortable, he had a long day at work, he had a headache—yes, a headache!

He loved her. He needed her. He couldn't believe his good fortune in marrying her. His parents adored her and seemed relieved in a way Hannah Lee didn't quite understand.

Their connection was intense and romantic, but not in a sexual way. Later, she saw how addicted she was.

Hannah Lee remembered an experiment from a college psychology class, about rats who were given food pellets in a random, unpredictable pattern. Those rats, compared to the ones given food on a regular schedule, pressed the food release lever endlessly, trying in vain to obtain what they wanted. They never gave up even though they rarely got the reward, addicted to the core.

There was something about getting what you wanted only part of the time that made you want it far more than was healthy. That was how she felt about Kenny, felt until that terrible day—the day she came home unexpectedly and found him in their bed.

With another guy.

That day she discovered he was gay but trying to go straight for the sake of his parents and his religious upbringing. And, for her. And all the pieces to the confounding puzzle of her short marriage fell into place.

At that moment, all the desire, the romantic longing, died. The rose-colored glasses she'd worn fell off, and she saw their relationship for what it was—a pathetic attempt on her part to be loved.

She'd always suspected there was something fundamentally wrong with her, that she was missing the gene for relationships and real love. Now, she knew that to be true.

Something inside broke, and that led to the handful of short relationships that had defined her life since then. And the many years of not dating, of staying far away from any risk of a repeat of the past.

CHAPTER TEN

PRESENT DAY

Hannah Lee woke up. She reached over and pressed the call button. Nurse Becca answered.

"Hi. Can you do something for me?"

"Of course, I'll be right there."

The door swished open, and Becca bustled over to the bed, smiling. "What can I get for you? Are you hungry? Thirsty? I think you're doing well enough that I can bring something besides water to drink, maybe apple juice or a soda."

"No—nothing to eat or drink. Can you call my friend for me? And give her a message?"

She gave Danielle's phone number to Becca, who left the room to place the call from the nursing station. She called Hannah Lee on the intercom and reported back that her friend was now on her way to the hospital. Hannah Lee felt some of the tension leave her body.

She closed her eyes and dozed lightly. Later, her eyes flew open as someone leaned over the bed. Warm arms encircled her fiercely.

"Hannah Lee! I can't believe you've been in the hospital for days, and I didn't know!" said Danielle, choking back tears.

"Um, let me breathe, okay, Danielle?"

"Oh! I'm so sorry, sweetie," said Danielle, pulling back and swiping away a tear. She pulled a chair close to the bed, sat, and took Hannah Lee's hand, gripping it tightly. "What happened?" she asked, worry pulling her eyebrows tightly. "And where's Ryan? Why isn't he here? *And why in the hell didn't he call me?*"

"I had an accident. I'm not sure what happened, but they tell me I was paragliding, and the equipment failed," said Hannah Lee, ignoring the other questions.

"*You?* Paragliding?" said Danielle.

"Right," said Hannah Lee. "It doesn't sound like something I would do, and I've lost a lot of my memory leading up to the accident, so—"

"What about Ryan? Where is he?"

"That's what I need to find out. They tell me he was here at first, but I haven't seen him all day. That's why I need the charger, so I can turn on my phone."

"Oh—right," said Danielle, fumbling in her bag and handing over a small package. Hannah Lee tore off the wrapping, and Danielle found a nearby outlet and attached the phone.

"It'll take a few minutes for enough power to turn on the phone," said Danielle. She peered at Hannah Lee. "Tell me about Ryan."

"I don't know what to tell you," said Hannah Lee, frustrated. "I tried to reach him this morning, but I haven't seen him all day, and my phone died, so I couldn't call again after that." Tears unexpectedly welled in her eyes.

"Oh, honey," said Danielle. "I'm sure everything's fine. He's probably been trying to call you but couldn't get through because of your phone."

At that moment, Hannah Lee's phone let out a chirp. She grabbed it and touched the screen, scrolling rapidly.

"What? It's Ryan, right?" said Danielle. Hannah Lee showed her the screen.

FREE FALL

Hi—it's me. I'm sorry I've been out of touch. They told me you were awake, eating, and doing physical therapy. One of my jobs went bad...Sorry...I'll be there @TEOTD or 2MORO. {heart emoji} Ryan

"What the heck does that mean?"

"It's texting code. I don't like it, but he uses it," said Hannah Lee, exasperated. "It means he will show up at the end of the day or tomorrow."

"Hmm," said Danielle, frowning. "I don't know what to say. I mean, I like Ryan and all, and he *is* your husband...but still." She blew out a breath. "Just seems like a pretty important thing to miss—*your wife in the hospital*." Her eyes blazed with indignation.

"I know," said Hannah Lee miserably. "I don't understand. And another thing," she said, hesitating.

"What?"

"There's no message from my parents, which means he hasn't told them about the accident. I'll have to call them later."

Danielle sucked in air. "What? Hannah Lee. That doesn't sound good."

They sat quietly, but Danielle looked like she was holding back steam.

"But he is my husband," said Hannah Lee dejectedly. Danielle shook her head sorrowfully, then changed the subject.

"What about the accident? What do you remember?"

"Not much. I have flashes of the sky above and looking down at the ocean on one side and the mountain on the other. I...I have moments where I feel jolted, no images, but I break out in a sweat and my heart races. I have this sensation of—I guess it's called *free falling*—nothing to slow the plummet to the ground."

"Shit, that sounds scary," said Danielle, concern lacing her features.

Hannah Lee's breath hitched, her heart palpitated, as a light sheen of sweat appeared on her body. She squirmed, suddenly terribly uncomfortable.

"I...I can't talk about it anymore, Danielle," she said in a tight voice.

She pressed her fingertips to her eyelids as if to block the images.

Nurse Becca walked into the room, still chatting with someone over her shoulder. She took one look at Hannah Lee and advanced quickly to her side, looking at the monitors behind the bed. "Your heart rate is way up," she reported.

"Okay, I don't know what you ladies were chatting about, but we need to get her calmed down," she said pointedly to Danielle. "It's time for your pain meds," she told Hannah Lee. "This will help you calm down and get drowsy."

She handed the small paper cup to Hannah Lee, who tossed the two pills in her mouth and washed them quickly down with water. Slowly, she felt the panic subside. Danielle watched her worriedly, and that soon became too much.

"Look, Danielle, I'm glad you came to see me, but I'm going to have to sleep some more. I'm really tired. And I want to feel rested when Ryan shows up."

"Of course." Danielle stood, leaned over, and gave her one more fierce hug, whispering in her ear, "I will be back. I'm not going to let you be here all alone. No way."

She turned reluctantly and left, pausing at the door to blow a kiss. Hannah Lee put up her hand automatically, caught it in the air, and pressed it to her cheek.

After Danielle left, Hannah Lee closed her eyes and drifted away.

✎

It was dark in the room again, only night lights glowing. Hannah Lee woke enough to see that she was alone in the room. No Ryan. She picked up her phone and looked. No texts. No calls.

What was happening? Why was he so out of touch? How could he not be there while she lay helplessly in the hospital, barely able to move? What kind of man does that?

What kind of relationship do we have, really? She wondered. Certainly not the one they had just a few short months ago.

FREE FALL

She saw herself again on their first date. It was an evening of wonder, of discovery, and of starting to believe, for the first time, that she might be loved.

CHAPTER ELEVEN

After sharing about her first marriage, Hannah Lee sat quietly, emotionally spent. She wondered if she'd just killed off any chance for a second date with the man in front of her. She noticed two things at that point.

One, Ryan sat quietly, watching her closely, his eyes catching a reflection of the remnants of sunset. Two, he held both her hands. And it felt good, so good. She felt calmed, held to the earth by the warmth of his hands, by the look in his eyes.

The look. It wasn't pity. It wasn't disgust. It was something she didn't expect—it was understanding.

In the years since her divorce, she'd never once shared the complete story of her relationship with Kenny, feeling too humiliated and embarrassed each time she considered spilling it to another person, even Danielle.

Humiliated because she was a smart woman, but she'd missed all the obvious signs of her husband's missing passion for her. Humiliated because she'd found out in the most embarrassing way.

Embarrassed because, deep down, it meant she was terribly

misguided and defective, missing the basic ingredients most people held in their emotional repertoire—the unnamable things that made you fit for a great relationship.

She didn't even know what those things were, but she knew she didn't have them.

And now? She hadn't imagined that anyone might...*understand* what it was like for her to love someone so much who turned out to have so little to give. Her parents seemed to feel sorry for her after the divorce, not understanding why she'd left someone so wonderful as Kenny, a man who clearly adored her.

Of course, she never told them the full story about Kenny. It didn't seem right to reveal his secrets.

The worst part was that he did adore her. He begged her not to leave, swore that he could repress his feelings for men, that he loved her, wanted to be married to her. And she believed him—that he really did love her, that he would try to repress his true feelings. Their friendship, their warm and tender connection, was undeniable. That part was real and so hard to give up.

How many wonderful evenings had they spent together, laughing, drinking wine, and playing like two unbridled children? Arguing over the best movies—her ranking over his ranking, 1 to 10. Kenny brought her coffee in bed on weekend mornings, followed by breakfast. He loved watching Rom-Com movies together just as much as she did.

He rubbed her back, her feet, and her shoulders after a long day at work. He poured a glass of wine, distracted her with funny stories about his co-workers. He was truly her *best friend*, and wasn't that what marriage was all about?

Someone once told Hannah Lee to choose the guy she could picture pushing her around in a wheelchair in her 90s. Kenny was that guy.

But she knew it would never work for her, that she'd never erase the images in her head of Kenny in the arms of another man, looking so...natural, and right. She knew he was meant for another kind of relationship—one he could never have with her.

And, if she was brutally honest with herself, the reality was that all that back-rubbing and foot massaging almost never led to sex. And she wanted sex, wanted a lover, and was terribly frustrated with Kenny. He was so good looking, so attractive to her, but so out of reach as a lover.

No, it wouldn't have worked, so she ended it.

"Let's go," said Ryan, pulling her to her feet.

"What?" she asked, startled.

"Let's get out of here." They walked to his truck, both quiet. During the drive, she said nothing, waiting for the other shoe to drop. He was taking her home, where he planned to dump her at the curb and take off as quickly as possible.

The truck stopped, and Ryan opened his door. She looked up and saw that they were parked near the beach. Her door opened, and Ryan reached in, gently removing her sandals while she sat frozen.

"We're going for a walk," he said. He helped her out of the vehicle, and within a couple of minutes, Hannah Lee's toes sank exquisitely into the still-warm sand of Carmel beach. She sighed as she walked.

Ryan took her hand, and they continued for a moment, then stopped. She turned her face to absorb the last of the sun's light and took a deep breath. Deep orange sat low on the horizon, a few dark, stray clouds spread their fingers above that, and the rest of the sky showcased deep blue and purple.

Hannah Lee never tired of California sunsets. She'd lived here for the past couple of years, but each day, it felt as if she'd just arrived. Wonderment bubbled up unexpectedly as she went about her day, and she sometimes felt like a child in a toy store, constantly noticing the ever-changing sky, the horizontally twisted, visually enthralling cypress trees, the year-round bloom of vibrant flowers.

"Hannah Lee," Ryan spoke to her but continued to face straight ahead, not making eye contact as they walked. "I'm glad you told me about your marriage. It helps me understand you better."

He paused and turned to face her, gently taking both hands in his.

"What you're also telling me is that you don't know what it's like to

63

have someone really make love to you."

"I—I guess that's true," she said.

"And you feel embarrassed that you married someone like that, someone who couldn't love you in all the ways you needed."

"Yes, I—"

"It's okay. I get it. I've made a few mistakes too. But here's the thing—I don't think it means something bad, that there's something wrong with me. I think you don't always know who you're with, not until much later when you're tested."

He gently took her hands. "I think it's time you quit blaming yourself, thinking there's something wrong with you," he said softly. "There's nothing wrong with you."

And he leaned in, brushed his lips across her cheek, then, cupping his hand behind her head, tilted it up. He brought his lips to hers, kissed her lightly at first, then much more deeply, pulling her body to his with his other arm. Electricity coursed through Hannah Lee's body.

After a moment, Ryan pulled back. "Let's go," he said softly.

Later, at her home in Carmel Valley, he slowly removed her clothes. She tried to be modest about showing her body, but he wouldn't let her.

"You don't get it, do you?" he asked softly, breathing in her ear as his hands roamed her body expertly. "You're beautiful, Hannah Lee."

She arched her back, gasping as he made love to her. He was right—she'd never experienced anything like this. She let herself fall into the full experience—the passion, the ecstasy.

Falling asleep in his arms later, she knew it was probably only one night.

She knew she could handle that. But as she drifted off, she allowed herself to dream for a moment that maybe this could be the first night instead of the only night. She smiled as her breathing slowed into sleep.

❧

The next morning, they sat outside, sipping coffee, and watched the sunrise.

A hummingbird flitted close, checking them out before zooming to the scarlet flowers nearby. A tiny tongue flicked the flowers, wings holding the creature aloft, suspended impossibly. Then, a flash of brilliant color as the bird disappeared. They turned to each other with delighted grins.

Hannah Lee sighed with complete and total pleasure. Her heart and body wanted to sit forever like this, immersed in the afterglow of the night before, the beauty of the early morning light. But her practical mind took over.

"Not to spoil the moment," she said to Ryan, "but we still don't know a lot about each other. So, what do you do?"

"I'm a contractor. I remodel homes."

"I should have met you before I did mine," Hannah Lee said, smiling. "Although Danielle did a great job, so I guess it's okay."

"Your home is beautiful," he said admiringly. "I'd like to get to know Danielle. I had a designer who helped me with that part of it, but he moved away a few weeks ago. I'm great at executing the construction plans, but design is not my strong suit."

He sipped his coffee. "And you?"

"Me? Oh—you mean work. I, um...I've been lucky. I worked for a company for many years, a manufacturing business, and I had a little stock. The business sold, and I was given a nice check. It, um, allowed me to move here and buy this house, remodel it. I have just enough money left over, so I don't have to work again for a while."

She felt her cheeks turn pink, and she kept her eyes averted, hoping he wouldn't notice.

"That's great," he said, his face tightening.

She looked up quickly. One thing she didn't want was for Ryan to think of her as a spoiled, entitled person with money. She didn't want him thinking they weren't on the same level and feel uncomfortable with her.

"I, that is, I still need to work," she said quickly. "I'm lucky—I have a little time to figure it out."

"Okay," he said slowly, studying her. "And what will you do—the next job, that is?"

"I'm not sure," she said, this time genuinely. The truth was, she was getting a bit bored. She didn't have quite enough to do, although she'd enjoyed the past couple of years relaxing for the first time ever.

"I've thought about going into retail. This place seems ideal for a charming shop, maybe even a vintage bookstore. I think—"

"Everyone does that here," he interrupted coldly. "That's the first thing they think of, opening a shop of some kind, or a restaurant. But it's not as easy as it looks. You're better off throwing hundred-dollar bills on the street. At least then someone would benefit."

Stunned, she didn't say anything.

"I'm sorry," he said, reaching out to take her hand, looking in her eyes apologetically. "I get a bit carried away sometimes. It's just that I've known a few people who failed spectacularly at retail. And other things."

She just nodded, searching his eyes. "It's okay," she said.

He looked relieved. Checked his watch. "I've got to go, got a job to get to."

He stood, and she followed him into the house to the front door. He took her in his arms and gave her a tender, passionate kiss that set her body tingling. Then, he released her and said, "I'll call you later," and left.

Hannah Lee stood in her great room, looking around slowly. She could still smell his scent in the air—slightly musky, maybe sandalwood. She closed her eyes and re-lived a couple of their most erotic moments, feeling herself blush again.

Then she thought of his response to her idea for a business and felt her stomach drop. She'd wanted him to catch her excitement, to ask more questions, to tell her that it was a great idea. No, more than that. She'd wanted to talk about it, show him how smart she was, as a businesswoman.

How egotistical. Just because she was successful before didn't mean she could re-create it here, now. She understood her old business so well—had worked in that industry her entire career. What made her think she could do that in retail? Ryan was right—it was entirely different, probably much harder.

Her thoughts turned to his final comment—*I'll call you later*. Would he? Did she want him to? She reminded herself this was a one-off date, the bonus an unexpected night of passion.

She knew it was unlikely there would be more. But she wished there could be. Oh, how she wished there could be.

CHAPTER TWELVE

PRESENT DAY

Soft light pressed on Hannah Lee's eyelids, and a chirp sounded nearby. She wondered why her phone alarm was going off. There was no reason to get up at a certain time, after all. She stretched—or tried to—and instantly felt the stiffness in her body, the lack of mobility in her pelvis and legs, the pain. Her eyes flew open.

Of course. She was in the hospital, not at home. It was morning, but what day? She picked up her phone and looked at the calendar function. *Saturday.*

She'd been in the hospital since Tuesday and only vaguely recalled seeing Ryan. Her stomach tensed with anxiety.

Then she noticed she had a text message. *OMW, ETA 15 minutes*

She blew out a breath. *Finally.* Her husband would soon be there. Wait—when was the text sent? She saw the time stamp—12 minutes ago. She desperately pressed the call button.

"Good morning! What can I get for you?" chirped the ever-pleasant voice of Nurse Becca.

"Um, a toothbrush? My husband is on the way and—"

"Say no more! Emergency toothbrush on the way."

The door flew open, and Nurse Becca scampered into the room, carrying a small tray and a toothbrush loaded with toothpaste. Hannah Lee grabbed the brush gratefully, gave her teeth a swift wash, rinsed, and handed everything back to Becca, who stowed it all away in the bathroom. She pulled a brush out of her pocket and gave Hannah Lee's hair a quick once over, then stood back.

"There! Now you're ready to see your sweet hubby," she beamed. "Call if you need anything else," she said as she swished out of the room.

Sweet hubby. Maybe not so much. She smoothed the blanket over her body, lay back against the pillow, and tried to be calm.

She thrummed her fingertips on the blanket, picked up her phone, and checked the time. The fifteen minutes had come and gone with an additional ten. *Where was he?*

Should she text and tell him she was waiting? Maybe he thought she was too out of it to notice whether he arrived or not, stopped to do errands, thinking it didn't matter.

She picked up the phone, debating whether or not to text him. She began typing, *can't wait to see you*...then stopped.

Something hardened in her heart. Ryan would get there whenever. Sending out another desperate plea when he'd clearly read the last one, as evidenced by his text this morning, didn't feel right. She was vulnerable enough.

Why keep reaching out to a husband who'd been absent for over 24 hours? While she was *in the hospital*?

She erased the text and dropped her phone on the bedside table. Picking up the television remote, she flipped to a random station.

While she lay there watching, she practiced the moves her physical therapist had taught her—flexing her toes up, then down, repeatedly; slowly bringing her knees up as far as she could, bending them slightly, which was all she could manage, then lowering them. She raised her arms over her head, flexed her fingers, made fists, brought them down.

She drew up her knees slightly again, this time squeezing her buttocks and lifting her pelvis from the surface of the bed. That lasted about a second before she lowered her body quickly. She was breathing as though she'd run a marathon.

The door opened, and she drew in a quick breath. But it wasn't Ryan. A hospital worker brought in her breakfast, set it on the tray, chatted momentarily before leaving.

Hannah Lee decided it was time to quit nibbling at food. She needed strength to recover, get out of this bed, and get back to her life. She ate everything, forcing herself to keep going until the tray was empty. She pushed it away, focusing again on her exercises.

The door opened and her heart lifted in anticipation, then dropped.

"Good morning. I see you're doing some of your exercises—that's great," said Seth, smiling. Hannah Lee repressed disappointment.

Seth took her through a grueling drill, pushing her to do more. He helped her sit up on the side of the bed, swing her legs over so that they hung down, then slowly lift each one and hold it. He allowed her to use her hands on the mattress for stabilization but not to hold herself up.

It was beyond difficult. She knew it was for the best, but as he left, she fell back against the pillow, exhausted and hurting. She reached for her water and drank for a long time.

Nurse Becca breezed into the room, bringing her pain meds, which Hannah Lee eagerly swallowed. She longed for pain relief, but also for the relief of her mind going fuzzy, sleep taking over.

Lying there, wondering about Ryan, unable to do anything about it, was agonizing. She'd never felt so powerless. The worst part was that she couldn't clearly remember what their relationship was like in the weeks leading up to the accident. Were they distant, like now? Was he absent a lot, like now?

If so, why? What had happened? They hadn't been married that long—they were still practically newlyweds. They'd loved each other enough to marry. Did they still love each other? *Did he still love her?*

Instinctively, she placed her hand over her heart, feeling a deep ache that wasn't physical. She knew that she still loved her husband, and that was almost unbearable in the face of his apparent abandonment.

Then there was the accident—what had happened? What was she doing paragliding? How had she ended up on the side of a mountain, critically injured? Where was Ryan that day?

Exhausted, Hanna Lee drifted into a much-needed respite from the endless loop of questions in her head.

CHAPTER THIRTEEN

The hospital room door opened, and Hannah Lee stirred as someone approached the bed. She opened her eyes just as Ryan took her hand and said, "Hello you."

"Hello, you," she responded, the unspoken question in her eyes.

"Listen, um, I'm sorry," he said, pulling up a chair, letting go of her hand. "I wanted to be here sooner, but I had an emergency at a job site. The plumbing broke, and all of a sudden, we had a disaster on our hands—with the potential of setting back the job for weeks, which, as you know, would be super expensive for me."

He said this in the familiar manner that intimated he wasn't ultimately responsible, that he resented having to deal with the problems of his work. It was a tone she recognized—one of the things she found baffling when she first encountered it in her husband. It was also a major point of difference between them.

Hannah Lee had always felt she was responsible for anything that went wrong at her job. After all, she was in charge. It was her decisions, or lack thereof, that created the issues at hand. She worked long hours for many years, addressing the problems that were inevitable in a small, growing business.

She'd sacrificed a personal life doing so, but she never once held resentment. It was her choice to run, and later, buy the business. She could have gotten a job and worked for someone else, someone who would have carried the responsibility for the entire enterprise. But she chose the path she traveled.

Ryan ran his own small business, contracting to remodel homes in the area. He was fine, cheerfully going to work, as long as nothing went wrong. But as soon as something did, his mood darkened.

Sometimes she felt as though he blamed her in some way. That he held her responsible for losing money when jobs went sideways or expected her to rescue him financially.

On those days, he came home exuding simmering anger. He drank more than usual then, interacted little to none with her, and usually stayed up late playing video games after she gave up and went to bed.

She squirmed inside, thinking about his business struggles and the stress he evidenced. Maybe she had let him down, failed to help when she could have offered so much. Perhaps that led to the distance between them that she felt now.

She sighed. "I understand."

He looked at her angrily. "Of *course,* you do. You're always so *understanding*," he snapped.

"What does that mean?" she asked, shocked.

He ran a hand over his face, stood, and turned away. Huffing a breath, he shoved his hands in his pockets. "Nothing," he said, his back still to Hannah Lee.

Nurse Becca blew into the room, talking to someone behind her. "Check on Mr. Graham, would you, Susan? He needs his medication and more water." She smiled at Ryan, "Hello, I'm Nurse Becca," she said. "You must be Mr. Winn. How is our patient?"

"Hello," said Ryan, turning around. "I'm Ryan. She seems okay," he said.

She checked the water pitcher, took Hannah Lee's pulse, and

looked at the tablet at the foot of the bed, seemingly oblivious to the tension in the room.

"It's almost time for more pain medication," she said. "And lunch is on the way." She looked from one to the other. "Ryan?" she said. "There's food in the cafeteria downstairs if you're hungry."

He shook his head, stared at the floor.

"All righty then," she chirped, turning to Hannah Lee. "Can I get you anything else?"

"No, thank you," said Hannah Lee gratefully. Becca turned and left.

"Listen, I've got to go," Ryan said, not making eye contact.

"What? You just got here," she said, alarmed.

"I'm sorry, Hannah Lee, I just have a lot of issues on this job, and I can't afford to bail out. Look, you're okay, right? Are they taking good care of you?"

"Of course, they are, but wait—" she said as he turned to go. He paused. "I—I love you," she said helplessly.

"Me, too," he said flatly. He didn't even look at her. He slipped out of the room and was gone.

Hannah Lee sat back in the bed, stunned. The room was so quiet.

Her phone rang. She picked it up, looked at the screen, and burst into tears. "Hi, Mom," she said, sniffling.

"Hannah Lee, what's wrong? I've been so worried about you. We haven't talked in days, and I don't get an answer at your house."

"Oh, Mom! You're so old school," laughed Hannah Lee through her tears. "Don't you know no one pays attention to the landline anymore? And nothing's wrong, I've just been busy."

"Well, of *course*, they do. I answer mine all the time. Though it's usually those telemarketers trying to sell me something. Robert says I should just hang up, but I don't think that's polite, do you? Anyway, sometimes they have something that sounds like a good idea, but your dad says I'm banned from buying things over the telephone. Or, from those Infomercials—the ones where they have a famous person, like

Susan Lucci, selling beauty products. The other day I saw—"

Hannah Lee's mom prattled on, and her daughter smiled, feeling a desperate sense of longing for the comforts of home. Her heart ached, and tears leaked as she listened.

She lay back and held the phone close while her mom talked about the neighbors, her cataracts, and the cruise they'd booked for the following year.

In the background, she heard her dad interrupt from time to time, correcting his wife. But it was done lightheartedly, and her mom swatted him away verbally with first "That's not true" and then "Oh, what do you know—you don't watch those infomercials—if you did, you would understand. They're so interesting! And the products—you can't find things like that at the mall. I'm definitely getting some of that hair line that makes women grow back the hair they've lost with no more frizzies. I need that before we go on the cruise, Robert, and you know that. It's going to be especially humid..."

Hannah Lee's tears gradually dried. She snuggled deep under the covers and let the conversation ramble, her eyelids heavy. Her dad came on the line and chatted for a bit, but he never had much to say. He didn't need to say much for Hannah Lee to feel cared for, loved.

Neither one of them asked where she'd been, and she didn't tell them she was in the hospital. They were so far away—she knew if she told them her situation, they'd spend too much money to get last-minute plane tickets, rushing to her side. They'd never let her pay for them, and she didn't want them to waste their money.

Soon, the conversation wound down, everyone said, "I love you," and Hannah Lee hung up. The tears started again as she lay there. She quickly swiped them away as Nurse Becca bustled into the room.

"Well, that was certainly a record short visit. I don't think I've ever seen anyone come and go so quickly." Becca had her hands on her hips, looking uncharacteristically stern.

"He had to go see about a job he's working on," said Hannah Lee lamely. "He's a contractor," she said.

Becca took her hands off her hips and crossed her arms. "That's the story?" she asked, obviously not buying the pitiful excuse.

Hannah Lee shrugged helplessly, unable to answer. Tears started to leak again.

"Oh, honey, I'm so sorry! I have to learn to keep my big mouth shut," said Becca. "Please, just ignore me. Now, where's that wonderful friend of yours—Danielle, right?" she asked.

"I'm here," said Danielle, pushing her way into the room, arms full of packages.

Nurse Becca beamed at Danielle. "Good! Our patient needs some TLC—you couldn't have come at a better time."

CHAPTER FOURTEEN

Danielle plopped down the bags and began pulling out various items. "Lavender sachet for under your pillow—it's supposed to help you sleep. Also, to help you sleep better," she said, displaying a black satin eye mask. Hannah Lee took it and fingered the silky fabric.

"Teabags—big assortment," she said, setting a very large tin on the table. "Plus," and she pulled out food containers with cheese, crackers, sliced deli meats, nuts, and bread. "I have a small smorgasbord of delectable items. I figure you're getting tired of hospital food."

"And," she said, looking around furtively, "your favorite wine," she said, pulling out a bottle of pinot noir.

"Danielle, I can't drink that," said Hannah Lee, laughing. "I'm on serious pain meds."

"Well, then, I will," huffed Danielle, twisting open the top. She looked around, found a plastic cup, poured some, and took a long sip. "Umm," she breathed.

"Actually, isn't that *your* favorite wine?" said Hannah Lee, smirking.

"Okay, maybe so. But if I'm going to sit here and play cards with you for hours," whipping out a card deck, "I have to make it a bit more entertaining."

Danielle opened the cards, took them out, and quickly shuffled them. Twenty or so cards flew on the floor. She sighed dramatically, picked them up, and shuffled again more slowly, then cut the cards. "Now, what's your pleasure? Speed? War? Sixty-six? How about Go Fish?"

She shuffled again, barely catching all the cards. She sat on the bed facing Hannah Lee, then dealt the cards.

They played War, laughing helplessly as they slapped down cards rapidly, piling them up.

"I won!" declared Danielle, picking up all the cards and splaying them out.

"Yes, you did," said Hannah Lee, laughing. "Thank you for coming to see me," she said quietly. "I needed this."

Danielle sipped from her third cup of wine and looked closely at Hannah Lee. "Are you ready to tell me about Ryan?" She hiccupped. "Crud. Sorry about that."

Hannah Lee sighed. "I'm really tired."

"Oh no—you don't get to do that, girlfriend," said Danielle, hiccupping again. "I know something's going on, and you're going to spill. Now." She reached over and took Hannah Lee's hand. "It's okay, sweetie. I'm here. We're going to get through this."

So, Hannah Lee spilled everything—Ryan's text, his visit hours later, his hasty retreat, the lack of any visible signs of actual love or concern for her. She wound down and lay quietly while Danielle fumed.

"That rat bastard," she said. "It was too good to be true, wasn't it? Showing up in your life like that, sweeping you off your feet, getting married so quickly."

"We dated for a few months before—" Hannah Lee said defensively.

"You know what I mean," said Danielle, disregarding the issue with a swipe of her hand. "Anyway, that doesn't matter. What matters is how he's treating you now. I'm not married, but if I were, I'd be furious if he didn't show up at the hospital. What happens if you ever have a kid? I guess he'd miss the birth and show up later with some lame story about a job that required his undivided attention!"

Danielle paced the room, drinking more wine, and talking with her hands. "Who the hell does he think he is? How dare he blow you off like this? I'm going down to that job site and—"

"Don't you dare!" said Hannah Lee, panicked. The last thing she needed was her best friend getting into an altercation with her husband. "Please, Danielle, promise me you won't do that! Ryan and I need time to work things out, that's all. I'm sure we'll get to the bottom of it. It won't help if you get in the middle of this—you know that."

Danielle stopped pacing and stood undecided. "I don't know, sweetie. Maybe if he realizes that someone's noticing how he's treating you, he'll get back on the ball. Maybe if I let him know how it's affecting you—I see the sadness in your eyes, the stress, at a time when you need nothing but support and love from your husband. I know you, Hannah Lee. You tend to stay quiet when you need to speak up if you think it will create conflict with someone you care about. Am I right?" She took another gulp of wine and burped.

"Um, Danielle? You're going to have to stay here tonight. I don't think it's a good idea for you to drive after all that wine." Hannah Lee waved toward the sofa.

"Yeah, maybe you're right."

"Danielle," said Hannah Lee hesitantly. "I'm having a little trouble remembering things before the accident. Can you tell me something? Did I talk about me and Ryan, anything about our marriage?" She didn't want to lead the answers.

Danielle frowned. "No, not really. You seemed okay with him, as far as I could tell. Why? Was there something wrong? Something you didn't tell me?"

"No, nothing in particular." The truth was, she couldn't remember clearly how it had been between them.

"Well, how about we get some rest and figure this out in the morning," said Danielle, plopping on the sofa. "Where's that nurse? Don't they have any extra blankets around here?"

"I'll get it," said Hannah Lee, punching the call button and making the request.

Nurse Becca came in with an extra blanket and pillow, took care of Hannah Lee's needs for the evening, told them good night, and turned down the room lights as she left.

As they lay in the almost dark, Hannah Lee whispered, "Danielle? I know it sounds childish, but would you just tell me everything's going to be okay?"

Danielle whispered back, "I promise you—if I have anything to say about it, everything will be okay. Now get some rest."

Hannah Lee's last thought was about how wonderful it would be if she could hear those same words, infused with love, from her husband.

❧

Hannah Lee slowly rose to consciousness, brought there by an odd buzzing sound in the room. The buzz droned, then caught, then droned again. She opened her eyes, oriented herself to the hospital room. Danielle lay splayed on the sofa, hair tangled around her face, one arm flung to the side, snoring.

Might as well let her sleep, after all that wine. Hannah Lee's heart warmed with love—Danielle was an amazing friend, a true giver with only the best of intentions. Not perfect—far from it. A perfectionist in her design work, she flipped to the other side of the coin personally.

Her dating life was a train wreck with a regular pattern. Step one—blow up the dating apps and go on a slew of coffee and wine bar dates. Step two—carefully select a guy, glue herself to him, rave about him, and declare, "He's the one!"

Within six to eight weeks, however, she uncovered all his terrible flaws, and that led inevitably to step three—dump him unceremoniously. Often with a text message. A couple of her past flames still pined over her, and in between 'serious' relationships, Danielle would hook up with one of her old boyfriends for a week or two of passion.

Yes, she was a bit of a man killer. But an amazing friend.

Hannah Lee had never used a dating app. She argued mightily over that with Danielle, insisting she preferred single life over using something so impersonal to meet a guy. Danielle argued that dating apps allowed you to have choices instead of what she called 'serial monogamy.'

Loud yawning interrupted Hannah Lee's thoughts. She looked at Danielle, who stretched and attempted to open her eyes.

"Ugh," she groaned. "Good morning, sunshine," she added in a less than enthusiastic voice, finally cracking open one eye and peering at Hannah Lee.

She pulled herself to an upright position on the sofa and held her head between her hands. "Oh, boy," she croaked. "Say, this is a hospital. Do you suppose I can get that nurse to bring me some aspirin?"

"I don't know why not," said Hannah Lee. "Meanwhile, you might try the hydration cure," she said, pointing at the water pitcher. Danielle lurched upright, grabbed the water pitcher, upended it, and drank straight out of it. Wiping her mouth, she declared it perfect.

Nurse Becca breezed in. She handed Danielle—who looked at her in astonishment—two aspirin and a cup of water. She smiled as Danielle swallowed the aspirin.

"How did you—"

"The night nurse told me about the wine party in the room last night," she said, smirking.

"Okay, so it's not magic, but it's close! Remind me to ask for you if I ever land in this hospital," she said to Becca admiringly.

Becca turned to Hannah Lee, beaming. "Good news, Hannah Lee. Today, you get the chance to get out of that bed and do some walking. Seth is coming in, and I've heard he's going to get you on your feet. Once you begin gaining mobility, you will be that much closer to going home."

Hannah Lee thanked her for the news, feeling hopeful about her release from the hospital but dread about what awaited her back home with Ryan.

"Don't get too excited, though. You've got a few more days with us. But we'll do our best to help the time pass—right, Danielle?"

Danielle yawned and nodded. Becca gave Hannah Lee her meds and refreshed the water, then left.

"Hey, kiddo," Danielle said to Hannah Lee, "I'm going to grab a bite to eat downstairs, but I'll be right back. It's Sunday, so I don't have to be anywhere."

Hannah Lee lay back on the pillow after Danielle left. She held her phone in her hand, trying not to feel so needy, but desperately wanting to see a text from Ryan. It was Sunday, after all. He never worked on Sundays, so he should be here with her.

Sadness clutched her chest, squeezing her heart, as she allowed her mind to take her back once more to their—was it a courtship? Or was it something else? At first, it seemed almost too good to be true.

CHAPTER FIFTEEN

The doorbell chimed, and Hannah Lee counted to three before pulling open the door. She smiled at Ryan, who reached out with a bunch of flowers to give her as he walked in. Wildflowers in various colors mixed with pink roses. She thanked him, held the flowers to her nose, and breathed in, briefly closing her eyes.

"You look great," he said, sweeping his eyes over her body. She wore white jeans and a black tank top, along with dangling turquoise earrings. She felt pretty after a day of sitting outside, the sun leaving her skin with a slight glow.

She quickly found a vase for the flowers and, after adding water, set them on the dining room table where she'd arranged two place settings and a candle. Chilled white wine sat in a bucket with glasses nearby.

"May I?" Ryan asked as he picked up the wine and corkscrew.

"Please," she said, smiling. He quickly removed the cork and poured the wine.

Dinner was simple—roasted chicken with brussels sprouts, crisp salad, and hot crusty bread with butter. They sat at the dining table and dug in. The wine flowed, and so did their conversation.

"How was your day?" asked Ryan, smiling. "No, wait. I have to say that I had a difficult time focusing today. I couldn't help but think about that position last night when you—"

"What? No, stop it!" she said, laughing. "I'm fairly embarrassed," she said.

"You shouldn't be. You are quite the delicious lover, sweet lady," he said, managing to make his comment simultaneously both erotic and romantic.

Hannah Lee blushed and looked down but felt pleased inside. She'd never been told anything like that before. She'd only seen herself as just attractive enough to get the occasional date. But as a lover?

After Kenny, she had a couple of very short relationships that involved sex, but in both cases, it was that dreaded scenario of too much to drink, clothes fumbled off and dropped on the floor, followed by the embarrassing morning after.

Nice as it was, she didn't want to linger in that conversation, so she asked, "How about your job—how is it going? What are you working on?" She was genuinely interested, having just gone through her own renovation.

"Good. It's a small job—a condo in Monterey," he said. He picked up Hannah Lee's hand and slowly stroked the back of it as he talked, sending a delightful chill down her spine. She squirmed pleasurably. He seemed oblivious to her reaction.

"It's a great little place—two bedrooms, with a view of the bay. The new owner wants it totally tricked out—new hardwood floors, open plan, all new high-end kitchen cabinets, and appliances." As he talked animatedly about the project, Hannah Lee watched his face, amazed that a guy with his looks was sitting here with her, in her house, holding her hand.

Ryan's hair fell over his forehead a bit as he talked. Occasionally, he used his hands to illustrate a point about the property he'd worked on that day as if painting architectural designs in the air.

Suddenly embarrassed, Hannah Lee zeroed in on Ryan's

conversation, realizing that she'd been far too focused on his physical attractiveness. She listened intently and offered a few comments. Then, her interest piqued as he delved into his vision for his business.

"...so, if I can ever swing an interim loan of some kind, I can work on a large complex, but right now, I can only do one unit at a time. It's a good enough business, but I would really like to expand and grow it, and that takes money." He stopped, sipped wine, and focused on her.

"Sorry about that," he said, "now is not the time to talk business." He leaned in, pulled her face toward him, and kissed her slowly, then pulled back. "Definitely no business," he breathed before teasing her tongue again with his. He stopped and stood, pulled Hannah Lee up with him, and led her into the bedroom.

It felt so good to be desired; touching and being touched, tasting, and being tasted, in ways she'd only fantasized about. He made love to her slowly, in no hurry, and leaving out nothing. She didn't know that kind of lovemaking was even possible.

Later, she lay in his arms, breathless, warm, and slightly sweaty, feeling the aftermath of heightened sensory stimulation.

This is impossible, she thought. *This guy can't really be here, with me, in this way. It can't possibly last.* But she decided to enjoy the relationship for as long as it lasted—tonight, tomorrow maybe— beyond that she couldn't see.

Hannah Lee drifted to sleep listening to Ryan's measured breathing, her legs entwined with his, their bodies almost as one.

❧

Three weeks later, after seeing each other every night, they sat on Hannah Lee's deck drinking wine, nibbling on cheese and crackers, watching the sunset. Hannah Lee sipped, or rather, gulped the wine, working up her courage.

"I really like working with Danielle," Ryan said. "She's already given me some great ideas about the remodel. She came up with these beautiful antique doors to put on the pantry—something I would never have thought of—and the client loved it." He glanced sideways at Hannah Lee.

"What are you doing? You've been staring at me all evening. I'm starting to think I've got a bat in the cave," he said, tilting his head back and looking cross-eyed at the end of his own nose. When she didn't react to his humor, he sat back and stared at her.

"Um, well, the thing is..." she trailed off.

"What?" he said.

She took another big gulp of wine and blurted out, "What are we doing?"

There. She took a deep breath, waited.

"Um, we're drinking wine. On your deck?" He shook his head, baffled.

Courage, Hannah Lee, she told herself. "But the thing is, I don't know what we're doing together," she said. "I mean, it's been wonderful—don't get me wrong! It's been, well, amazing, these past few weeks. It's just that...I mean...well, I thought you'd be gone by now."

He raised one eyebrow. "Gone?"

"Yes. Gone." She blew out a breath.

He stared at her, shrugged, looked confused.

"As in moved on. Over and done."

How much clearer could she possibly be?

"Oh." He took a sip of wine, gazing into the distance.

Hannah Lee sat awkwardly as the silence between them stretched.

"Well, if that's what you want," he said carefully, still looking away.

"If I...what? No, that's not what I want," she said frantically.

"Well, you brought it up. I was sitting here enjoying being with you, watching the sunset, and you brought up the fact that you expected me to be gone." He sounded utterly cold, distant as the hills beyond the canyon.

Hannah Lee's chest tightened. She reached for his hand, but he sat still, unresponsive to her touch. "No, Ryan, that's not what I meant. I want you here."

"Really? You've got a funny way of showing it."

Panicked, Hannah Lee sat frozen. Tears formed in the corners of her eyes, and she turned her head away quickly so he wouldn't see them. Her chest literally ached. In a shaky voice, she said softly, "Ryan?"

Nothing.

"I'm sorry. That's not what I meant," she said sadly. "I guess I just couldn't believe that someone like you would really want someone like me. I thought maybe it was a fling to you, a passing...I don't know...a short-term thing. I guess I thought if I brought it up, maybe, I mean, I guess I was trying to give you an easy way out. But I also thought, maybe, you would tell me I'm crazy, that of course, you're not going away."

She stood. "Excuse me—I've got to go in," she choked, turning to go, hiding tears.

"Hannah Lee. Wait."

She stopped.

"You *are* crazy."

Her shoulders slumped. She turned away again.

"Of course, I'm not going away," he said, suddenly behind her, circling her waist with his hands from behind, nuzzling her, kissing her neck.

He turned her around, pulled her close, and kissed her, tasting her tears. He kissed her harder, then led her into the house and gently pushed her onto the sofa, where she lay breathlessly.

Ryan unbuttoned his shirt, tore it off. His jeans went next.

Hannah Lee sucked in air as he unzipped her shorts, tugging them off along with her panties. He lowered himself over her, kissing her, touching her, and tasting her with urgency. He was relentless—almost rough—and her body responded in kind. They exhausted each other, leaving each other thoroughly spent.

Later, as they lay in each other's arms, Ryan whispered, "Hannah Lee. Don't you get it? I'm not going anywhere."

Her heart swelled with love. Her brain lit with visions of the future. That was when she knew she'd fallen deeply, totally in love with Ryan.

A few weeks later they were married.

CHAPTER SIXTEEN

Danielle blew into the room, talking as she walked. "Cafeteria food at the hospital—that's worse than the food we ate freshman year." She flopped on the sofa, grabbed her bag, rummaged around, and pulled out a brush. After running it through her hair, she pinned it up.

"So, what's on the agenda today?" she asked.

"More rehab," said Hannah Lee.

"Maybe I'll go home during your physical therapy, shower, and change, then come back," offered Danielle.

"You really don't have to come back. I'm fine. It was huge for you to show up yesterday and spend the night with me."

Danielle hesitated but spoke firmly. "I'm coming back—unless that worthless husband of yours shows up. If he does, text me. Let me know when he leaves."

"Okay. Thanks again."

"Sure, sweetie." Danielle gave her a hug and left.

That day, Hannah Lee's physical therapist, Seth, worked with her to sit up, step into a walker, and take a few steps around the room. Her arms felt weak, and the pain intensified during the walk, but she made it around the room. After that, she did exercises while sitting on the side of the bed and lying down.

More pain meds helped, as did a few bites of lunch and a nap. But when she woke up, there was nothing from Ryan. Danielle was sitting on the sofa, reading.

"When did you get back?" asked Hannah Lee. "I'm sorry—I guess I slept right through it."

"No problem, dear—it was time to catch up on a little light reading." She held up the book—*Fifty Shades of Grey*.

"Oh, Danielle! Are you really reading porn?" laughed Hannah Lee.

"Well, everyone else, it seems, has already read it, so I'm just catching up." She threw down the book and stood, stretching. "So, where is he?"

"I haven't heard from him," said Hannah Lee hopelessly.

"Scum."

"Danielle—he's still my husband. For all we know, something's happened to him."

"We should be so lucky."

"Danielle! Please don't say things like that. I need your support, and if you can't give it—"

"Of course, you have it," said Danielle. "I'm sorry. It's just so infuriating that you're so...so loyal. He doesn't deserve you."

Hannah Lee picked up her phone, explained what she was doing, and sent a new text to Ryan. *Where are you? If I don't hear from you in the next few minutes, I'm sending Danielle to find you.*

Immediately after hitting 'send,' little dots appeared on the screen. They hovered for a bit, indicating he was writing a response; a long one, or one that took him a long time to compose. Finally, it appeared on her screen.

No need to do that. IOMW to see you. Long day, lots of issues with the job. I know—it's Sunday, but.

She put down the phone, unsure if this constituted good news or bad.

"Well, he's okay. He's on his way here. I don't know how I feel about it. Did he respond because I threatened to send you to find him? Or was he going to show up anyway?"

"Don't worry—we'll find out when he gets here. Cool your jets, sweetie," said Danielle, as Hannah Lee opened her mouth to protest, "I won't say anything. Much. But you'd better ask him." She shot Hannah Lee a determined look.

Fifteen minutes later, the room door swung open, and in walked Ryan. He seemed surprised to see Danielle, especially after she gave him a look that radiated anything but welcome.

"Ryan—what a surprise," she said tersely.

"Uh, hello to you, too, Danielle," he said, frowning. He turned to Hannah Lee, gave her a small hug, and asked, "How are you feeling?"

Hannah Lee's stomach dropped. Ryan's demeanor was that of a solicitous friend, not a husband. "I'm better. Physical therapy went well today, but—"

"I know. I couldn't get here any sooner," he said defensively.

"I just meant—therapy went well, but they're saying I won't be going home for a few more days. But I'm making progress, so that's good."

"Asshat," whispered Danielle.

"What did you say?" asked Ryan, bristling.

"I said," Danielle said too loudly, "that your absence today was noted. Not to mention yesterday and the day before that." She stared at him, daring him to speak.

"Danielle," said Hannah Lee, pleading.

"I'm here now, so you can take off. I'll take care of my wife," he said coldly to Danielle, who crossed her arms and stayed planted.

"Danielle," Hannah Lee said gently, "It's okay. You've had a long day here, so why don't you go get some rest?"

Danielle peered at Hannah Lee. "Will you call if you need me?"

"Of course. Thank you. Give me a hug, okay?"

Danielle hugged Hannah Lee, glared one final time at Ryan, and left. The tension hung in the air.

Ryan pulled up a chair, sat by the bed, and took Hannah Lee's hand, stroking the top. He pressed his forehead to the back of her hand and let out a deep breath. Not making eye contact, he spoke.

"Listen, baby, I know you're mad, and you have every right. I haven't been here for you like I should. I thought I needed to take care of business because it really was an emergency situation, but that's no excuse. I—remember when we talked about our families?"

She nodded, bewildered at the abrupt switch in subject.

"When my parents had the car accident, they didn't die right away. Well, my dad did, but my mom didn't. She was in the hospital for a few days, on life support, barely alive. Sitting there with her, watching the machines breathe for her, not knowing if she would ever wake up— those were the hardest days of my life."

Feeling terrible for being angry with him, Hannah Lee took his hand and held it tightly.

"Oh, Ryan, I had no idea. How awful that must have been for you."

He nodded his head once. "So, when I saw you in ICU, it all came back. I had a panic attack, felt like I was back there with my mom again. I had to get away, not from you—from the feelings. But it's no excuse," he said, looking up briefly, then averting his eyes.

"I understand, really I do," she said. "Please don't feel bad. I've been very well taken care of, and you—well, I get it."

He was quiet for a moment. "Anyway, I'm here now, and I'm not going to let you down again—I promise," he said adamantly. He reached over, touched her cheek, and tucked a curly strand of hair. "Are you in much pain?" he asked softly.

"Not anymore," she said, feeling the tension leave her stomach for the first time in two days.

They sat for a few minutes, holding hands in the quiet.

Nurse Becca entered the room. Ryan looked up and met her inquiring look. "Thanks for taking such great care of my wife," he said. "I've taken care of some things so I can be here more—a lot more."

She simply nodded and went about her business. After telling them the doctor would make a visit the following morning, and Ryan letting her know that he wanted to be there to find out about Hannah Lee's status and prognosis, she left.

As Hannah Lee drifted off, Ryan sat by her, lightly stroking her arm. "Don't worry, honey, I'm here now. I'll be here when you wake up."

She slept deeply, dreamlessly, for most of the night.

CHAPTER SEVENTEEN

Hannah Lee hung in the air, suspended at an impossible height. At first, it was glorious—azure sky above, white puffy cotton ball clouds lower, the ocean stretching out to the west, small west coast mountains below. From this height, the water was smooth, reflecting the sun, almost like glass.

Suddenly, as she watched, the lines that attached her harness to the sail fell away in slow motion—just dropped. She fell, rapidly, wind whipping her equipment and her body, taking her breath away.

She reached for the parachute ripcord, desperately feeling for the small handle that should have been there. *Nothing*. Her fail-safe wasn't there.

She screamed as the ground rushed toward her. *Oh God, I'm going to die*, she gasped. Screams ripped from her throat just as she...

❧

"Hannah Lee! Wake up. You're having a bad dream," said Ryan, shaking her lightly. She jerked awake, breathing rapidly, pulse racing, her throat dry and raw.

Ryan peered into her wide-open eyes with concern. She shook all over, feeling first hot, then cold. She tried to take a deep breath, but it caught in her throat. She squirmed with panic.

Why couldn't she stop the panic? She looked around the room slowly, taking in the environment, forcing the message into her brain—*I'm here, in the hospital, not hanging in the sky, not plummeting to my death.*

While the hospital wasn't the best place in the world, it was safe. *I'm safe*, she commanded her brain. *I'm safe.* Gradually, her pulse lowered, and her breath extended deeper into her lungs.

"Ow," said Ryan, pulling away his hand. She realized she'd been gripping it tightly, hanging on for dear life.

"I'm sorry," she said, taking another deep breath. "I was dreaming about the accident." She looked at Ryan. "I think I remember some of the details about what happened. Have you found out anything—while I've been in the hospital? Did you talk to the...the paragliding people?" she asked urgently.

"No—I've been too busy, and I figured it was just a freak accident," he said. His face tightened as he studied her.

"But what if it wasn't?" she said, shaking her head. "I remember the harness disconnecting from the sail. That's not supposed to happen, is it?" she said.

He frowned. "No, but I'm sure that's not what happened. Those instructors are licensed and bonded—they put these things together all day, every day. Safety is their number one concern."

She concentrated, trying to capture the memories—if that's what they were. But what if the details coming back to her now were merely the products of a dream?

"Hannah Lee," said Ryan, getting her attention. "I'm sure it was an accident, and no one's fault. Paragliders sometimes hit the sides of mountains, like the one where you were found. It's hard to judge the distance and control the landing, especially if there's a sudden updraft or downdraft." He sounded firm, adamant.

How could he be so sure?

"But why would I have tried to land on a mountain? Why wouldn't I have gone to the landing site—come down there? That makes no sense." She tried to remember taking off, but that was still a blank. She tried to remember where she was headed, where the landing site might have been—no dice.

"What was I doing paragliding anyway?" she asked. "That's not something I would have wanted to do. That was your thing—your hobby, not mine."

"You don't remember?" he asked skeptically.

"No, I don't."

He looked thoughtful for a moment. "Well, you wanted to go paragliding because you said you wanted to experience—just once—something that is important to me. Remember the big discussion we had about how my hobby was taking up too much time and keeping us apart?"

She felt confused, completely lost. "That doesn't sound like me," she offered weakly. "I don't have a problem with things like that. I respect your need for a hobby that I don't share—I would never resent that."

But he shook his head. "No, you did have a problem with it. You said you felt bad that you'd never even given it a shot, that you'd never tried it to see if you liked it. I tried to talk you out of it, but you were insistent."

What? Again, that didn't sound like her. Insistent about wanting to go paragliding? *No, that didn't sound like her at all.*

But she couldn't remember clearly before the accident. She'd lost all memory of that day. She had no idea what she did that morning, let alone what had led up to her hanging in the sky.

Not only had she lost her short-term memory, but she'd also lost long-term memories of the weeks leading up to the accident. It wasn't that she didn't remember anything. It was more that those weeks hid in a fog. There were no clear details, no specific events.

Since those weeks were blurred, maybe something did happen to stimulate a desire to share Ryan's hobby. Maybe he was right—maybe they'd been spending too much time apart, so much so that her fear of heights was overshadowed by her fear of losing Ryan.

That was one thing that emerged, now, from the blur of those weeks. *She'd been terrified of losing Ryan.*

❧

Later that morning, Dr. Hudson stopped by, met Ryan, talked about her recovery process, and needs going forward. It was Monday, and later, Ryan went to work, promising to come back in the evening.

Hannah Lee pushed herself hard that day, but it was frustrating. As hard as she tried, the best she could do was two rounds in her room with the walker, followed by sitting and reclining exercises. All of them seemed so tedious, so microscopic, yet so painful. When would she regain her ability to move around freely?

❧

Danielle stopped by at lunch and noticed something.

"Why so down, sweetie? Is it Ryan again?" she glowered.

"No, it's not Ryan. He's been great. It's just that everything seems to be taking so long. I never realized how wonderful it is to just walk without pain. You know me—I'm not a big exercise person, but I do love walking. Now, it's an effort to get to the bathroom. And—can I say this—I *really* don't like sponge baths." She blew out a breath. "Sorry. I have no right to complain. The truth is I'm lucky to be alive."

"Yes, you are," said Danielle, unexpectedly tearing up. She grabbed Hannah Lee and hugged her hard.

"Danielle," said Hannah Lee.

"I'm okay," said Danielle, standing and swiping away a tear. "It's just that—well, I couldn't deal with it if anything ever happened to you." She grabbed tissues from the table nearby and blew her nose loudly.

"Same with you," said Hannah Lee, slightly embarrassed. They'd known each other since college, and they were best friends. But she'd

100

never seen such an emotional display from Danielle—nothing like this, except over one especially notable breakup in college.

Danielle blew her nose again, and they both laughed. She stayed through her lunch hour, then left.

CHAPTER EIGHTEEN

Ryan was true to his word—he returned to the hospital that evening and stayed all night. He was solicitous, helpful, and sweet. *He was back*—the Ryan she remembered from dating and early marriage.

Minus the passion, of course. She was, after all, in the hospital and injured in a way that would most likely prohibit sex for a while. But that wasn't uppermost in her mind. Between the pain, the effort to do her rehab exercises, and exhaustion, she had a full plate.

It wasn't fun—doing rehab, taking pills, and falling into a restless sleep. While the pills helped, the side effects weren't so great. She didn't like the woozy feelings and lack of mental clarity. But she was determined to get to the promised point of recovery that would enable her to go home.

The next few days flew by, filled with physical therapy, naps, more therapy, sleep at night, and meals. Ryan was there every morning when she woke up, and although he left during the day to work, he was back in the evening. They watched television together, played cards, and slept.

Danielle came during the day, strategically avoiding Ryan, and vice versa. *I'm going to have to get those two to make up*, thought Hannah Lee.

Slowly, her strength built, and she obtained her doctors' release once she ambulated up and down the hallway. She finally managed a shower, though that was with supervision by Nurse Becca.

She felt a keen sense of loss as she said good-bye to Becca, who hugged her and smiled through a bit of moisture in her eyes.

But above all, she was thrilled about going home.

❧

Hannah Lee dropped on the sofa in her great room, exhausted but pleased beyond words. She looked around slowly, drinking in the beauty of the light, the incredible view, and the tasteful bits of art scattered around the room. She sighed joyfully. *Home!* At last.

Ryan opened the door, carrying all of her things—crutches, walker, and a bag full of medication. After putting everything away, he joined her on the sofa.

"I'm so glad you're home," he said. "And now that you are, you're going to get better so much faster. Right?" He pulled her close, held her for a moment. "I need to tell you something." He looked worried, and Hannah Lee's stomach clenched. "I know how much you value your privacy and the peace and quiet of this place, but..."

"What?"

"Well, I think you need a little extra help while you're recovering, so I hired someone."

"Ryan—"

"Now, before you say anything, can you just meet her? With an open mind?"

Just when she'd felt so much joy, so much relief, at being home, now she felt anxious. The thought of someone she didn't know hovering about—in her kitchen cooking, making tea or coffee, pulling out her drawers and utensils. And making her bed, which she knew she'd be unable to do for some time. Ryan could do those things, couldn't he?

"Why can't you take care of things?" she asked. "It's just for a short time anyway," she said, not believing her own words.

"I can, when I'm here," he said, "but I have to work during the day—you know that." The old attitude crept into his voice—hints of being put out, obligated unreasonably to earn a living, and resentful.

There were so many things they'd never talked about. That she had money and he didn't. That she didn't have to work, and he did. That it was her house, paid for in full, before they'd met. That she had never entertained the idea of selling it and getting a place they could afford together.

Her house, not really *their* house. Before Ryan, the house had been her greatest joy. It was her sanctuary, her reward—the physical embodiment of life after business. Life with no more worry about making payroll, no longer the constant concern about the high risk of owning a business or potential fines from the FDA.

She loved the house and assumed Ryan did as well. He admired it extensively when they first dated. Later, she wondered if the house might be a glaring representation of their financial divide.

Before she and Ryan married, she went home to see her parents. They'd met Ryan and were happy for her, but she wanted some time alone with them to make sure she wasn't making another mistake. So, she asked for their advice.

<hr />

"There is one thing," said her dad. He hesitated, looking uncomfortable. "What about the fact that you have money? What is his situation?"

Hannah Lee had told her parents she'd sold her business and pocketed some money. But she never told them how much. They knew she'd paid cash for her home in California and that she didn't have to work.

"His situation is fine," she said. "He has a contracting business, and he seems to do well."

"Does he know your situation?" he asked, unaware of the full truth of it.

"Yes, he does, and we've talked about it. He seems comfortable with it." *Not exactly true*.

"What about the house?"

"What *about* the house?" she said, thrown off.

"Well, the house you live in is important. Best scenario is to get a house that didn't belong to either of you before you got together, one that is yours as a married couple. It's a territorial thing—it's yours, and he's allowed to live there vs. it belongs to both of you."

Sell her dream house? *Give up her special sanctuary?* Hannah Lee couldn't imagine that, so she pushed back, reassuring her parents it wasn't an issue.

"That's so old-fashioned, Dad," she protested. "This is the twenty-first century. If he had a house before we met, I bet you wouldn't say these things." Stung, her parents offered no more advice. She felt bad about it but let it be.

She wanted them to be happy for her, and they were, somewhat. But they seemed a bit guarded with Ryan leading up to the wedding. Later, after the wedding and during their periodic visits, they seemed more relaxed with him, but she hadn't forgotten their hesitance.

Maybe they'd seen something she hadn't.

CHAPTER NINETEEN

Now, she wondered. *What if the house was an issue?*

And money. They never talked about money or the house. They'd tiptoed around those subjects for so long she wouldn't know where to begin. Besides, now wasn't the time.

Hannah Lee suddenly felt exhausted. Ryan's attitude about work and her need to recover were at odds.

"What is it?" he said.

"Nothing," she told him, curling up on the sofa. "I'm tired—doesn't seem like much, going home, but I feel like I need a nap."

"Let me get your meds," he said, standing up. She closed her eyes. "Here," he said, giving her two pills and a glass of water.

She sat up partially and swallowed the pills, then lay back down. Ryan covered her with a soft throw, leaned over, and kissed her cheek as he told her he was leaving for work. She closed her eyes.

After he closed the front door, she opened her eyes. She felt the distance between them again. He was pulling away, now that she was home, her recovery well underway.

She felt helpless, both emotionally and physically. It was almost more than she could bear and vastly different than how she'd felt before the accident.

How did you bring back a love that slowly drifted away? How did you warm another heart when it grew cold?

But she knew the answer. *You didn't.*

Love is either there, or it is not. The heart doesn't respond to grasping, neediness, fear, or pain. She wiped away the one tear that slipped down her cheek and gradually fell into a restless, drug-induced sleep.

⚮

The doorbell woke Hannah Lee. It took a moment to realize where she was—on the sofa in her house. The bell rang again. She struggled to get up and realized the walker was nowhere nearby, nor were the crutches. Helpless, she stared at the door, wondering where Ryan was, just as someone gave up on the bell and knocked tentatively.

"Come in!" she called out, something she would never have done in the past. The door opened slowly, and a slender, diminutive figure slid into view—round face, brown skin, ebony eyes, dark hair pulled into a long braid down her back. She wore a vivid green tee shirt and slim jeans with sneakers. She carried a fabric bag, which she set down near the door.

"Hello," said Hannah Lee.

"Hello, Mrs. Winn?" said the mystery girl, who seemed terribly shy.

"Yes, that's me. You might close the door."

The girl's eyes flew open, and she turned to close the door, slamming it, then apologizing— "I'm sorry."

"It's not a problem. Um, why don't you come over here? What is your name?"

"My name is Graciela," she said with a slight Spanish accent, approaching the sofa. "Mr. Ryan sent me."

"Encantado, Graciela," said Hannah Lee. "Mi nombre es Hannah Lee." *Pleased to meet you, Graciela. My name is Hannah Lee.*

Graciela nodded, smiled, and dipped her head.

"Por favor, llámame Ella." *Please, call me Ella.*

"Hablas inglés?" enquired Hannah Lee.

"Sí. Yes, I do."

"Bueno," said Hannah Lee. "That's good because I've used up most of my Spanish." She smiled, and Ella smiled in return.

"Well, Ella, I've never done this before, had someone work for me in my home, except for Lucia, who cleans once every two weeks. So, where do we start?"

"Um, Ms. Winn—Hannah Lee—I'm not sure. Your husband says you need help because you've been in the hospital."

"Yes, that's right. Let's start with the walker. I need to go to the bathroom." She pointed to the walker, which was standing near the doorway to the bedroom.

Ella retrieved it and brought it to her, then hovered nearby while Hannah Lee pushed herself up, took the handles, and began to walk. She stopped and said, "While I'm in the bathroom, could you look in the refrigerator and see if there's anything for lunch—maybe salad fixings?"

When Hannah Lee emerged from the restroom, Ella presented her with a nice salad, along with a tall glass of iced tea. She beamed when Hannah Lee thanked her.

"Now, how about you? Have you had lunch?" asked Hannah Lee, taking a bite of salad.

"No, ma'am, but I have something," Ella said, fetching the fabric bag. She pulled out an apple and a sandwich but seemed uncomfortable eating with Hannah Lee. She tucked the food back in the bag. "I'll clean the kitchen first and eat later."

Hannah Lee ate half the salad, then pushed the rest away, asking Ella to put it in the refrigerator for later. She rose, hobbled to the sofa, picked up the bag with her meds, and took it back to the kitchen. She extracted two pills and swallowed them with iced tea.

Ella seemed distressed at not being able to wait on her, but Hannah

Lee explained that her physical therapy required her to move around as much as possible. "You can take care of the big things, like grocery shopping and cooking."

Hannah Lee made her way to the bedroom for another nap. She gazed out the sliding doors at the beauty of the canyon, her eyes following a bird of prey circling high in the sky.

She sighed. Ella seemed sweet and helpful. Though it pained her to give up her privacy, she felt relieved not having to handle the details of the household for now. Maybe Ryan was right. Maybe this was for the best.

She had no idea when Ryan, who'd left the house again, planned to return. *Working*, she justified to herself. But still. She picked up her phone—no texts or voicemails. Nothing.

But she couldn't think about that now. The pain ebbed and flowed, and right now, it was flowing. Gradually, the pills took effect—the pain subsided enough for some degree of comfort, and sleep took over.

✇

She had a light dinner—leftover salad. She hobbled around the house with the walker and invented things for Ella to do—wash tee shirts and underwear, fetch medication and water, make a large pitcher of tea so she could get a glass every now and then. It was exhausting trying to come up with a long enough list of chores to keep someone occupied for an entire day.

Hannah Lee waited for Ryan, but evening came and went. Ella helped her draw bathwater, and she soaked for as long as possible, luxuriating in the bubbles. More pain pills, then bed. Thankful for the opiate haze, she drifted off, though restlessly.

✇

Hours later, Ryan slipped in the front door as Ella slipped out. Hannah Lee didn't hear him, didn't even know he was home. She didn't see him shower, washing away the scent, or carefully stuffing his clothes in the bottom of the laundry basket. She didn't stir when he quietly slid into bed next to her and lay still staring at the ceiling.

CHAPTER TWENTY

Hannah Lee was going stir-crazy.

She'd been home for six long, grueling days—six days of daily physical therapy with Seth, daily list-making to create enough tasks for Ella, and distress over Ryan's almost total absence. Thanks to the opiate haze, she often was unaware when he came home.

Sometimes he left before she got up so that the only evidence that he'd been home was his dirty clothes in the hamper and the wet towel next to the shower.

Their relationship had deteriorated into long periods of silence punctuated by occasional bickering over his absence.

❧

"Where are you going?"

He froze and turned slowly toward her. "I'm taking care of my business, Hannah Lee. Like I've told you a hundred times. Why do you keep after me? You know it's like this—I never know when homeowners are going to show up, wanting me to go with them to look at progress on their second home here in Monterey." The last was spoken with traces of contempt.

"I get that, Ryan, really I do. But every evening? Without fail? You haven't had an evening off since I got home. I like Ella—she's sweet and does a great job, but *I miss my husband.*"

"I guess now I'm supposed to feel guilty because I have to take care of my business! I hired Ella to make sure you have everything you need. Is there anything you don't have—*anything else you need?*" he asked, eyeing her coldly.

"Yes. I don't have you," she said, turning away to keep him from seeing the tears forming in her eyes.

"You have me. This is temporary," he said, softening his tone.

"Yes, I'm sure it is," she said, not meaning to sound sarcastic.

"What is that supposed to mean?"

"Nothing. I'm sorry, Ryan. I'm tired and a bit restless. I've been cooped up for a long time." Now she sounded self-pitying, not at all like herself. This recovery period had sucked all the gratitude and joy out of her.

"I know," he said, picking up his backpack and heading for the door. "I'll see you later."

No goodbye kiss, no hug.

❧

How could this happen? What—and when—was the real sea change? Hannah Lee struggled to remember their relationship in the weeks leading up to the accident, but all she got were snippets. Often vignettes of their life together appeared at night in her dreams. But were those real, or were they invented by her brain on opiates?

She'd been thinking a lot lately. Her life felt out of control. She felt like she'd wandered into a maze with endless twists and blind turns, no exit in sight.

It wasn't like her to feel this way. She'd always found a pathway to the outcomes she wanted in business. Relationships weren't business. But she was still the same person with a solution-oriented brain.

She had so many questions, most of them unanswerable. Her mind had been running in circles, trying to get answers, for weeks. Now, it was time to do something. She picked up her phone, wrote a short text, threw it down, and waited.

Ella showed up with groceries from the list Hannah Lee had given her the day before. She went into the kitchen to put things away, then headed for the bedroom to tidy things and gather laundry.

Over the past few weeks, Hannah Lee had drawn the conclusion that Ella's main job was to substitute for Ryan, not just in household chores, but in presence. Her husband was gone, and in his place was Ella, who did a fine job, but who wasn't her husband.

The doorbell rang. Hannah Lee quickly hobbled over with her walker and opened the door. Ella ran into the room, but when she saw that she wasn't needed, her shoulders slumped.

"It's okay, Ella, I got it," she told her. "Um, could you bring us some tea?" Ella brightened and headed to the kitchen.

"Hannah Lee! It's so good to see you," said Joe Thatcher, flashing a huge smile. He was in his early fifties, fit and trim, with a shaved scalp and wire-rimmed spectacles. He had a warm, friendly face and intelligent eyes. Juries liked him, judges liked him, and he almost always won his cases because he was brilliant at family and estate law.

She'd known Joe since college and had hired him to represent her in the sale of her business because she trusted him and because the acquirer was based in California. "Joe," she said, hugging him warmly, showing him in. "Thank you for coming over on such short notice. Please, sit," she said, hobbling to the sofa and indicating he should sit with her, which he did.

"Of course! But what happened—you are way too young for a walker," Joe said, smiling like it was a joke. But his smile disappeared as Hannah Lee told him about the accident.

He shook his head. "I had no idea. I would have come to the hospital, been here much sooner to see you."

"It's okay, Joe. I didn't want a lot of people knowing. It's better this way. But I do have something I want to run by you."

"Shoot," he said.

"You've been my attorney for a long time, Joe, so you know I wouldn't bring this up unless I had a good reason." She hesitated, chewed her lip.

"What? What is it?"

She blew out a breath. "Joe, I'm concerned about how the accident happened. I'm not sure it was an accident."

Joe's face tightened. "That is a serious allegation. What makes you think that? Have you reported this to anyone?" He took out a legal pad, but she asked him to put it away.

"I'm not sure I want anyone to do anything at this point, Joe. But you're my friend as well as my attorney, and right now, I want someone to hear me out. Someone who can be objective and tell me what they think. What *you* think."

"Okay, tell me. I won't do anything or take any legal action without your permission. But, if it sounds like a crime has been committed, I may be obligated to report it," he said.

She told him about the dreams she continued to have—about the lines separating, free-falling, the ground rushing up to her, waking up just before hitting the side of the mountain. She told him the dreams seemed real in a way that was different than most dreams—everything so crystal clear, the sequence never varying.

"I think my mind is replaying a tape, a real tape, of what happened that day. I want to know, Joe, what really happened. But what do you think, so far?"

"Let me back up and ask a few questions first. Have you had a neurological workup, and if so, what did they find?"

"Yes, and there's no evidence of brain injury. But I've had short-term memory loss. I can't remember anything from a few days prior to the accident all the way until I woke up in the hospital. They say it's a result of the trauma and that I'll eventually get some or all of the memories back."

"Okay."

"But, Joe? The thing is, I can't be sure about the dreams since I don't have real memories. That's why we're talking—I'm not sure if I'm losing my ability to tell what's real and what's not. That has me worried."

"Understood," he said thoughtfully, but he looked like he had a mental checklist. "Now, have you heard from the paragliding school? Anyone call, check on you, ask about your condition?"

"Nope, not a peep. Do you think that's a problem?"

"What about law enforcement? Did anyone come by your hospital room and ask you any questions?"

"No—what does that mean? Should they have done that?"

She never even considered that law enforcement should have talked with her after the accident. She never considered calling law enforcement herself to discuss her concerns about the accident. She'd been far too busy trying to get through each opiate-hazed day, pushing herself through rehab.

CHAPTER TWENTY-ONE

Joe tapped a finger on his knee. "It seems odd to me," he said. "Whether the school is culpable or not, I would expect them to check on you at the very least."

Again, she'd never thought about the paragliding school. *Why hadn't they called and checked on her?*

They sat in silence, both thinking.

"How about asking Ryan to go to the school, make some inquiries?" Joe suggested. "I can do it, but it might be strange at this stage."

"No, you're right—it's better you don't."

She twisted her mouth, looked down.

"What's the problem, Hannah Lee? Is there something going on with you and Ryan?"

She looked up quickly. "No, of course not. It's just that he's really busy right now with his work. But I'm sure he can find the time if I ask him."

"Good. I think that's a good place to start. It's highly unlikely it was anything other than an accident, considering the fact that law enforcement hasn't acted already. I'd say that's a good sign. For now, try to relax your mind about it."

She nodded. Maybe Joe was right. She was recovering from injuries, had nothing else to occupy her mind, and had begun to invent scenarios, perhaps out of sheer boredom. Or perhaps the pain of feeling Ryan distance himself had stirred up other fears, irrational fears.

"So, tell me about your injuries and recovery process," said Joe.

She talked about physical therapy for a moment, then switched subjects and asked about his family. Joe had a daughter just starting college and a son in his freshman year of high school. He spoke about them with pride. She found herself tuning out, thinking about having Ryan ask the school more about her accident.

They finished their conversation, and Joe looked ready to leave. Before he could, she touched his arm. "There's one more thing, Joe. I—this is really awkward, but I have to ask. Do you think anyone at your office could have told Ryan about the new will and trust, about the money?"

Joe's face tightened. "What do you mean? He already knew, right?"

She sat very still, a sense of unease raising the hair on her arms. She slowly shook her head.

Joe wiped his hand over his face, looking shocked. "I thought you told him. He showed up at my office a few weeks ago, telling me he wanted to do his will. He claimed to have a small inheritance from his parents—they both passed, right?"

She nodded. "Yes, but that was many years ago. I can't imagine any inheritance from them that he'd still have today. He seems to operate his construction business on a shoestring budget."

She stopped, feeling embarrassed. She never talked about Ryan's finances to anyone, and besides, it sounded ridiculous even to her. Why would her husband have to operate on a tight budget?

Joe looked at her oddly.

"I know that sounds strange, but we keep our finances separate. It was something we decided before we were married."

Joe nodded. "Of course."

"What else did he say when he came to your office?"

"He made a comment about the trust you set up for him, something about how it wasn't necessary. It seems a bit odd now, like he wanted me to think the money wasn't important. And maybe like he was fishing for information about the trust."

He sat there, remembering. "He made a reference to the amount of your business sale proceeds. I figured you'd told him your financial situation long ago. So, I didn't think anything of it."

She felt confused. How could this be? Ryan didn't have access to her financial information. All of it was held by trust officers at her bank, and her personal links and passwords were in her laptop, which was secured by facial recognition software.

"Where did he get that information?"

"I have no idea. He already knew the number, and when he said it, I just nodded, so that means I confirmed it. I'm sorry, Hannah Lee. I shouldn't have done that. I assumed you'd told him all about the trust." Joe looked stricken.

She sat quietly, unsure about so many things. *What did this mean?* Ryan—going to Joe's office without telling her. Ryan—saying he wanted a will to benefit her. But he didn't have anything to leave her, did he? He constantly claimed he teetered on the edge with his business—barely enough money to pay the subs, just enough profit to pay his personal bills.

"Joe, it's okay," she said. "I'm not mad at you. It was a slip, a small slip. It could have happened to anyone." But she felt like the bottom had dropped out, that Joe had slipped in a way that may have already had huge consequences.

"I'm going to recommend another attorney for you. We will still be friends if you'll have me, but you should have someone else who...I mean, you can't help it, but you'll never feel the same about our professional relationship." He looked undone. She didn't know how to make him feel better, so she sat quietly.

"What else can I do at this point?" he asked, gray faced.

"Nothing. I have to think about all of this, think about what to do."

She walked him to the door, said goodbye, already feeling like she'd lost a friend. That was ridiculous, of course—he'd always be a friend. But he was right—it wouldn't feel the same professionally.

And that meant one less person she could rely on to have her best interests at heart. Yes, she'd get a good referral—someone highly competent, no doubt. But that person wouldn't be her friend, wouldn't be someone she could count on personally.

CHAPTER TWENTY-TWO

There were so many unanswered questions. What really happened the day of the accident? Why did Ryan pump Joe for information about her estate? Because that was what it looked like.

How did he know? If he opened her laptop and tried to find the information, he wouldn't be able to get in, not easily.

Hacking a personal laptop would be difficult but not impossible. She rarely used it, and it was kept in a drawer in her home office. It would be easy for him to slip it out, take it to someone to crack the passwords, and see everything. All of the information about her money.

Her money. It was clearly an issue, one that should be cause for joy, for relief, for celebration. Instead, it was becoming a huge block in their relationship. Because she couldn't imagine having that conversation now.

Hey, Ryan, you know when I told you I made some money from my business, bought a house, and didn't have to work? Well, the truth is, I'm so wealthy I can't think of enough ways to spend it. The truth is, I didn't want you to know that.

The truth is—I wanted you to marry me for love.

What an idiot I've been, she thought, as tears welled up and coursed down her face. In her quest to marry for love, she withheld her real circumstances. She thought Ryan was a self-made entrepreneur, like her, so she figured he'd want to be independent, run his business as he saw fit, not be dependent on her.

She thought they were like-minded and that it would all work out great. They lived in her home, which was paid for, so their living expenses were low. He wouldn't have any worries on that score.

But, instead, she saw with painful clarity, they were not like-minded. Ryan seemed resentful of his clients and their wealth, of his need to go out and work every day. He wasn't grateful, relaxed, and joyful about their lives together.

He was distant, tense, and absent, more so daily.

She couldn't bear this line of thinking. Her husband loved her. *Didn't he?*

Hannah Lee felt a presence and looked up to find Ella hovering nearby, looking worried. She approached, handed her a glass of iced tea, and placed a box of tissues nearby. That small gesture opened the flood gates, and Hannah Lee sobbed. Ella sat beside her, patting her knee, while the grief poured through.

Afterward, awkwardness descended. Claiming fatigue, Hannah Lee went to her bedroom and closed the door. She pulled up a throw and stared at the ceiling.

This couldn't be what it looked like—that Ryan was after her money. She was tired, she was in pain, and she was on opiates. Her judgment was skewed by isolation and loneliness. Her memory was shot, and therefore, questionable.

The accident was just that—an accident. There was no way her husband wanted her dead, would deliberately set up a horrific accident just for her money. That only happened in the movies, right? Having those kinds of suspicions was twisted. *It's the opiates*, she thought.

Her heart ached with longing—to feel his touch, to nestle in his arms, to hear his soothing voice telling her not to worry, that everything was okay. She wanted to go back to that place and time when the two of them were tightly bound by unshakable love. Or so it seemed.

∞

Their honeymoon, an almost magical interlude, was spent driving around wine country—Napa and Sonoma—staying at small, charming inns. They visited wineries, did tastings, and Hannah Lee bought cases of wine. Every time Ryan took a sip or two, closed his eyes and said, "mmm," she followed up with an order.

Ryan tried to stop her. "You're spending way too much on wine."

But she brushed him off with the excuse that she'd saved up a small slush fund for this purpose. "I don't splurge often, and when I do, I like to stock up. Besides, it's our honeymoon! I'm celebrating the fact that I found the most wonderful man in the world. Just think—every time we open one of these bottles, we will re-live our honeymoon."

She was blissful, glowing—totally swept away on a romantic tide. They made love every day, slept wrapped around each other.

One day, sitting on the veranda of a winery, Ryan looked at her wonderingly. She was talking about books she'd read recently and something about sitting on a non-profit board years ago. It was supposed to be a funny story, but she realized with chagrin that it made her sound self-important.

"You're amazing," said Ryan, and she blushed, looking down. The last thing she wanted was to elevate herself.

"No, you really are," he said, reaching out to take her hand. "I don't mean the board seat or the books. I mean the thoughtful way you speak, the words you choose. That look in your eyes. You're not like anyone I've ever known before. You truly are amazing."

Uncomfortable, she tried humor. "Well, of course, I am! Isn't that why you married me?"

But he shook his head, smiling.

After their honeymoon, Ryan threw himself into work. For a while, their life together clicked along. He seemed content and came home, ready to hang out with her. They were close, or it seemed that way to her.

Still, something was missing. Their conversations never went below the most superficial elements. They talked about news and weather, about Ryan's jobs, his clients, and the latest book she'd read. She shared snippets from her family and updates on Danielle.

He didn't have any family to reference. He came into her life completely unencumbered by prior attachments. While he knew other contractors in the area, and certainly sub-contractors, he never spoke of college friends. He never spoke of friends.

To Hannah Lee, this didn't seem strange. She was an introvert too, so preferring one's own company to others was not a new concept.

Never one to socialize much, and totally consumed with her business, she hadn't made friends over the years, other than Danielle. Yes, they went out for wine and 'girl time' periodically, and Hannah Lee enjoyed their time together. But mostly, she enjoyed her beautiful home—her sanctuary.

Ryan being friendless made him seem more like her, but now she wondered if that were true. After the first few weeks of married life, he began to appear restless. He came home from work, ate dinner with her, and when she retired to read, he seemed at a loss.

When they first met, he seemed like an avid reader, someone who'd be content snuggling on the sofa with her at night, but now? Now, he was the guy who worked and went elsewhere. When did that start—the going out at night, with his construction friends?

She had a few memories—vague impressions—of sitting in the house alone at night, wondering when Ryan might come home. Digging deeper, she felt an uneasiness that threaded back prior to the accident. But she couldn't construct a timeline.

Remembering their honeymoon week again, Hannah Lee touched

her wedding band, slowly twisted it around, and thought about their life now—Ryan gone every evening, her body and heart in pain, her mind muddled by drugs and uncertainty.

Now what? Confusion reigned—her brain couldn't get a handle on what was real and what was not. She had no idea what—if anything—to do next. Anxiety coursed through her body, leaving her shaken.

What was that exercise she used to do when business problems seemed insurmountable? When she was tightly wound and lost sleep at night.

"Get out of the day-to-day, go to a quiet environment, or do this at night. Focus on your breath, meditate, and after that, give your brain something to work on in the background, not the foreground. Give it the command to create a solution to the problem, as if it were already solved."

Hannah Lee's executive coach, Leah, had given her the exercise.

"Remember, you already know everything you need to know to solve the significant issues of your life and business. Your brain will reveal this to you when you achieve a state of relaxation so the solutions can emerge, and when you tell it to do so."

She closed her eyes, inhaled slowly, and exhaled slowly, deeply. She breathed in slowly again, and exhaled slowly, focusing on her breath, imagining the air flowing in and out. She did it again, and after that, breathed normally while doing a meditative 'body scan.' That took a few minutes.

She drew in one final, long deep breath, and gave herself the command.

I remember. I remember everything that happened, and I know exactly what to do next. I will easily solve the problems of the accident and my marriage.

She repeated it to herself several times, feeling herself drift off to sleep.

⁂

Hannah Lee woke from her nap feeling refreshed and determined. She picked up her cell phone, searched her contacts, found the one she wanted, but paused.

Once she took this step, it meant a significant move away from Ryan. Instead of turning to her husband, the one person she should trust more than anyone else, she'd be turning to someone else.

If Ryan found out, and if her suspicions proved to be unfounded, he wouldn't understand. His heart would be broken, and his trust in her—well, she could probably count that gone. Forever.

She pushed the call button, heard ringing, and a voice from the past answered. "Hannah Lee. I'm so glad you called."

CHAPTER TWENTY-THREE

Matteo booted his computer and quickly booked a flight to San Jose, planning to drive to Carmel from there.

He envisioned Hannah Lee laid up with severe injuries, barely able to move around, in pain. But what got his blood boiling was the thought that she might be at risk in other ways. That someone, perhaps her shiny new husband, might wish her harm.

For the hundredth time, Matteo said a silent prayer of thanks—for meeting Hannah Lee all those years ago, for working for her for so many years, and for the enormous, good fortune that had turned out to be in his life. For the blessing that *she* had turned out to be.

In his wildest dreams, he never imagined that he'd be rewarded for his job as operations manager with a four-point-six-million-dollar check.

There was that meeting years earlier when Hannah Lee informed him and other key managers that they'd been endowed with small shares of the business. But they all looked at each other and smiled, having no idea what that might mean.

She made a fun joke out of it, bringing them all together for a catered dinner in their conference room. She started by solemnly declaring that she needed to introduce the new owners of the business, her new partners. This caused a mild surge of anxiety around the room.

She pulled up a slide deck on a large monitor. The first slide said, *New Owners Dinner*. She paused dramatically, then moved to the next slide.

Everyone at the dinner was on the slide—their photos and names. They looked around in confusion. She smiled broadly and said, "*You* are the new joint owners!"

That was just like Hannah Lee. She didn't need to endow them with shares. They already loved her, loved working at the company. Retention of key people was 100%. No one wanted to leave, and everyone worked together, sometimes for long hours, to ensure the success of the business.

But she gave them shares, perhaps not knowing herself how valuable they might be years later. Later, Big Pharma showed up with BIG checks and she decided to sell the business.

She handed them their checks after the transaction closed—smiling, tears in her eyes, thanking them profusely for their years of service. It was a hug-and-drip fest that day. The next day, she called them into her office for private conversations, asking them one by one if they might be willing to stay for a couple more years with the new owners.

Everyone agreed, including Hannah Lee. So, everyone stayed on a few more months, until Big Pharma one day sent a hotshot new executive team to run the business.

Hannah Lee, Matteo, and a handful of other executive-level managers were thanked and dismissed with large severance packages. The rest of the employees were given 'stay bonuses' and remained, though with misgivings. Many of them had worked for Hannah Lee for most of their careers.

The executive team going away party was especially bittersweet. They were all multi-millionaires, all set for life. They all knew they'd scored big. But never going to work again as a team? Many couldn't fathom it.

No more going out for dinner again as a team, to celebrate their success. No more pranks pulled on some unsuspecting person's birthday. No retreats to wine country for planning sessions, complete with dinner in a vineyard.

That was a bitter pill to swallow—the finality of it, the loss of a place to go each day, to feel productive, and to feel part of something good. Everyone was relatively young, ranging in age from mid-30s to late 40s.

Matteo was far too young to sit around with nothing purposeful to do. So, he found ways to stay active. And now, he had a new sense of purpose. He jumped up and got into action, quickly packed what he needed, and left his three-bedroom luxury condo.

Later, sitting on the plane sipping a glass of red wine, Matteo thought about his life—the winding pathway since working for Hannah Lee. From the joy of newfound wealth, and the bittersweet parting from Hannah Lee, to his all too brief marriage and abrupt divorce. Now, perhaps, back to Hannah Lee.

TWO YEARS EARLIER

Matteo raised a glass of Patrón on the rocks to Shelly, now wobbling as she pressed buttons on her phone to call a shared ride. Shelly beamed, hugged Matteo one last time—the third drunk hug—and turned to Hannah Lee, who endured an uncomfortable hug.

"Bye, bye, and let's shtay in toushh!" Shelly was their CFO, or former CFO, and a bright ray of sunshine everywhere she went. She'd been brilliant at the due diligence phase of their transaction and all phases of the sale, including helping to negotiate their exit packages.

Without her, none of them would have fared so well. She would, no doubt, continue her skyrocketing career—if she wanted it—working for private equity or another fast-growth firm. In her early 30s and wealthy, she could write her own ticket. Shelly sashayed out of the restaurant, the rest of the team having already left the farewell dinner.

Finally, Matteo had Hannah Lee to himself. They moved to the bar and sat side by side. He buzzed from the alcohol and the proximity to

Hannah Lee. "Quite a ride, huh?" he said, cutting his eyes to her.

"It's been amazing," she said, still with that I-can't-quite-believe-it's-true look. The look she'd had since they closed on the company sale a few months earlier. Avoiding a full-on stare, Matteo gazed at Hannah Lee as surreptitiously as possible.

She had shoulder-length, unruly brown hair, a heart-shaped face, and intelligent, hazel eyes—deep blue green with hints of brown. She had a habit of pulling her full lips to one side and frowning when she was deep in thought.

At the office, she wore black framed glasses that gave her a demure librarian look. Tonight, she wore no glasses, giving him an unobstructed view of her eyes and face.

She was almost slender—but the slight rounding effect of a few extra pounds enchanted him. Her skin was flawless and slightly rosy, especially her cheeks after she returned from vacation and a little sun. Normally, she wore her hair pulled back, but tonight it fell around her shoulders.

Hannah Lee was the type of woman who carried herself well, who effortlessly commanded focus from others, and put people at ease. Her intelligence was her most distinguishing characteristic, followed by her innate kindness.

Hannah Lee wasn't classically beautiful. Her face was nice but not stunning. Her hair, though, was...well, Matteo had longed to run his fingers through her hair for far too long.

But what really set her apart, in Matteo's eyes, was her presence. There was something about Hannah Lee that drew subtle attention. When they went through due diligence to sell the business, more than one sharp-dressed guy stole looks at Hannah Lee.

Even tonight, sitting at the bar, a couple of guys gave her the slow once-over but then noticed Matteo's intense stare and hastily backed off. She, however, was oblivious to the attention she attracted.

Matteo was wildly attracted to Hannah Lee, but also keenly aware of how unwelcome his advances would likely be. Hannah Lee was a true professional. While she always treated her employees and leadership team with kindness and care, she didn't encourage close personal relationships with any of them, including Matteo.

But now, their working relationship was officially over. Was it time, he wondered, for more?

CHAPTER TWENTY-FOUR

"So, what are your plans now, you and Chloe?" asked Hannah Lee, reading his mind, not for the first time.

Many times, as they worked together, they'd finished each other's thoughts, almost read each other's minds. Their working relationship had been nothing short of amazing as they riffed on the company strategy and execution plans. Of course, she'd pick up on his thoughts about Chloe. Hopefully, she wouldn't pick up on his other thoughts.

"Not sure yet. I'm not really sure where we're going," he said lamely.

"What do you mean? I thought you two were going strong," she said. "Didn't you tell me you were going to propose? I could have sworn I saw you looking online at diamond rings the other day." She grinned impishly at him.

"Yeah, well, I was, but—"

"Uh oh," she said, arching one eyebrow. "Are you avoiding commitment?"

"Maybe."

"Why? Chloe seems like a great girl."

"She is. But—"

"But what? See, this is what I don't understand. You're not the first guy I've known who meets a great woman, spends time with her, she falls in love, and then he fishtails out of there. I will never understand men and the odd things they do *after* getting involved with a woman.

"I mean, why bother starting something if you're not going to go the rest of the way?" She shook her head and looked over Matteo's shoulder, taking another small sip of wine.

He sat a bit surprised. That was the most she'd ever opened up with him. It could have been the wine, or maybe it was the fact that she no longer had to worry about seeing him at the office the next day.

"So, what is it, Matteo? Can you enlighten me about why men do that?" Hannah Lee gave him the same look that she'd often worn at work when trying to solve a complicated business problem.

"What about women who break it off with guys?" he said a bit defensively.

"And how often do you hear about *that* happening?" she said challengingly.

He thought about it and couldn't come up with a good story.

"Right," she said, nodding her head once. "It's almost always the guy who departs in a hurry, either before or shortly after the engagement, and sometimes, right before the wedding."

She shook her head gently. A curl fell over her forehead, and she brushed it aside. Matteo's heart skipped a beat.

"Anyway," she said a bit sorrowfully, "relationships are just too complicated. I certainly don't have a knack for love."

What could he say to that? He'd found it baffling that Hannah Lee had been single the entire time he'd known her. He opened his mouth to tell her how amazing she was, how any guy would be the luckiest man alive to have her.

"But you, Matteo," she said softly before he could speak. "You are such a good guy. I think any woman would be lucky to have you. What is it? Why aren't you happily married, with two or three adorable kids?"

"I could ask you the same question," he said.

Her eyes tightened. She looked down. "I just prefer my life to be quiet, uncomplicated," she said. "If I'm being honest with myself, I knew I didn't have it in me to run a business all day long, with all the risks and uncertainty, people's jobs on the line, and come home to—to problems and issues."

He let that sit. *So, men represented "problems and issues" to Hannah Lee.*

Later, he walked her to her car. As she reached for her door, he gently stopped her. She turned to him. He stood so close he could see the rise and fall of her breath in her chest. He reached out with his right hand, slid it slowly around her waist, lowered his eyes to her lips.

"Matteo," she said softly, her voice tinged with uncertainty.

He paused and, at the last minute, moved into a nice, brotherly hug. He felt her relieved breath and pulled back. "I hope I didn't make you uncomfortable," he said.

"You didn't. It's just that—"

"I know."

They stood awkwardly for a moment.

"I know we'll stay in touch," she said, as he simultaneously spoke almost the exact same words. They both laughed softly.

"Doing it again!" she said, looking up at him, smiling.

"Always," he said, feeling a catch in his throat.

He watched as she got in her car, giving him a little wave as she drove away. He felt a deep heaviness as if he'd lost a part of himself, something dear and irretrievable.

He'd been so close to what he'd wanted to do for months—finding out if Hannah Lee shared his feelings. Though she'd stopped him and seemed relieved, he'd swear on a stack of Bibles that she felt the same energy he felt—the chemistry, the attraction, the heat. He re-lived the moment, her beating heart, the smell of her hair, the feel of her waist.

As he drove home, he wondered why he didn't feel the same way

135

about Chloe—the intensity of emotion, the longing, the need to protect. *What was wrong with him?* Chloe was gorgeous—the kind of girl most guys dream of marrying. *Wasn't she?*

CHAPTER TWENTY-FIVE

Matteo eased open the door, slid in quietly, dropping his keys on the entryway table.

"Matteo?" called out a girlish voice. Chloe. He slumped.

In the living room, she sat on the sofa with her legs tucked underneath. Coco, her Pomeranian, looked up eagerly at Matteo, but when she tried to jump down to run and greet him, Chloe held onto her like a small, fluffy security toy.

"It's okay, Coco. It's just Matteo," she cooed, petting the dog's impossibly thick fur. Coco snorted loudly, barked twice, and whined. Chloe frowned. "No barking, Coco."

Chloe was beautiful, with long, tan legs, a slender, toned frame, big blue eyes, and long dark hair. She was mid-twenties—*too young*, his Mamá had assured him. "You need someone with a good head on her shoulders," she'd said, shaking her head. "Like that Hannah Lee, you work for," she'd added knowingly.

Women. Even his mother seemed to know things about him that he didn't.

"Where have you been?" Chloe asked accusingly.

Coco looked sharply at Chloe, tongue out, panting slightly.

"It was the company going away dinner. I told you about it three days ago."

Coco looked sharply at Matteo. "Why wasn't I invited?" she asked petulantly, beginning to look fragile.

"No spouses—significant others—were invited. I told you that too," he said.

"But it was your last company dinner! I just don't understand that Hannah Lee—she's anti-social or something. Or maybe she has a thing for you and didn't want me there! I swear she doesn't like me. I can tell."

Her voice rose, not only in volume but in pitch. Chloe had a little-girl voice and look that he found utterly charming in the beginning, but which now grated. She ran a money-making fashion blog—her all-American model good looks a valuable social media asset. He thought that was charming as well, in the beginning. But as time went on, he began to see her lack of depth.

At this point, Coco looked like an observer at a tennis match, her tiny, furred face moving swiftly from Chloe to Matteo and back again. She whined, and Chloe shushed her.

"Calm down," he said to Chloe, raising his hand and lowering it slightly as if to turn down the volume of her voice and her emotions. But that only inflamed her.

"Calm down? Calm down! I've been sitting here for hours waiting for you! Since when does a *'company dinner'*"—here she made dramatic air quotes—"take seven hours!"

Coco barked once, whined, and Chloe shoved her off of her lap. Coco ran to Matteo, who picked her up gently and petted her soothingly.

"It wasn't seven hours. It was..." he checked his watch. Oops—it was actually almost eight hours. But Chloe didn't know what time he'd left for the dinner.

"Anyway, I'm tired," he said, turning toward the bedroom, taking Coco with him.

"Where are you going?" she demanded, voice now laced with the beginnings of tears. "I'm talking to you, Matteo!"

"I'm tired, Chloe. I'm going to bed."

"Wait." She sounded slightly mollified. "I have something important to tell you."

"Can't it wait until tomorrow?"

"No, it can't."

With a heavy sigh, he sat beside her, still holding Coco. When he met Chloe, he thought she was a true animal lover. She seemed totally enraptured with her tiny dog, carrying her everywhere in a 'dog purse.'

But later, he realized Coco was more for show and for her blog. It seemed as long as Chloe's mood was up, her dog was adorable, but when Chloe sank into her petulant moods, Coco became an unwanted accessory.

"You haven't even kissed me," said Chloe, gazing at him soulfully with her big, blue eyes. He smelled her shampoo—some kind of floral-like essence. Her skin glowed, and she'd allowed one strap of her tiny, black tank top to slip from her shoulder.

He leaned in and gave her a perfunctory kiss, but before he could pull back, she placed her hands on either side of his face, pulled him in, and kissed him slowly, her tongue darting in and out.

He kissed her back, but after a minute or so, gently pulled away. "What is it you wanted to talk about?"

She sighed, opened her eyes dreamily, and smiled. "I have some news."

"Okay," he said, anticipating an announcement about her business, such as gaining 5,000 new followers.

She reached down beside the sofa, picked up her designer bag, rummaged around, and pulled out an envelope. She handed it to Matteo triumphantly.

"What is this?" he asked, still holding the unopened envelope. There was something lumpy inside. He felt an unexpected rise in tension.

"Open it," she said gleefully.

He sat for a moment, frozen. He hated surprises. Chloe knew that. When he remained grim-faced, her smile began to drop.

Not wanting any more drama, he tore open the envelope, and something fell out. He caught it and stared at it. It was a little larger than a standard thermometer, white plastic, blue on one end, with a little window. In that window, he could see two faint lines that formed a cross.

He looked blankly up at Chloe, whose smile had grown. "What does this mean?" he asked, already knowing the answer.

She playfully punched his arm. "You know what it means, you big silly. We're pregnant!" She threw herself into his arms and began kissing him again. He kissed her back but without enthusiasm, feeling his entire insides drop.

"Aren't you happy, baby?" she cooed, nuzzling his neck. "You're going to be a dad! You're going to be a *great* dad," she said emphatically.

"Of course, I am," he said. "This is...as my mom would say, a baby is always a blessing." He worked to put as much love and enthusiasm as possible into his voice.

"I'm so excited, Matteo! I've already started sourcing a few lines for maternity wear. I am going to be a role model for pregnant women. I'm going to show them that you can look beautiful and glamorous all the way to the delivery room. None of this eat-everything-in-sight, get fat as a pig—that is not for me. And baby wear—once we know the gender, I can start with those products as well. It's going to be so fun, don't you think, sweetie?"

She babbled on about her blog, about fashion and make-up, while Matteo sat in stunned silence. To think he was ready to end this relationship and would have done so in a heartbeat if Hannah Lee had given him any indication that he had a chance with her.

But that was over. He'd been called to love—this woman about whom he'd been so ambivalent, and who now needed him. And the child growing within, toward whom he now felt a surge of protectiveness. The baby who needed him even more.

CHAPTER TWENTY-SIX

PRESENT DAY

Hannah Lee, sitting on the sofa in the great room, wiped the sweat from her brow. She fought the pain and shivered under the blanket despite the heavy sweatshirt she wore. Her heart raced, her breath shallow. Her thoughts ran the gamut from determination to hopelessness.

The front door swung open, and Danielle called out, "Hey! Your BFF is here bringing goodies!" She carried a large food bag smelling suspiciously like burgers and fries. She set it down on the coffee table in front of Hannah Lee, who jumped up, yelped in pain, then sat back down swiftly, and lost it. Her stomach purged its contents on the rug.

"Dang, girl! What the heck? Oh, Hannah Lee, you're sick! Why didn't you tell me?" Danielle was frantic. She ran to the kitchen but was intercepted by Ella, who brought towels and went to work cleaning up the mess.

Hannah Lee sat back on the sofa gasping for breath. "I'm okay, really," she said weakly.

"You're white as a sheet! You're anything but okay," said Danielle, sitting beside her friend, putting her hand on her forehead. "You don't feel feverish. Have you called your doctor?"

Hannah Lee shook her head. "I don't need to. I just need to keep going. I'm—" she hesitated, blew out a long breath.

"What? Are you pregnant?!" Danielle's eyebrows flew up, Ella sat back and stared at Hannah Lee, and all activity stopped.

"No," said Hannah Lee, "not even close. I'm getting off the pain pills. It's just withdrawal. Not to worry—according to my research, this will pass in a couple of days."

Danielle looked far too relieved, which felt wrong to Hannah Lee. "You don't have to look so happy about it," she said sarcastically. "It wouldn't exactly be a tragedy if I had a baby." She stared at Danielle, eyes narrowed.

Danielle's hands went up. "Whoa, there, girlfriend. I didn't say anything."

Hannah Lee reined in her irritation. It wasn't Danielle's fault that everything seemed to set her off. She'd felt like this since yesterday when she stopped taking the pain pills. It wasn't like her at all. She was always so unflappable, so even keel. So much so that she sometimes was accused of not being emotional enough.

She could hear her mother saying, "Hannah Lee—it's okay to get mad about being left out of the sleepover with the other girls." But she only shrugged and went back to her room to read. She figured she'd get invited the next time, and meanwhile, she had that great book waiting to be devoured. Always unruffled, so easy going.

Not today. Coming off opiates was far more difficult than she'd imagined.

Danielle waved a hand in front of her eyes. "Hellooo. Anyone home?"

Snapping back to the present, Hannah Lee sighed. "I'm sorry. It's been a little difficult the past few hours. I just can't stand taking the pills anymore. I don't like feeling fuzzy headed. I can't focus, can't figure out what's going on. The worst thing, though, is that I still can't remember what happened that day! Or for a couple of weeks before.

And taking these pills makes it worse, I think. So, I'm getting off of them."

"Understood," said Danielle. "I take it you're not exactly hungry," she said, eyeing the burger bag.

"No, I'm not, but you go ahead," she said unconvincingly. She'd probably hurl again if that bag were opened in her line of sight.

"Uh, no thanks," said Danielle. "I think I'll just put it in the kitchen for later."

"Wait," said Hannah Lee, grabbing Danielle's arm. "I need to talk to you about something, and we have to do it now."

"Sure," Danielle said, sitting back down.

Hannah Lee bit her lip. "The thing is, um." She stopped, looked around, then suddenly made a resolution. She stood up, grabbed her walker, and said, "Let's go."

"What?" Danielle stood as well.

"Let's go somewhere else—anywhere else. I've been cooped up here forever. I can't stand it another minute."

Danielle nodded her head. "At your service, ma'am! I thought you'd never say it."

As they made their way to the front door, Ella appeared, concern marring her pretty face. "Where are you going, Ms.—Hannah Lee? Mr. Ryan says you need to stay here and rest."

"It's okay, Ella. We're just going out for a bit," said Hannah Lee.

Ella looked worried, chewed her lip.

"What is it?" asked Hannah Lee, stopping to take a good look at Ella. She seemed unusually distressed.

"Um, Mr. Ryan—he says I have to take care of you all day while he's working. He says he is paying me for that."

Danielle gawked at their interaction, but Hannah Lee ignored her and smiled at Ella. "That's okay, Ella. I will make sure you are paid for all your hours. If you could just take care of the laundry while we're gone, that would really help."

Using the walker, she turned and headed determinedly for Danielle's SUV. She climbed in awkwardly while Danielle put her walker in the back seat and took the driver's seat. As they backed out, Hannah Lee watched Ella, still standing in the doorway looking concerned. "Is it just me or was that an odd level of concern for my wellbeing?" she asked.

"More like an odd level of needing to keep an eye on you," said Danielle sourly. "I'd say your husband is behind it."

"I'm sure it's nothing," said Hannah Lee, waving her hand dismissively.

"If you say so. Now, what is it you want to talk about?"

But Hannah Lee didn't feel like talking right away. "First, let me get some coffee in me before I spill my guts."

CHAPTER TWENTY-SEVEN

"So, what's up?" asked Danielle. They'd settled in at a private table in the corner with coffee and scones.

"I've done something, and before you judge, or comment, let me just tell you the whole story first. I'm not sure about my instincts right now, so I need you to be as objective as possible. It's important because I may be making decisions that will be life-changing, and I want to make the best ones." Hannah Lee blew out a breath, feeling the tension rise.

Danielle rolled her eyes. "Speak," she said, waving her hand in deference. Hannah Lee knew that was typical Danielle—for *yes, I will suspend judgment and listen with my mind open, at least partially.*

"Do you remember the guy that worked for me years ago, my number two person on the team? Matteo."

"I don't specifically recall a guy like that."

"Well, never mind. Anyway, I called him, and he's on his way here."

Danielle cocked a brow, waited.

"I called him because I want him to help me figure out a few things. I feel odd about it, too. It's a big ask, to get someone to jump on a plane and travel across the country for...what I have in mind."

"And exactly what do you have in mind?"

Hannah Lee outlined her plan, unsure of every step. But she couldn't keep it inside. She needed to share it with her best friend if for no other reason than simple moral support. Or even to argue about it, if that's what it took for her to feel more confident.

"What is the reason for this, sweetie? What's really going on with you and Ryan?"

"What's going on is that he's out all evening, sometimes most of the night, supposedly for work. But it doesn't seem right. He's never kept hours like this before. I can't exactly follow him around, not like this," she said, waving toward her walker.

Danielle sat uncharacteristically quiet.

"What? What are you thinking?"

"I've been thinking about this for a while. So, I'll just say it. What do you really know about Ryan? I mean, besides the obvious. Who is his family? Where is he from? What is his real background?"

"I know everything there is to know!" Hannah Lee snapped back.

"See, that's why I haven't asked this before," said Danielle. "I knew you'd be defensive about him. I didn't say anything when you got married in such a Godawful hurry, but now—now something doesn't feel right, and I can't keep quiet. I guess I'd rather speak up and know I did than stay quiet and regret it. So, go ahead—get mad." She sat back in a huff.

Hannah Lee reached over swiftly to touch her hand. "I'm sorry. I have no right to be defensive about Ryan. He's the reason we're having this conversation. I guess I haven't wanted to think about these things." Hannah Lee felt a catch in her chest, tears welling. She never cried so much in her life before the past few weeks, ever since the accident.

"Oh, crap. Don't cry, Sweetie," said Danielle. "We don't have to talk about this."

"No, I'm fine. I just can't seem to stop crying lately," said Hannah Lee, rooting around in her bag for a tissue. Finding one, she blew her nose. "We do need to talk about it," she said finally.

"Okay," said Danielle. "So, think about it—what do you really know about Ryan?"

Hannah Lee thought about it. *What did she know?* "He grew up in a military family—his dad was career, Army, I think."

"Where?"

"All over. No particular place."

"Have you met them?"

"No. They were both killed in a car crash years ago."

"How convenient."

Shocked, Hannah Lee stared at Danielle. She'd always felt tremendous compassion for Ryan—that he'd lost his parents so young and didn't have siblings. She didn't feel close to her sister, but they were cordial and enjoyed catching up during holiday visits. And her parents were the best, always there for her. She'd always felt lucky to have a family.

"Hannah Lee. How do you know Ryan's story about his family is true? Did you confirm any of these things before you married him? In your position, you can't afford to just take someone's word for who he says he is, right?"

"I—no, I didn't." She sighed. "I felt so strongly that he loved me for me. I didn't want to do what so many wealthy people do—hire a private detective, snoop into someone's life without their permission. And if I'd told him I was doing that, I don't think he'd have forgiven me. I'm fairly sure it would have crushed our relationship right at the beginning."

Danielle studied her, saying nothing.

If Danielle knew the real extent of Hannah Lee's wealth, she'd probably explode with suspicion, mirroring her own growing suspicions.

But that seemed premature. In fact, this whole thing seemed wrong. *What kind of wife was she?* "You know, this is probably a terrible idea—asking Matteo to come out here and play private detective, spy on Ryan. What was I thinking? It must be the drugs—it's destroyed my judgment." Hannah Lee felt tiny beads of sweat forming on her forehead, arms, and legs.

"I've got to call him, tell him it was a mistake," she said, suddenly feeling ridiculous. She grabbed her phone to cancel Matteo's visit.

Danielle reached over and gently took the phone away, stopping her from aborting the mission. The percussion in Hannah Lee's chest gradually slowed, and her sweat glands stopped producing.

But her mind continued to swirl in confusion. She'd never been like this before—insecure, frightened, unsure of her own thoughts and motives. "I've always been so level-headed, so even keel. I feel so disoriented, so confused. I'm not sure what's real and what's not. That's why I called Matteo. I need someone to help me understand all this. He was my right-hand man for years—I've never known anyone so capable of figuring out the most complex problems."

Hannah Lee looked up swiftly. "It's not that I don't think you could help me, but since people around here know you, I was afraid it would get back to Ryan."

Danielle waved away the concern. "It's okay. He sounds like someone who can help, and I think it's important for you to follow through. You have the best instincts of anyone I know, Hannah Lee. But why haven't we talked about Matteo before?"

"He was a huge part of my old life, before I sold the business. It was so hard leaving that life behind, giving up my job, and saying good-bye to all my employees. They were like family. I spent more time with them than anyone else. It was far more than a business to me. They *were* my family."

She stopped, tears forming. *Oh God, here come the waterworks again*. "I had to somehow just, I don't know, put it in a box, place it on the shelf. Do you know what I mean?"

Danielle shrugged.

"For me, the only way I could move forward was to do that, and Matteo went in that box as well." Hannah Lee stopped, and her thoughts turned to Matteo, about their last meeting, and the parking lot, *the almost-kiss*. "But now that I've called him, I can't stop thinking about him. I'm afraid I've been a terrible friend."

"Wait—I thought he was an employee," said Danielle.

"He was, but he could have been more than that. If I hadn't compartmentalized that part of my life, I'd have had Matteo as a friend after we both left the business. He could have been a good friend, a *best* friend—he was that kind of guy. I trusted him one hundred percent."

Danielle stared at Hannah Lee with raised eyebrows. "Whoa. What are you saying? I mean, I hear the word 'friend,' but I'm getting a whole different vibe—way more than friendship—when you talk about this guy."

Hannah Lee was surprised by the insinuation. "No, it's nothing like that," she said, as she felt warmth rising, her cheeks deepening in color. "Anyway, I heard later that he got married, and so did I. We are officially and forever in the friend zone."

Danielle stood. "Let's go, girlfriend."

"Where are we going?"

"We don't have to wait for Matteo. We're not exactly damsels in distress, you know. Let's do a little sleuthing of our own."

CHAPTER TWENTY-EIGHT

They pulled up in front of a construction zone—a full renovation of a large, rambling house in Carmel Valley. Three pickup trucks were parked haphazardly on the street. Workers milled about carrying tools or clipboards.

"Wait here," said Danielle, beginning to climb out of the SUV.

"No! I want to go with you," said Hannah Lee.

"It's dangerous here. You can't exactly get around easily, and the place is filled with boards and nails and—"

"I'm going with you," insisted Hannah Lee. She climbed down from the passenger seat, hobbled to the back door, opened it, and pulled out her walker.

Danielle rolled her eyes. "Okay, Ms. Independent."

Danielle walked confidently up to one of the workers and asked a question. He pointed toward the unfinished interior of the house. She waited for Hannah Lee to catch up, and they went in together.

A tall guy with long bleached hair in a low ponytail stood talking to one of the workers, giving instructions. He turned to the two women as they approached. "Danielle!" he called out, striding to them. He shook Danielle's hand, grinning.

"Did you come out here to show me up on my design work?" he said teasingly.

"No, Scott, not today," she said, grinning playfully at the good-looking guy.

"So, how can I help you?" he asked.

"I'm...Scott, this is Hannah Lee, Ryan Winn's wife. We were wondering if you could tell us where he's working today. He forgot to tell her. You know how it is," she said, oozing charm.

"Of course," Scott said, taken in by Danielle at her best. "But he's not working on a job right now. I saw him yesterday and asked him about it. He said he didn't have anything at the moment, that he's in between jobs." He glanced at Hannah Lee with an embarrassed expression.

Hannah Lee's stomach dropped. *How could Ryan not have a job right now?* He was gone all day, every day, and every evening as well—supposedly working on a huge, time-consuming job. This couldn't be true—something was wrong. But before she could ask, Danielle sent her a subtle signal to be quiet.

"Of course, he is," said Danielle, still oozing charm. "Things have been a bit hectic with them lately since Hannah Lee's accident. That's why I'm helping out. Um, do you happen to know when Ryan finished his last job?"

Scott looked puzzled. Danielle was trying her best to be subtle, but even Hannah Lee knew her line of questioning was odd. This would never work.

"It's just that Hannah Lee has been in the hospital, and she's in treatment, and their focus hasn't been on Ryan's work, it's been on her recovery," explained Danielle. "And, well, she realized today that she just had no clue what was going on with his work. She's feeling better now, so we thought we'd surprise him."

Danielle delivered this completely unbelievable monologue with a slightly flirty smile, one hair flip, and a hand on her hip. And, judging by Scott's look, he bought it.

Amazing, thought Hannah Lee. She'd never really seen Danielle in action with a guy, and it now dawned on her that she was watching a master at work.

"Sure. Wait a second," Scott said. He turned to one of the workers nearby and yelled, "Hey Kevin! When's the last time you worked on a job with Ryan Winn?"

The guy stopped, seemed to think about the question, then nodded. "It was, oh, about five or six weeks ago. Wait—it was definitely over six weeks ago because we did that condo in Monterey at least that long ago. Why?"

"No reason. Hey, thanks, man," said Scott as the guy nodded and walked away. "That's Kevin. He's one of Ryan's sub-contractors, one of the best at his trade, and he also works for me. Ryan never does a job without him."

Hannah Lee felt light-headed. This couldn't be true. Ryan, *with no job for over six weeks?* Ryan, leaving the house for hours at a time, not showing up at the hospital, all with the excuse of work that he apparently didn't have?

"Are you okay, Ms. Winn?" asked Scott.

"She's fine," said Danielle, taking Hannah Lee's arm and steering her out. "Thanks, Scott—you're the best!" she threw at him over her shoulder.

Back in the SUV, Hannah Lee slumped against the door. Her heart was heavy, her mouth felt dry, and she felt nauseated. Sweat began gathering on her brow again.

Danielle started the vehicle. "Let's get you home. You're white as a sheet. How do you feel?"

"How do I feel? I feel like I've been gaslighted for weeks. Maybe for longer than that," said Hannah Lee, choking on the words. Her insides began to rise, nausea rolling.

"Pull over! I'm going to be sick," she said. Before Danielle could fully stop, she threw open the door and left the remaining contents of her stomach on the side of the road.

CHAPTER TWENTY-NINE

Back at the house, Danielle sat in front of Hannah Lee, holding both of her hands, peering anxiously into her eyes. "I'm so sorry. You must be devastated. What are you going to do?"

Danielle stood and began pacing, gesturing wildly with her hands. "This is not good. He's lying to you. It's been weeks—*weeks* that he said he was on jobs while he stayed away from the hospital. *Weeks* he stays away now at night. I can only think of one good reason for that," she said, stopping in front of Hannah Lee.

"Actually, it's not a good reason, but it's the only reason guys do things like this. You know he has someone else, don't you? *He's having an affair.* That scumbag!"

Danielle's face flushed with anger. Hannah Lee sat quietly in shock, remembering Kenny, walking in on him with someone else. The possibility of Ryan having an affair—not a short fling, but something that may have been going on for some time—was too much to bear.

"Come on. Let's get your bags packed. We're getting you out of here. Now," declared Danielle.

"Ms. Winn? Hannah Lee?" The small voice interrupted them. Ella stood in the entryway of the bedroom wing. She wore a concerned expression.

How long had she been there? What had she overheard?

"Yes, Ella?"

"Is there more for the day?"

"No, you can go. Thank you for taking care of everything," said Hannah Lee.

They sat quietly while Ella gathered her things and departed.

"Great," said Danielle. "You know she's going to say something to Ryan."

"What? Why would she do that?"

"He hired her, didn't he? Housekeeper, maybe. Caretaker, perhaps. But *definitely* a spy, someone to keep tabs on you."

Hannah Lee's stomach twisted again. Could that be true? Could Ella be a spy for Ryan? Would she tell him whatever she overheard? She seemed so kind, so devoted to Hannah Lee after only a short time.

Danielle was suspicious of Ella and saw Ryan as a lying, cheating scumbag. Danielle didn't know about the accident—that it might not have been an accident at all. She didn't know the motivation for the possibly-not-an-accident.

Hannah Lee could hardly think it—*an attempt on her life.* If that's what it was. If Danielle knew, she'd never let Hannah Lee stay there. And she needed to be at home. She hunched over, holding her arms around her waist. Her mind whirled.

"Come on, we're going," persisted Danielle.

Hannah Lee looked up at her best friend. "No," she said slowly.

"What? That's crazy! You can't stay here with him!"

"I can. I need to. We don't know the full truth yet. He is my husband, and he deserves the benefit of the doubt. There could be other reasons he's staying away and telling me he's working when he's not. Sometimes, people who are out of work lie about it because it's embarrassing." But she didn't believe her own words. She knew, deep down, it was something far worse than that.

"Maybe. It's a long shot, but okay, I'll give you that one. Maybe he's out *not working* all day long, for *weeks*, because he's *embarrassed*," huffed Danielle.

"Please, Danielle. Let me handle this my way. Matteo's on his way here, and we'll get to the bottom of whatever is going on."

Danielle stood with her arms crossed, shaking her head at Hannah Lee. Finally, she grabbed her bag and headed for the door. "Please. Please call me if you need anything," she said before leaving.

❧

Hannah Lee jerked awake but didn't open her eyes. She was sprawled on the living room sofa, with a throw covering her, and her eBook nearby, presenting the picture of a wife who fell asleep reading.

Not a wife who was secretly waiting up for her husband.

She willed her breathing to remain slow and listened. Something had interrupted her sleep. Ryan tiptoed into the house, then gently closed, and locked the front door. Clearly, he was trying to avoid waking her.

She stirred, stretched, and opened her eyes in mock surprise. She hated being deceitful like this. "Ryan?" she called out.

"I'm here," he said, reversing directions as if he were coming from the bedroom.

"How long have I been here?" she asked, feigning ignorance about his whereabouts.

"A while. I thought I would let you sleep," he said. But he stood near the bedroom door, didn't come near her. "I'm just going to take a shower, and then I'll help you go to bed."

"Wait, Ryan. Where have you been all evening?" She peered at her watch and looked up at him.

"I was out on a job."

"Oh? Which job?" Testing him.

"Just another remodel. It's not much of a job, and I didn't think it was worth talking about." He turned around and headed into the bedroom.

Still lying, she thought with dismay.

157

Who is this man? Who did I marry? The questions swirled.

Danielle's questions earlier came to mind. How well did she really know Ryan? How could she love someone enough to get married yet not really know him? Even worse, how could she love and *feel loved* by someone she didn't know?

This wasn't the first time she'd experienced the unbearable pain of her belief in someone tearing apart. Like the impact of an earthquake, she felt the foundation of her marriage—the love, trust, and commitment she thought they shared—slowly crumble. Her chest hurt and her eyes leaked tears.

What kind of person does this—blindly trusts anyone who gives her the slightest attention? She should know better. After what happened with Kenny, how could she have taken a risk like this? She was terrible at love, a poor judge of men.

Then a far worse thought occurred. If she didn't really know Ryan, she didn't know what he was capable of doing. The cold finger of profound doubt touched her heart, and she shivered.

CHAPTER THIRTY

On my way to your house, read the text.

Not my house—meet me at the coffee shop, she texted back, providing an address.

Hannah Lee looked up at Danielle. "He's on his way."

"So, what's the plan? How are you going to do this?" Danielle asked.

"I'm not sure. Don't be offended, Danielle, but I need to talk to Matteo on my own. I don't want you in the middle of this in case it goes terribly wrong."

Danielle huffed out a breath. "Just a minute, girlfriend. I'm already in the middle of this, and I don't really care what happens if Ryan finds out. I can handle it, thanks very much."

Hannah Lee suddenly felt tired. "I know that. But please, let me have this time alone with Matteo. You can stay until he gets here if you want to meet him," she conceded.

"At the very *least*," said Danielle. "More tea?" she asked as she jumped up for refills.

"Sure," said Hannah Lee. While Danielle was gone, she looked at her text thread with Ryan. Nothing, as usual. He'd disappeared early that morning before she woke up. The persistent ache in her chest threatened to spread.

Focus, she told herself. *Remember, you don't really know the whole story.*

She felt achy all over, so she searched her bag and found an over-the-counter pain reliever. She quickly swallowed three. She'd graduated from a walker to a cane, thankfully. Hopefully, soon, the pain would be gone—the pain in her body, at least.

The door to the coffee shop swung open, and she looked up quickly. Not Matteo.

"Here you go. And I got you a scone to help settle your nerves. You look a little peaked. It's light and will hopefully make your stomach feel better." Danielle placed the scone and a cup of hot tea in front of Hannah Lee, who thanked her. Danielle nodded toward the scone with raised eyebrows.

Hannah Lee didn't feel like eating. Her eyelids felt heavy and her throat was dry. But she took a small bite to appease her friend.

"So, what does he look like?" Danielle asked, scanning the crowd.

"Well, he's medium height and has brown hair, brown eyes," she said lamely.

"Well, that describes about half the guys in here already," Danielle smirked, which annoyed Hannah Lee, but she let it go. She was tired, utterly exhausted. She'd barely slept after Ryan came home, after their surreal encounter.

Against her will, Hannah Lee felt her eyelids close.

∞

Soft laughter and conversation woke Hannah Lee. She was leaning against the cushions, slumped to one side, and the unmistakable feel of drool caused her to quickly swipe her hand across her mouth and sit up.

She felt slightly disoriented. A man spoke animatedly to Danielle, his back to Hannah Lee. He turned around. "Hannah Lee?" a deep male voice said softly.

"Matteo!" she cried, and then literally cried. Solid, muscled arms encircled her while she wept uncontrollably.

"It's okay. I'm here," he said.

She pulled away, wiping her eyes. "I'm sorry," she said. "I've never cried so much in my life, and just so you both know, I will *never* come back to this place again," she said adamantly, sniffling. Matteo and Danielle looked at each other, and stifled smiles.

"What?" she said.

"Hannah Lee. There's almost no one here but us," said Danielle, throwing up her hands. Hannah Lee quickly took in the almost empty coffee shop and sighed.

"Well, at least there's that," she said.

They seemed to have connected while she snoozed, Hannah Lee noted with a tiny stab of jealousy. Danielle had her flirty game on, and Matteo looked even better than she remembered. After a few more minutes of banter, Hannah Lee tilted her head toward the door behind Matteo's back, and Danielle got the hint.

"I'll leave you two to catch up," she said, standing, "but I expect a full report later," she said firmly, giving Hannah Lee a look. They made plans, and before leaving, she leaned down to give Hannah Lee a hug and whispered in her ear, "You didn't say he was drop-dead gorgeous!"

Hannah Lee waited while Matteo refreshed her tea again. She took another nibble of the now hard scone and quickly chewed and swallowed the dry bread.

Matteo sat down at an angle to Hannah Lee on the sofa and asked, "Where do you want to start?"

"First, we start with you." She sighed. "I want you to know that I'm sorry for not staying in touch. It's just that I—"

"It's okay," he said. He watched her closely. "The phone works two ways, you know. So does email. I've been busy, too. And I'm not mad at you, not at all. I'm glad you called."

"Tell me about you, your life since we last saw each other. You're married, right?" she asked. "I heard you and Chloe were expecting a baby, and that was a couple of years ago, so that means the baby is—oh, Matteo. What have I done? I've dragged you away from your wife and new baby!"

She felt terrible. How could she be so selfish?

"Relax, it's okay," said Matteo. His eyes took on a pained look. "I'll catch you up." He recounted the main facts of the past couple of years, but many of the details he seemed to gloss over. Hannah Lee didn't press, reserving her questions for another day, or perhaps, never.

❧

Matteo couldn't share all the details of some of the most painful moments of his life. Maybe someday he'd tell Hannah everything, but not now. He gave her the highlights even as he re-lived it anyway.

TWO YEARS EARLIER

After telling Matteo about the baby, Chloe focused on the next item on the agenda.

"I can't decide, sweetie. I thought, let's get married right away so I will still look stunning in my wedding dress. Or let's wait until after the baby is born, a couple of months later—after I've lost the baby weight. But I *have* to look amazing on my wedding day, Matteo. It's part of my brand. And we have to figure it out soon, or I won't have time, either way, you know, to, like, pull it all together."

She continued to talk as if he weren't even there.

Matteo's head spun with the baby news, and now the talk of weddings and dresses. Vaguely, he noted that she spoke in terms of 'her' wedding, 'her' choices.

There was nothing about him, his feelings, or what he wanted. It was simply understood—this was the next stage of his life as well as hers.

And he knew it. There was no way his Mamá would approve of him waiting months after the birth to marry the mother of her first grandchild.

He insisted that they marry as soon as possible. But what about a proposal? His mouth felt dry as he anticipated getting on one knee to ask this woman to marry him. A woman whom he didn't deeply love.

It was a priceless moment he'd thought of having one day but had recently allowed himself to fantasize about having it with an entirely different woman. The same woman who'd stopped their first kiss before their lips touched, who had never done anything to indicate that she returned his feelings.

Time to get on with real life. Or rather, life with a social media star. There were some interesting moments over the next few weeks, all captured on Instagram, Twitter, and various other social media platforms. Everything was orchestrated by Chloe and her P.R. army, with Matteo in the background, or foreground, depending on the publicity angle.

It all felt fake, beginning with the choreographed 'surprise' proposal at a strategically chosen restaurant that paid a large fee for Chloe's big event. Dinner with the most expensive champagne in the house was comped, of course.

Chloe chose the massive, flawless, diamond ring he presented to her, also heavily discounted, though he'd protested mightily. He could afford it, but she considered the discount another feather in her publicity cap, so he let it go.

Four weeks after looking at the small, plastic indicator that had changed his life, Matteo exchanged vows with Chloe in front of two hundred fifty people, barely any of whom Matteo actually knew.

It was during their honeymoon at a beautiful seaside resort in the Bahamas that Matteo began to suspect something was wrong.

CHAPTER THIRTY-ONE

Chloe only nibbled at breakfast, skipped lunch, and barely touched dinner. She looked pale, seemed tired all the time.

"What's wrong?" he asked the afternoon of their second day.

He'd asked her to go outside, sit under an umbrella on the beach with him. She declined just as she'd done the day before. She held her abdomen and complained of cramping.

Alarmed, Matteo asked, "When did you start feeling this way?"

"I don't know. An hour ago?"

But a short time later, she perked up, said she felt better, and everything seemed fine until the day after they arrived home.

Matteo waited patiently in their living room while Chloe dressed for dinner. He flipped through channels on the television. But after a half-hour, he looked up and wondered what was taking her so long.

"Chloe?" he asked, rather loudly. "I'm waiting."

No answer. Coco trotted into the living room, looking distressed. She barked twice, spun around, and raced back toward their bedroom. This was not like her; she normally wasn't skittish around Matteo. He got up to check on Chloe.

Walking into the master bedroom, he heard Chloe call out.

"Matteo! I've been trying to call you." She sounded like she'd been crying.

"What is it? Let me in," he said as he tried to open the bathroom door but found it locked.

"I can't right now," she said, openly crying.

"What's wrong?" he said, alarm raising the volume of his voice. "Are you okay?"

"No, I'm not," she said, wailing.

He pushed the handle down sharply and shoved the door again, but it wouldn't budge.

He looked on the top of the door frame for the tiny key. He grabbed it, stuck it in the little hole, and twisted. The handle turned, and he let himself in.

Chloe sat on the floor, crying. She looked up at him, tears streaking her cheeks, mascara running. He got a glimpse of blood on a towel on the floor, and large drops on the floor.

"I think I'm losing the baby!" she cried out.

He rushed to her, but she pushed him away. "Stop! It's so gross! Just get me some towels, quick!"

He did, and she insisted that he leave the bathroom while she cleaned up.

He waited in the bedroom until she came out slowly, holding her abdomen, and crawled up on the bed. She looked pale and sick.

"I'm calling for an ambulance," he said, picking up his phone.

"No, don't do that. Just take me to the clinic."

After arguing one more time, he gave in. He helped her to the car while she held her belly, occasionally moaning.

Later, the doctor called Matteo into his office and explained that she'd had a miscarriage. Matteo demanded to know what went wrong, what caused it. The doc insisted there was nothing specific, that sometimes the fetus develops incorrectly, such as with chromosomal abnormalities, and the body lets it go. He explained that a significant number of first pregnancies ended this way, but that didn't help Matteo's deep sense of loss.

Because the miscarriage was incomplete, they went home with medication, which Chloe took to cause her cervix to open and the rest of the tissue to emerge. It was a brutal process that took several hours. Chloe bled extensively and cramped fiercely. She cried, and Matteo watched helplessly, bringing her hot tea, cool towels, changes of pads.

The next day, as Chloe lay in bed crying, she declared that pregnancy was the most godawful experience, one that she never wanted to go through again.

Shocked, Matteo told her she was just reacting to the miscarriage, that she'd feel differently later. He couldn't imagine not trying again to have children.

"You can say that all you want, but you're not the one going through it!" she said venomously.

After that, their relationship deteriorated rapidly. Chloe withdrew emotionally and refused to talk about or process what had happened. She wouldn't even acknowledge the loss.

Instead, she told Matteo that since it was so early in the pregnancy, they couldn't really call it a baby. It was a mass of tissue that left her body, and thankfully, she was back in great form. She focused on her business.

Matteo silently grieved the loss of his first child, perhaps his only child and only chance to be a father. He knew his relationship with Chloe was deeply damaged, but he didn't know what to do. Instead, he focused on networking with some of his old colleagues, exploring opportunities to serve on boards, and searching for a new business to buy.

The inevitable day came when he arrived home and found Chloe packed and ready to leave, clutching Coco in her doggie purse. She was cold and matter of fact as she laid out her terms. She'd keep all her money from before their brief marriage and all of the value and rights to her enterprise. He'd keep his.

Matteo asked once if she'd reconsider. She stared at him with those beautiful blue eyes, raised her eyebrows, and said, "Really?"

As she drove away, he realized that he only asked her to reconsider because it was the right thing to do. But he wasn't disappointed by her negative answer. He was drained, empty, and void of feeling.

The divorce was fast and fairly painless since there was nothing to fight over. After that, Matteo occupied himself with sitting on a couple of boards. It kept him busy, but he lacked the strong sense of purpose he'd had when he and Hannah Lee worked side by side.

Then she called.

PRESENT DAY

"I'm so sorry," said Hannah Lee, placing her hand on his. How awful for Matteo. She felt terrible for him. But also, she felt terrible for herself. How could the two of them have gone from the high of selling the business, of taking away so much wealth, to this?

Of course, none of what had transpired in their lives had anything to do with money. *Or did it?*

He looked up. "Don't be. I deserve what happened. I didn't exactly marry Chloe with my heart in the right place."

"Of course, you don't deserve to lose a child," she said adamantly. "You'd have made a great father," she added. Realizing her faux pas, she quickly corrected, "I'm sorry—I meant, you *will* make a great dad. I'm sure you'll meet someone new and, well, you know."

"Sure," he said, but he didn't look convinced. Changing the subject, he said, "Now, let's get to you."

She took a deep breath and talked nonstop for the next hour. She told him all about how she met Ryan, got married, and felt happy until a few weeks before her accident. She told him about the mountain, the hospital, the physical therapy, pain, and now getting off of opiates.

She told him about not having clear memories of the weeks leading up to the accident.

She chose not to reveal what she'd discovered talking with her attorney, that Ryan knew all about the money. She wasn't sure it meant anything, and she didn't want to completely smear Ryan in Matteo's eyes.

She told him about Ryan's disappearance all day and evening since she came home from the hospital and about not being on a job. He listened attentively, stopping her at times to ask questions.

Then she got to the reason for calling him. After she explained, he nodded. "Why do you think Ryan is doing these things?" he asked.

"I don't know—it's completely out of character. At least, I think it is."

He sat silently, leaving the obvious unsaid.

"I guess the truth is that I don't really know him as well as I thought," she admitted, once again embarrassed at finding herself in this position. *How could she be so stupid?*

"You want to find out what he's up to, maybe even who he really is. I think I understand. But why didn't you call a private detective?" he asked. "Why me? I'm not experienced in things like this."

She bit her lip, hesitated. She didn't have a good answer, just a feeling. "I'm not sure. I think partly because this is a small town, and there's a good chance that if I hire someone, it will get out. But also, because I'm not sure I'm doing the right thing," she said, feeling the doubts resurface.

"If it turns out I'm wrong—if it turns out I've made a mistake, that Ryan hasn't done anything wrong, then I may well have wrecked my marriage for nothing. That scares me to death."

Matteo looked at her intently. "There's one thing I know about you, Hannah Lee. You have the best instincts of anyone I've ever known. If you think something strange is going on with your husband, there is. And if you need my help figuring out what it is, I'm here, and I will."

Still, she hesitated. This was a step she couldn't take back, one that would send her irretrievably down a path that would change her life.

Her instincts were not what they'd been when she ran her business, and that was the only way Matteo knew her. This was personal, and since the accident and the opiates, she didn't trust herself. She needed someone else's perspective.

She didn't have any other ideas for how to move forward. She couldn't continue to sit in her house, inventing things for Ella to do, doing physical therapy, and waiting for Ryan to show up.

"There is one more thing to consider," Matteo said. "I might find out things that you won't appreciate. I could be the bearer of bad news," he added, hedging.

"It's okay," she said. "I want to do this," she added, feeling the flutter in her chest, and realizing it wasn't going away anytime soon.

THE CLOSING

The assistant looked at the documents, scanning them for errors.

This Business Sale Agreement, hereinafter referred to as "Agreement," is entered into and made effective as of the date set forth at the end of this document by and between the following parties:

—, a corporation, incorporated under the laws of the state of Texas, who will hereinafter be referred to as "Seller," having a primary address at..., and—, a corporation, incorporated under the laws of the state of Delaware, who will hereinafter be referred to as "Buyer," having a primary address at...

The assistant recognized the buyer—a well-known international pharmaceutical brand.

WHEREAS, Seller desires to sell Seller's business and Buyer desires to purchase the business through the sale of assets

("Assets") involved in the operation of the Business...based on the terms and conditions stated herein...

NOW, therefore, in consideration of the promises and covenants...

On and on, through paragraphs of legal jargon.

Then, the money clause.

The Purchase Price shall not be assessed as a price per Asset and shall, instead, be assessed as an overall purchase price for a buyout of all of the Assets. The overall Purchase Price is...

The assistant's eyes grew wide. *What could be worth that much money?*

Later, the assistant carried all the documents into the conference room and approached the sharply dressed guy at the head of the table. The assistant placed them in front of the guy, who smiled, straightened his tie, and said, "Shall we begin?" There were several men around the table, all well dressed in suits and ties.

The assistant noticed a woman sitting to one side of the head of the table. She wore dark slacks and a cream-colored blouse. She had thick, wavy hair pulled back in a low ponytail and small glasses perched on her nose. She looked nervous—more like deer-in-the-headlights.

Must be a legal assistant.

She looked young, maybe in her mid-30s. She was cute, although not exactly gorgeous. She wore no ring on the third finger of her left hand, something the assistant noted.

The assistant hovered outside the glass-walled conference room, periodically summoned to make copies of documents and bring fresh water. At one point, the assistant took a position in the back of the room, within earshot, and with a clear view of all the players.

Once the closing got underway, it became clear that the woman was the seller. She read each page of the agreement closely, then handed it to the sharp-looking, bald guy sitting to her left, who also scanned it closely. Her attorney presumably.

The other suits around the table looked impatient, but she never once looked at them, didn't notice how her slow perusal of the documents affected them. They attempted small talk, but she ignored them, concentrating on the pages in front of her.

The closing took about an hour. Once the seller signed all the required documents, the notary officially stamped them with a seal.

At that point, the seller looked up and around the room as if coming back from a long journey, nodded once, and said, "That's it, I believe."

The seller walked around the table slowly, shaking every hand and thanking each person. She declined someone's offer for a celebratory dinner that night, claiming exhaustion.

She and her attorney left together. After that, the assistant ushered in the buyers, and the final steps of the closing took place.

The assistant knew there was anonymity to the day, that no one would remember the temp who showed up that morning to replace the full-time assistant who'd called in sick.

Awareness dawned later while watching television mindlessly that this was a unique opportunity, one that had provided some extremely valuable information. Thinking of the check—it was a crazy amount of money—and the seller. She'd seemed *nice*, something the assistant recognized with a trace of contempt. She was young and maybe a little bit vulnerable.

A plan began to form. It was a good, solid plan.

But then life got in the way. It was months before the temporary assistant arrived at the target destination.

CHAPTER THIRTY-TWO

RYAN, BEFORE THE ACCIDENT

The bartender set a beer in front of Ryan. He took a grateful long pull and grabbed a handful of bar nuts. It had been quite a day, filled with problems. Finally, a chance to sit and do nothing but stare at the game on the TV over the bar. No one to talk to or answer to, just himself. He let out a breath and began to relax.

"Hey, Ryan, buddy! What's up?" Uh oh, reverie broken. It was Scott, an acquaintance, and local general contractor.

"Hey, Scott. Just having a beer. You?"

As Ryan turned toward the voice, he was immediately captivated by the girl with Scott. She was slender, toned, and wore skinny jeans with a white tank top that showed off her tan. She was in her late twenties, with long, slightly curly blonde hair that hung down her back in a loose braid. She sported a rose tattoo on her upper left arm and wore no makeup.

She was stunning.

"Ryan, this is Kari. She's a friend of Lauren's who's new in town. We're having dinner tonight. Kari, Ryan."

Kari held out her slender hand to Ryan, so he took it. Immediately, he felt a frisson of energy. It went straight through his belly and below the belt. He shifted uncomfortably and let go of her hand. "Nice to meet you," he said.

"You, too," she said, flashing a movie star smile and looking him full on with eyes the color of the sea.

Scott had turned away and was scrolling on his phone. He turned back to Ryan and Kari. "Uh, oh. That's Lauren. She's coming down with one of her migraines and won't be joining us. I'm gonna have to bail for tonight, Kari."

She hesitated, and Ryan jumped in. "I'd be glad to show you around a little, maybe grab a bite," he said to Kari.

"Are you sure?"

"Sure," he said. "No worries, Scott. I'll take good care of her."

"Hey, thanks, man. I've got to run and get Lauren's meds before the pharmacy closes. I'll see you later, Kari." He turned and left in a hurry.

The bartender approached, asked Kari what she wanted. She looked at Ryan's beer and said, "I'll have what he's having."

⌘

After catching up on how they each knew Scott and Lauren—she, a college roommate of Lauren's, he from construction work—they sat quietly for a moment watching the game. Ryan was on his fourth beer and felt himself gradually losing his inhibitions.

"So, what brings you to this area?" he asked.

"I needed a change," she said enigmatically, gazing at Ryan. He felt that frisson again.

She stared at him for a moment, searching his eyes, then asked softly, "Have you ever wanted to just bail out on the life you have? You know, start over, do something totally different, find new people? Get out of the complications you have?"

He nodded slowly. He had, and in fact, he'd done it.

"I, like, had to do that," she said. She suddenly looked a little sad, and Ryan's heart tugged a bit.

"What was it?" he said.

She looked down, bit her lip, looked up, and gave him a penetrating stare. "Why are you asking? Are you just making conversation, or do you really want to know?"

Her question was so direct that for a moment, Ryan was blown back. *Did he really want to know?* Yes, he did, suddenly very badly. He reached out, touched her arm, felt a slight shock, and pulled his hand away slowly.

"Whatever it is, if you feel like telling me, I really want to hear it."

She leaned toward Ryan, lowered her eyelids, and said, "I had to get away from a guy." She sat back, gazed into the distance, and began talking. Her eyes reflected fear, pain, and sadness as she spoke.

"He was wonderful at first—pursued me non-stop, sent flowers, took me out, did, like, everything a woman wants. By the third date, he told me he loved me and wanted to marry me. I thought I loved him, too."

She paused, wiped away a small tear in the corner of her eye. "Are you sure you want to hear this?"

"Yes, I do. If you're okay with talking about it," he said, wanting her to continue. He was enthralled by her and didn't want their time to end.

She nodded, then continued. "One night, I went out with a couple of girlfriends. It was our tradition; we'd been doing it forever. We went to a nice bar, got our martinis on, had a great time. All of a sudden, my phone blew up with text messages. It was him. He said he was watching me. Followed by little hearts.

"I texted back some hearts. I stupidly thought that was sweet. I looked around and saw him, sitting a few tables away from the bar, staring at me. He gave me this little wave." Her hand lifted briefly, mimicking.

"I was totally charmed. But I will never forget what Megan, my best

177

friend, said. *That's not normal. He's a stalker. You'd better get away from him now while you still can."*

She turned back to Ryan and gave him a penetrating gaze. "Are you sure you want to hear the rest of this? It gets pretty hairy."

"I do," he said, and really meant it.

"Let's get out of here," she said. "Where can we go to talk?"

After Ryan paid the tab, they walked out into the Monterey twilight, and he drove her to a home he'd remodeled. It was in the final completion stages, and he used his passkey to get in. They sat in the empty living room on the beautifully finished hardwood floors. Ryan gave her his jacket, and she gratefully draped it around her shoulders. She resumed her story.

Kari wound up bailing early on her girlfriends that night, deciding to hook up with the guy, Eric. It was a passionate night, their first time to sleep together. The next morning, he was extra sweet. Then, over breakfast, he started asking her questions.

Who were her girlfriends? What did they really do on girls' night? Had she ever met a guy on one of those nights and hooked up? How many guys had she slept with?

Offended, Kari left in a huff, thinking she'd break up with him. But within two hours, a huge arrangement of flowers showed up at her work with an apologetic card attached. That afternoon, he texted asking to see her that night.

She did, and that was the start of their pattern. Things would go great for weeks at a time, and then, something would set him off. *Some guy stared at her too long in a restaurant. She spent too much time texting one of her girlfriends—were they talking about him? Was it really a girlfriend? Or was it a guy?*

She kept her phone password-protected so he couldn't see her texts and calls, but this became an ever-increasing issue. *Why was her phone password-protected? What was she hiding?*

Eric went in and out of these jealous moods. For days at a time, he was loving, sweet, passionate—everything a woman wanted. Then, his mood descended into a dark place, and that's when he'd show the ugly side.

One day, she decided she was going to 'start over'—wipe the slate clean and reassure Eric by giving him more access to her life. She erased all of her text threads with friends, some of which contained references to him. She also deleted the contact information for all her past boyfriends (there were quite a few). Then, she removed the password from her phone.

That night, as a 'gift' to Eric, she presented her phone to him, telling him he could freely check it at any time. She was happy with her decision, believing it would relieve his anxiety.

Instead, he took it, scrolled through her contacts and texts, and threw it back at her violently. He could tell she'd deleted most of the information, which only made him angrier. *Clearly, she had something to hide. Did she now own a burner phone with the real information? How stupid did she think he was?*

They sat at a local restaurant the night it happened. He left abruptly and drove away. Her phone lay shattered on the floor, and other patrons averted their eyes. She had no way to call anyone and no ride home. Humiliated, she asked the waiter to call a friend whose number she knew by heart.

⚮

Kari stopped talking for a moment. Ryan waited, not touching her but wanting to, desperately.

"This is the worst part, and I'm afraid to tell you," she said, tears welling in her eyes.

"Only if you want to," he said softly.

She sat for a moment, silently brushing away tears. The house where they sat had disappeared to Ryan. He saw only one thing—her, all of her.

CHAPTER THIRTY-THREE

She told him everything about that night. How, after she found her way home, dropped off by her friend, she fell into bed, exhausted, and cried herself to sleep. In the middle of the night, she felt a presence in her room. Before she could react, he was on her. He ripped off her tee-shirt and panties and forced himself on her. She tried to stop him, but he wouldn't. It was rape, plain and simple.

The next morning, he apologized profusely. She tried to break up with him at that point, but he cried and told her the sad story of his childhood. How he grew up with little contact from his mother, no father, sent to live with an emotionally cold aunt, yada, yada.

She felt sorry for him at that point. But that wasn't the worst of it.

She felt humiliated by the rape and didn't think anyone would believe her, so she didn't tell anyone, even her closest friend, Megan. After that, the idea of leaving him became increasingly difficult. She felt isolated and broken.

✂

Kari stopped talking. The last light of the evening sun streamed through the windows lighting up her eyes, and she turned them to Ryan. Her lips were full, flushed from emotion.

Ryan felt a surge of anger toward this animal of a guy. *Who was he?* Maybe he could find out, do something about him. "That guy deserves to get hurt, badly," he said heatedly.

She drew back a bit.

"How did you get out of it?" he asked gently, holding back his anger.

"The last straw was when he threatened my friend, Megan. We hadn't gone out in weeks, and she was texting me every other day, asking how I was. I made stuff up—I was sick with a cold, I had a headache. Finally, she texted that she was on her way to my house to see if I was okay, so I said yes. She came over, and I told her about everything but the rape.

"At that point, I wasn't even sure if it was rape. Nothing like that had happened again, and he'd begun saying things like, *we got carried away*, and *sometimes sex is a little rough*. So, at that point, I doubted my own sanity. I wasn't even sure of my perceptions about that night."

Another surge of anger coursed through Ryan's blood. "What did Megan say about the rest of it?" he asked tightly.

"She said she was going to help me get away. We started hatching a plan that night at my apartment. We got on my laptop and started doing some research, trying to figure out where to go."

The door flew open, and there stood Eric, face flushed with anger.

"Well, if it isn't the douche bag," said Megan sarcastically. "Just one thing you need to know before the doorknob hits you on the butt on your way out— you're never going to hurt Kari again."

He grabbed the computer, saw the search window, knew what it was. He grabbed Megan roughly by the arm, frog-marched her out of the apartment. She struggled but was no match for his strength. He shoved her so hard at the doorway that she stumbled, almost fell.

FREE FALL

*"I will kill you, little girl, if you ever come near Kari again and try to
break us up!" he hissed before slamming the door in Megan's face.
He turned to Kari, advanced on her menacingly. "And as for you,"
he said in a low voice.*

❦

Kari's lip trembled as she fought back tears. "That night, he told me in
no uncertain terms what he would do to me if I ever left him. Basically,
I'd end up in small pieces in the ocean. I've never been so scared in my
life."

"What happened to Megan?"

"She was terrified. But she told me later she was still going to help
me get away. That's when I knew I needed to leave on my own, make
it look like she had nothing to do with it. So, I staged a friend break-up.
I sent her a handful of foul texts, telling her that I didn't want anything
to do with her again.

"I spent the next few days sucking up to him, so he'd calm down,
and made my exit plans. I took all my savings out of the bank, in cash. I
sold my car, got cash for that too. I cut up all my credit cards. When I
left, it was on a bus, ticket paid for in cash. I left no electronic trail."

"Do you think that's enough? Could he find you again?"

"I don't think so. He'd have to hire a private detective, and I don't
think he'll do that." She stopped. She drew her knees up to her chin,
wrapping her slender, bare arms around them. "You know what the
worst part is?" she whispered, voice breaking.

"No, what?"

"That I lost Megan." She began to cry.

Ryan moved next to her, put his arms around her, and drew her
into his chest. She sobbed, clinging to him. He held her closer, tucking
her head under his chin. It was tempting for him to nuzzle his nose in
the sweet fruity scent of her hair.

She gradually stopped crying but remained nestled in Ryan's arms.
"That's the first time I've cried about any of this," she said. "I've been

183

so focused on getting away, I haven't let myself feel any of it."

She looked up at Ryan, now just inches away from his face. He felt all of his molecules dancing.

Her eyelids lowered, and she moved closer to him, her lips almost touching his. She breathed in and out once, and he smelled an intoxicating combination of beer and spearmint.

He stayed perfectly still as if she were a small, wild animal, who might run away. And who needed to feel totally safe.

She slid her hands around his neck and brought her lips to his. She kissed him slowly at first, then with more passion. He kissed her back, but let her lead.

Their kissing intensified.

Minutes later, Ryan lowered her to the floor on his jacket.

Never once did he give a thought to Hannah Lee, not then. Not until much later.

❧

That night, Ryan drove Kari to Scott and Lauren's house, where she was staying temporarily. He turned off the engine, and they sat in his truck. She asked him quietly. "You're married, aren't you?"

He nodded, looked ashamed.

"Figures," she said, as she swung open the passenger door of the truck and got out. "Just my luck—I finally meet a dream guy, and he's married," she said, blowing out a breath and hugging herself against the cold night air.

"At least tell me I'm not one of your many affairs or one-night stands," she said, looking up at him.

"Of course not," he said. "Look, I know it sounds unbelievable, but...I want to see you again."

She was quiet, looking down. He got out of the truck, went around to her side, took her in his arms. She let him hold her.

"Please. I can't stand the thought of not seeing you again, and I know that sounds bizarre since I'm married, but—" He hesitated for a moment, then, impossibly, blurted, "Do you believe in soul mates?"

"I'm not sure," she said hesitantly.

"I do, and I think I just met mine. My wife is a good person. It's just that I met her at a weird time in my life, and I think I, I probably married her for the wrong reasons."

"Isn't that what all married guys say to their girlfriends?" she asked lightly, teasingly. But her face reflected the vulnerability of someone waiting for the ax to fall, and it wrenched him.

He blew out a breath. *Of course, she'd say that.* What reason did she have for believing him?

But she did say 'girlfriend.'

"Look, I don't know how I'm going to do it, but I'm going to show you I mean what I'm saying. It's just that it's complicated with my wife, and I know that's lame, but please, just give me a chance."

"Maybe," she said, sliding out of his arms. She turned and walked away.

He stood there watching her go, knowing his life had just changed.

CHAPTER THIRTY-FOUR

Ryan's hands shook as he pressed Kari's phone number. It rang repeatedly, and her voice mail picked up.

"Hi, this is Kari. Tell me everything." Then a throaty laugh, and a beep. He hung up.

He called her several times that day. No answer.

Look at me, he thought. *I'm acting like her stalker boyfriend.*

They'd been seeing each other over the past two weeks. Now, it appeared she'd ghosted him.

He got out of his pickup truck, walked onto the worksite, leaving his phone behind. Maybe if he couldn't see it, he'd quit trying to call her.

Hours later, he wrapped up work for the day, sat in the truck, and powered up his phone. His heart lurched when he saw the voice message indicator. He pressed the icon, listened.

"Hi, it's me," she sounded a bit breathless. "I'm sorry I didn't get your calls earlier. I had to think things over. I'm still not sure about all this. I, well, I'm not sure what to do." There was a long pause. "I guess I'll see you around." Another pause. "Oh, I got an apartment today.

187

There wasn't much to move in, so, anyway. Bye."

He sat back, feeling his heart thudding. *She called.*

Did she want to see him? Did he want to continue seeing her? What about Hannah Lee? He hesitated. He got out of his truck, began walking. He started to run, couldn't stop. He ran recklessly along the two-lane highway that wound through Carmel Valley, not caring when random cars approached. He passed by the beauty of the rolling hills, the cypress trees. But he didn't really see.

He ran until he was completely winded. He didn't know where he was. He stopped, put his hands on his knees, hung his head, and drew in deep breaths. Sweat dripped off of his forehead, ran down the back of his neck. Slowly, his heart rate normalized.

He held up his phone—one bar. He punched the button to return Kari's call.

"Hi," she said.

"What's your new address?" he blurted.

⸎

Later, they lay entwined in her bed, facing each other. He ran his hand through her hair, touched her face, gazed into her eyes.

"This is crazy," she said.

He kissed her and began touching her. She playfully pushed his hand away, but he persisted until she began to moan. As they made love again, she looked into his eyes and whispered, "Please, don't hurt me."

He made love to her urgently, feeling something new, something he'd never felt before with a woman. That time, at the moment of maximum ecstasy, he told her, "I love you," the words pouring from deep within his body and soul.

Later, as she slept, he thought of Hannah Lee, how deeply hurt she'd be. He'd told her he loved *her*, was committed to her. But this was different.

He had no idea what to do about Hannah Lee, but one thing he knew for sure. He would do anything to keep Kari in his life.

~~~

"Tell me about Hannah Lee," she said softly, her head on his shoulder, slender hand playing with the hair on his chest as they lay entwined.

"No, that's not right," he said.

"Yes, it is. I need to know about this amazing woman who got you first."

He squirmed, feeling uncomfortable with Kari for the first time. She gently held him in place with her legs, wrapped herself more firmly around him.

"Oh, no, you don't. We need to have this conversation. You know everything about me—it's not fair that I know so little about you, especially your wife."

He sighed. This was bound to happen. They'd been seeing each other for weeks, off and on. He never knew when he'd get a chance to be with her. Some days, she avoided him, saying that she wasn't sure about their affair. Other days, she called him over, urgently pulling him in the door, saying she'd missed him terribly. They'd make love exquisitely.

On their off days, he felt like he was going crazy. He didn't want to be like the stalker ex, so he only called a couple of times. But he obsessed about her, wondered what she was doing. He fantasized about seeing her again, holding her and kissing her, making love.

He couldn't blame her, not really. He was the married guy, committed to someone else. Of course, she'd eventually get tired of his excuses. *It's complicated. I can't just leave, not right now.* It was only a matter of time before he'd lose her. He couldn't bear that thought.

It was time to give her the whole picture of his life and his marriage. It was only fair that she knew, so she could make her decision about him with a full deck of cards. Might as well get it over with.

"You're not going to like me when I'm finished," he said.

She looked up at him with her amazing eyes and said, "No way."

"Way," he said, but he wasn't joking.

So, he told her everything. He told her how amazing Hannah Lee was—her intelligence, her ability to make things happen, her business, and her success. He told her how he'd met his wife, how they got married after only a few short months.

Then he told her things about himself, who he really was—all of it.

She went still as he talked. Her legs were no longer entwined with his, and her expression was closed off, distant. No surprise.

She pulled herself up in the bed, her back against the pillows, the sheet pulled up to cover her breasts. She ran her fingers through her hair, looked away.

"I told you," he said, a deep heaviness in his chest.

"Told me what?"

"That when I was finished, you wouldn't like me anymore."

She shrugged. "This isn't about like or not like. This is about...soul mates."

Huh? But he didn't say anything, just sat up next to her and faced her. His heart thumped. He felt terribly exposed.

She fixed her gaze on him intently. He tried to prepare himself for the blow.

"What you've told me makes everything clear. I thought you were, like, this golden guy—*perfect*, too good for someone like me," she said softly.

"What? I'm so far from perfect—" he began.

"That's what I mean. It turns out you're like me—not perfect after all." She leaned in, kissed him slowly, pulled back. "We're the same. And now I know we're meant to be together."

His heart felt like it would burst as he gathered her in his arms, clung to her, and, embarrassingly, cried. He didn't know what he would have done if he'd lost her by telling his real story.

It was the first time he'd ever revealed all of himself, the full, unvarnished truth. It felt amazing and terrifying. It felt free. *He* felt free.

That night, for the first time, when he said, "I love you," she said it back.

CHAPTER THIRTY-FIVE

"Now," said Kari. She began to lope toward the drop-off, and Ryan and his instructor followed. His heart raced, and he was sure this was the stupidest thing he'd ever done. He fixed his eyes on Kari, who was already airborne, as his feet lifted off the ground.

Ryan squeezed his eyes shut for a moment, then opened them. He was hundreds of feet in the air. He drew in a huge breath, blew it out, then really looked. He took in the magnificent vista of Carmel Valley stretched out below—the lush, rolling hills dotted with trees and homes. His pulse raced with exhilaration.

He sat slung back in a harness that wrapped under and around the lower half of his body, his legs dangling. The instructor, Bruce, sat close behind him, guiding their slow glide with two looped hand grips that attached to slender lines feeding upward to the sail over their heads. Ryan gripped the crossbars on either side of the harness.

"You okay, buddy?" asked Bruce. He spoke loudly to be heard over the wind.

"Yeah!" said Ryan. And, amazingly, he was.

When Kari suggested they go paragliding, at first, he said no. No way would he go up in a flimsy flying apparatus, his life in the hands of some unknown instructor, no matter how experienced.

But she'd rolled her eyes at him, one hand on her hip. Then she sighed and nailed him right in the heart. "Fine. I'll find some other guy to fly with. I mean, it's only *my world*, something super important to me."

She was right. Paragliding was her hobby; one she'd indulged in for years. Somehow, she found something in it that fueled her life. He couldn't expect her to be in his life unless he was willing to be in hers. So, he acquiesced, although not without dread. She flew solo, but Ryan had to fly tandem with an instructor.

Now, he understood why Kari loved it. It was extraordinary—the wind flowing underneath the canopy of the sail, the complete peace, aside from the occasional instructions from Bruce. But no mechanical sounds, no traffic—none of the usual loud pulse of humanity.

The most amazing part was the visual experience. On his right, a small road zig-zagged down a hillside, at the top of which sat a series of homes, each of which, he thought, had far-ranging views of the valley.

Straight ahead, he could see the marine layer that sat on the ocean near Carmel. In the foreground, rolling hills were dotted with the occasional tall conifer but mostly deciduous trees such as sycamore, cottonwood, and willow. Working in construction had given him a certain familiarity with all types of wood.

Ryan felt totally alive, his senses tingling. Here, he had an unparalleled birds-eye view. He'd flown many times, but commercial airlines flew at 30,000 feet, offering an ill-defined view of earth far below. He'd flown once in a helicopter, and it afforded this kind of view, but the noise of the rotors was deafening, and the small, plastic windows were slightly foggy.

This was magnificent. He couldn't soak in the experience enough. His grin spread, and he felt himself opening to life itself.

Occasionally, he saw a small amount of acreage devoted to growing grapes, no doubt destined for a winery. He let himself imagine for a moment that one of those small farms belonged to him and Kari.

He fantasized about the two of them tending grapes by day and sipping wine by night in front of a fireplace with a view of the valley. He saw them together, every night, wrapped in each other's arms. There'd be no need to get up at midnight, dress, drive home, and sneak into bed with another woman.

Gradually, they glided closer and closer to the ground, and before he wanted it to be over, Bruce gave him instructions for landing. All too soon, Ryan felt his feet on the ground, and the solidity of the earth once more. But Kari waved to him from a distance as she landed, and his heart lifted. She made her way over to him once she unstrapped.

"Was that amazing or what?" she asked, her cheeks glowing, her smile wide, and her blue-green eyes lit with joy. He swept her into a huge hug and whispered in her ear, "It was beyond anything I thought it would be. Thank you." But the instructors were looking at them, so he quickly released her. Her smile dropped.

❦

Ryan picked up and looked at his cell phone for the umpteenth time, swore softly at the blank screen. No call, no texts. He paced the floor in a hotel room. It was nice, but the view was even better—the stunning coastline and the promise of a gorgeous sunset.

He'd told Hannah Lee he needed to scope out a project out of town, that it would take all day. He wanted to have dinner with the potential client, so he wouldn't be home until the following day.

What he craved was uninterrupted time with Kari. They'd been seeing each other for weeks but always in short snippets of time, never a full night together.

He glanced at the ice bucket with chilled champagne, chocolate-covered strawberries nearby. He quickly typed a text—*where are you? Waiting here—it's been two hours.*

He unmuted the television and mindlessly watched a hockey game. He heard a vehicle pull up outside and sprang out of the bed just before he heard the knock at the door. He pulled it open, and Kari rushed inside. She threw herself in his arms, shaking.

"What's wrong, baby?" he asked, pulling her shoulders away so he could see her tear-streaked face. She shook her head wordlessly, tears welling in her eyes. He led her to the bed, and they lay down together.

He held her tightly, asking again. "Tell me, please."

She whispered. "It's him. Eric. He found my cell phone number somehow, and he's been calling."

Rage burned in Ryan's chest. "Let me see your phone. I'm going to stop this," he said vehemently, sitting up.

"You can't find him that way," she said quickly. "He's using a burner phone. There's no way to trace it. And he's too smart to send a text. It's only phone calls. He never leaves a message."

"Then, how—"

"The first time he called, I didn't know it was him, so I picked up," she said. "He warned me that I had to take his calls, or else. I let some of them go, but then I picked up, so he wouldn't get mad."

She took his calls so he wouldn't get mad? Ryan felt enraged and bewildered. "But I don't get it. Why would you take his calls? So what if he gets mad! Let him get mad; that just makes it easier to nail him, charge him with something, right?"

She looked down, her cheeks pink. When she looked up, she had a thousand-yard stare. "You don't understand."

"That's right—I don't! You're letting him manipulate you."

"Really." She went silent.

"Kari, this is crazy. We have to do something, call the police."

"You mean, *I have to call the police*, don't you? Because you can't. They'd want to know who you are, who I am to you, why it matters to you," she said pointedly.

He felt instantly ashamed. Once again, he was letting her down. He got off the bed, paced around the small room.

"I will report him," he said firmly. "I just have to figure out how to do it anonymously, so they don't know who I am. I can give them a false name—that's one way. I can say I overhead you in a bar, and found out your name, and I'm reporting what I heard because I don't think you'll do it—you're too scared of the guy."

"Ryan, that's ridiculous. The police won't fall for that. They'll keep asking questions and expose the lie."

"No, it can work," he insisted. "I have to do something."

She sat up, and she stared at him. She got off the bed, took her phone, stuffed it in her bag, and went to the door, her back rigid.

"Wait! What are you doing?" Ryan asked, rushing over. He placed his hand on the door to hold it shut as she twisted the knob to open it.

She faced him. "You know what, Ryan? This is really not your problem. You have your—your wonderful life with Hannah Lee, and yes, I know it's 'complicated,' but my problems are not yours."

She twisted the knob again, giving him a hard stare. He moved his hand, let her open the door.

She turned around again. "Anyway, I'm just a good time for you, right? We had a great vibe, but maybe it's time to move on." She left while he stood mutely, watching her go.

He was left with nothing but the scent of her hair, which hung there for a moment with a subtle essence of flowers. He picked up the champagne, popped the cork, watched the foam run down his hand, then took a drink from the bottle, shaking with impotent anger. He poured more, walked out onto the balcony of the room, and continued to drink.

❧

Two hours later, he heard a knock on the door through the haze of too much alcohol. He'd fallen asleep on the bed, still in his clothes. He dragged open his scratchy eyes, let them close again, and rolled over.

The knock turned into pounding, and then he heard her call out. "Ryan? It's me." And then, "Fine. I'm leaving since you don't want to—"

He scrambled up, flung open the door, and there she stood—tall, lithe, and somehow so vulnerable. The exterior light created a halo around her hair.

She threw herself in his arms, whispering, "I'm sorry. I shouldn't have left like that. Are you mad at me?"

He pulled her into the room, onto the bed, and made love to her, whispering how much he loved her, how glad he was to have her back. He felt the way a heroin addict must feel, getting a bump, the high coursing through his veins.

The shaking stopped, and he felt safe again. They fell asleep wrapped in each other's arms and legs. He couldn't get enough body contact, enough emotional enmeshment.

The next morning, he woke alone, and found a short note on her pillow.

"Had to leave. Let's talk later. Love you, K."

CHAPTER THIRTY-SIX

PRESENT DAY

Matteo parked the rental Ford two streets away from Hannah Lee's house, killed the engine, and got out quietly. He walked carefully but casually, paying attention to the possibility of neighbors, careful not to be seen.

He approached their house, aware of the gravel crunching underfoot. They lived on a hill in Carmel Valley, with winding country lanes that advanced in elevation, no shoulders, or curbs.

He checked the address and knew he'd arrived as he spotted Ryan's Ford F-250 Limited. *Nice*, thought Matteo. He made his way to the truck, leaned over, and quickly placed a small device on the inside of a rear wheel well.

He stepped back quickly, turned, and walked leisurely down the road. Step one complete, but he felt a bit slimy. He'd never done anything like this, and deep down, he believed in the basic premise that people are entitled to their privacy.

Behind him, a door opened.

He glanced over his shoulder in time to see Ryan, or a guy who fit the description Hannah Lee had given him, open the door to the truck, climb in, start it, and back out of the driveway.

Crap. What if Ryan drove this way and spotted him? But Matteo had parked uphill from their house, and Ryan drove downhill in the opposite direction.

❧

Matteo sat in the car staring at the cell phone app linked to the tracker. He waited until the indicator showed that Ryan was several blocks away, then started the vehicle and proceeded. It was easy to follow the tracker. At one point, the red dot on Matteo's smartphone screen stopped and didn't move. He pulled over and waited. The dot stayed put, so he continued.

Matteo pulled into the parking lot of an apartment complex. Since the tracker wasn't that precise, he couldn't be sure exactly where he might find Ryan's truck. After driving around, he found it parked in front of one of the apartment buildings. Matteo pulled into an open spot. Ryan's truck sat parked three spaces down.

The complex was nice: two-level buildings with wood siding, lots of pathways, and lush landscaping. Trees formed canopies over the pathways.

He sat for ten or so minutes, wondering if Ryan had made a brief stop for some reason and might emerge from the building. After more than fifteen minutes, he decided to leave after making a note of the address.

❧

Later, from his room at a local motel, Matteo booted his laptop and logged into the tracking website. Leaving that window open, he opened a new one and began another kind of research.

There were countless websites that offered the ability to find out anything about anyone, as long as the name you had was a real person. For a small fee, you could view a person's life history, including criminal records, marriages, divorces, bankruptcies, and more.

Many people thought it was safe to put everything about

themselves on social media, and those people were the easiest to stalk. Unfortunately, people up to no good either didn't post on social media or invented false identities, making it more difficult to access their real information.

If Ryan was his real name, Matteo could find out everything he wanted to know about him. If not, if he'd assumed another identity, that would be an entirely different path and a far more expensive one.

He logged into one of the more popular sites for finding the history of a person and put Ryan Winn into the search box, no specific location. Immediately, over 1,300 records popped up. He narrowed the search to Carmel and then Monterey. Only five records for Ryan Winn. One showed a definite linkage to Hannah Lee.

So far, it appeared that Ryan Winn was his real name.

Next, he searched again, narrowing to Texas. This time over 90 records appeared. Hmmm. He'd have to find a way to search with more specific criteria. No problem. He had an unlimited budget, so he began using it.

⊰⊱

Four hours later, Matteo stood up and stretched. He hadn't eaten all day, though he'd been drinking lots of coffee. His stomach growled, so he decided to check on Ryan's current location. He opened the window on his computer for the tracker and saw it was moving.

Fifteen minutes later, Matteo drove past Ryan's truck in the parking lot of a restaurant just as the driver's side door opened. He whipped into a parking spot and pulled up his digital camera with telephoto lens to focus on the vehicle.

Ryan walked around the truck and opened the passenger side door. Out stepped a beautiful blonde who reached up and kissed Ryan before turning to walk toward the restaurant. Ryan took a quick look around and followed her at a discreet distance.

Gotcha.

Matteo's blood boiled. The guy was definitely cheating on Hannah Lee.

He envisioned her face, the look of doubt, her fear of offending her husband, her concern over wrecking her marriage by *checking up on him.*

And that solidified his plan to find out everything he could about Ryan, and to put together such a detailed, compelling case that Hannah Lee would never again suffer from doubt about her husband.

Matteo no longer felt slimy; he felt justified. If he couldn't have her in his life, in the way he wanted, at least he could help her move on with her life, away from this scumbag. That gave him a large measure of satisfaction.

Matteo followed them into the restaurant, at a distance. At the hostess stand, he requested the open table closest to Ryan and his mystery date. He lucked out and snagged a seat one table over from them, caddy corner. It was close enough so he could study their faces and body language. And maybe more.

He quickly put in his drink order. Then he pulled out earbuds, put them on, and opened the special app. Placing the phone on the table with its microphone pointed toward their table, he pretended to study the menu while watching Ryan and the blonde out of the corner of his eye.

He adjusted the app to filter out background noise and picked up their voices. He knew he'd picked up the right table because the audio on his headset matched the movements of their mouths.

CHAPTER THIRTY-SEVEN

"This is a bad idea, Kari," said Ryan. "What if someone who knows me sees us?"

Kari. Now I have a name, thought Matteo. A first name. Not much good without the last name.

"So what?" scoffed Kari. "We have a cover story."

"What, that we know each other from paragliding? Remember, we're trying to keep that on the downlow. In case she starts wondering how she ended up on that mountain. Which I'm still wondering as well," he finished, giving her an odd look.

Kari's body language changed. She stiffened, and when Ryan reached over to touch her hand, she pulled it away. "This is the second time you've said that. Go ahead. Why don't you just get it off your chest?" she said coldly.

Ryan blew out a breath and slumped, looking defeated. "I'm not questioning you," he said. "I'm sorry. It's just that—in spite of everything, the last thing I want is for her to—"

"I know," said Kari. "Me, too."

The last thing he wants is for her to...what? Thought Matteo. *And what did these two have to do with Hannah Lee's paragliding accident?*

He felt a cold sensation in his heart, followed quickly by anger. He had to stop himself from doing what he wanted to do, which would have left Ryan on the floor of the restaurant. That would be one way to get quick answers, but it might not be the most helpful to Hannah Lee. He squirmed and continued to listen.

Their lunch arrived, and for a moment, neither talked as they ate.

"What are we going to do?" asked Ryan.

"I don't know," said Kari, looking at her plate.

"We need to do something about Eric," he said pointedly.

"There's nothing we can do," she said, stabbing her salad with her fork. "I have to figure something out. It's my life," she said with finality.

Ryan stared intensely, grabbed his wine glass, and took a gulp. "Fine. Maybe you're right."

She looked up quickly, searched his eyes, her fork poised above her plate. Suddenly, her body language changed. She moved her eyes to Matteo, who quickly shifted his eyes down to the menu. But not before her striking blue-green eyes had bored into his and he'd seen her expression.

"Let's get out of here," she said, laying down her fork. "I'm not hungry."

"Me neither," he said, signaling the waitress. He got the check and quickly threw cash on the bill. They both stood and left.

⚬✺⚬

Matteo watched them through the window of the restaurant. They stood by Ryan's truck for a long time, talking intently. At one point, Kari gestured toward the restaurant.

Busted. He knew it, and now he'd have to take extra precautions to complete his mission.

They couldn't possibly know his identity or his purpose, but now, he couldn't show up at Hannah Lee's house or check out Ryan up close. That was too bad. He wanted multiple avenues to understand the guy and meeting him personally would have been one of the richest.

FREE FALL

Matteo was a student of body language and verbal expression. He'd taken multiple management courses that dealt with how to understand people. Plus, he'd always had the ability to read people. Or so he thought.

After witnessing Ryan with his little honey, Matteo had no doubts. Hannah Lee's husband was having an intense affair, not a fling. Even worse, it was beginning to look like Hannah Lee's accident might not have been an accident.

He needed to know more about Ryan, and he needed to find out about Kari. He had to be more careful, so they didn't realize what was happening. He hoped that whatever suspicions Kari had would blow over.

And who was Eric?

Knowing if he left now, it would only confirm suspicions, Matteo ordered lunch. He did a little bit of searching using his phone and dug into the burger and fries when they arrived.

❧

Back at the motel, Matteo booted up the tracking website. Ryan's truck was back at the apartment building, and now he was fairly sure who lived there. He looked up the management company for the apartments, dialed the number, and waited.

"Hello," said an efficient female voice, "this is Monterey Management."

"Yes, I'm interested in the apartments on Surfside. My friend, Kari, lives there. I'd like to know if you have an available unit like hers."

He heard a keyboard clacking. "Yes, of course. Kari Montague. She lives in one of our one-bedroom plans. We have one other available right now. When would you like to see it? We're here all afternoon."

"Um, tomorrow is better. How about 1:00?"

"Yes, of course. Your name?"

He gave her a made-up name and phone number, then signed off. It was amazing how much you could find out with a question that sounded like you knew something.

Bingo. Now he could begin part two of his research.

203

❦

Hannah Lee waited, sitting in her living room. She and Ryan called it the Window Room because of the amazing views. She gazed out at the canyon, now shadowed by dusk. Her heart felt heavy, and she felt more alone than ever before. Not the way she'd felt alone years before when she was single. Back then, being alone was a respite from long, stressful days.

Now, it was different. There was something terribly isolating and frightening about feeling alone while married, while supposedly joined with someone who'd vowed to stand by her, to love and protect her.

Her phone rang, and she picked it up.

"Hello," she said softly. She listened for a moment. "Yes, okay. No, I'll meet you there."

She hung up and pulled up a ride-sharing app. After entering the information, she rose, took her cane, and made her way out of the house and into the night.

No one saw her leave because no one else was there.

CHAPTER THIRTY-EIGHT

Matteo and Hannah Lee sat together in First Class, but Hannah Lee declined the offer of alcohol and food. Instead, she sipped hot tea and sat quietly with her eyes closed. She was tired, but mainly she wanted to avoid conversation.

What do you say to the guy who'd uncovered so much about your husband—information that exposed numerous lies? Information that showed Ryan had lied about everything important, about who he was.

She felt humiliated and bewildered at the same time. She'd missed so many clues, so much that might have warned her.

The night before, they'd sat at the coffee house while Matteo showed her everything he'd discovered. First, her husband was no doubt cheating on her with a beautiful blonde.

Second, almost nothing about his background was true.

His father wasn't in the military, and his parents were very much alive. That's where they were going. Hannah Lee was about to meet her in-laws, the ones who were supposedly dead.

That morning, she'd told Ryan she had to leave on business. There were details about her old company to sort out, in keeping with the consulting agreement she'd signed years before. She told him she was headed to Texas to do that. It was the first lie she'd ever told her husband.

Luckily, her destination was in Texas. Oddly, it turned out that Ryan grew up not terribly far from her former business.

Ryan had moved away from Texas many years ago. He'd lived in various parts of the West coast, leaving a trail of failed business ventures in his wake.

While she didn't know all the details of Ryan's financial history, a disturbing portrait emerged. It appeared that he had a history of getting into ventures that promised rapid wealth while taking high risks with his own or others' money.

He'd been in everything from multi-level marketing to failed franchises. He had a large, unpaid student loan debt. He'd bankrupted out of at least one business in the past.

Hannah Lee felt bad for him. It was a form of gambling for some people—the pursuit of wealth, not through hard work and diligence, not through following a passion, but through scheming.

No wonder he was so negative about her idea of opening a shop in town. Now she could see his overall malaise about work, his resentment toward her for not needing to work.

The familiar sense of guilt surged, about achieving her wealth while others did not. She'd never aimed for money, not at that level anyway. The satisfaction of solving problems and running a business well—that was what got her out of bed each day. She'd enjoyed the journey, most of the time, and never dreamed the endpoint would be what it was.

❦

Stepping out of the airport terminal, the Texas heat took away Hannah Lee's breath. She'd forgotten how hot it could be in August, having grown accustomed to the mild Carmel weather. She almost lost her resolve, not because of the heat, but because of the fear. Not knowing the truth was awful, but the prospect of knowing was terrifying.

She stopped and asked Matteo if they were doing the right thing.

He spoke to her with a quiet urgency, explaining again the things he'd discovered and the dark theories he held.

It didn't seem real, her life now, where it was headed, and the deep uncertainty that was now her daily experience. She'd built her new life on an overriding sense of being on the right path, on a belief that if she tried again, if she trusted again, it would turn out well.

But deep down, she knew there was something wrong with her. Despite all of her accomplishments, and from the outside they were numerous, she was fundamentally insecure. She didn't trust herself. Look at all the mistakes she'd made personally.

~~~

Matteo pulled the rental car to a stop. Hannah Lee peered ahead, checking the address. "This is it, or, rather, that's it," she said tiredly, pointing.

"Okay, let's go," said Matteo, starting to open his door.

"No, Matteo, I need to do this myself," she said. "Please," she added, laying a hand on his arm.

He sighed and relented. "At least let me pull up closer," he said, but she declined. She didn't want Matteo sitting there watching every move up close.

It was awkward, but she managed to move up the street using her cane. The lots were tiny, the mobile homes not far apart. She was surprised at how anchored they appeared, like regular houses. Most of them had a modicum of landscaping, with freshly mowed postage-stamp lawns, and siding that looked freshly painted.

Her destination was at the end of the row—siding painted sky blue, white trim, and a few small bushes around the foundation. It looked older than some of the other homes, less tidy, more tired. The paint on the outside trim peeled a bit, and the grass looked mostly dead.

She reached the door and knocked. She could hear a television inside, turned up loud. No one came to the door, so she knocked louder.

"Just a minute!" someone yelled.

The door jerked open, and a man who appeared to be in his seventies, wearing a faded tee-shirt with an old-fashioned Budweiser logo, stood in front of Hannah Lee, frowning. He was bald on top, with an untidy fringe on the sides and a silver mustache that needed trimming.

"Who are you?" he asked gruffly.

"Who is that?" called a woman's voice.

"I don't know!" he yelled back, still staring at Hannah Lee.

"I'm...my name is Hannah Lee Winn," she said, practically stuttering.

"*Winn?*" he said, screwing up his face. "Is this some kind of joke?"

He started to close the door, but she put out her hand to stop him.

"No, I'm afraid it's not a joke. I'm Ryan's wife, your daughter-in-law. Please, may I come in for a few minutes?"

He stared hard at her for a moment, then mumbled something before motioning for her to enter.

Once inside, she waited for her eyes to adjust. The interior of the mobile home was dark, lit only by the ambient light of a large, flat-screen television, faced by two faded dark blue easy chairs. One was empty, and the other was overfilled with a large woman.

She wore a faded shirt with a floral design and large, flowing cotton pants. Her hair was salt and pepper, somewhat curly, and messy. On the TV tray next to her sat a glass filled with what looked like iced tea.

Next to her chair was a walker.

While slightly shabby, the home was neat and tidy. Careworn, perhaps like the people who lived there, she thought.

There was no obvious place for Hannah Lee to sit, other than to take the man's chair, but he promptly sat in it. They both stared at her, the television still blaring. It was tuned to a home-shopping network.

"Um, thank you for talking with me. Do you mind lowering the volume?" she asked. Her normal, confident voice was missing, but she managed to speak over the TV. The man picked up the remote and muted it.

She took a breath and began to speak.

CHAPTER THIRTY-NINE

She turned to the woman first. "You're Joann, right?" she queried, to which the woman said, "That's right, and who are you?"

"I'm Hannah Lee, Ryan's wife," she answered, extending her hand to Joann, whose eyes had gone wide with shock. The woman made no move to shake her hand, so she dropped it.

"And you're Fred," she said with more certainty.

"That's right."

The two of them looked at each other and shrugged. Fred took over the conversation. "So, why are you here without Ryan? Where is he?"

Hannah Lee didn't know how to answer that, so she hedged.

"Um...I'm not sure. He...he and I haven't been in touch lately, and there are some things that...don't quite add up. I...I really came here to find out more about him because..." she sighed. This sounded completely stupid, and as she spoke, she could see their faces shutting down.

"Oh, shit," she said uncharacteristically. "Can I sit down somewhere?"

"Get her a chair, Fred," said Joann pointedly.

Fred got up slowly and dragged over a wooden chair from the small dinette nearby. She lowered herself in it and tried to gather her thoughts.

"Look, you're Ryan's parents, and I don't have any right coming here under false pretenses, so I'm just going to be straight with you. Ryan told me a lot of lies when we met, and one of them was that you were both dead. Clearly, that is not the case," she said, beginning to feel beads of sweat gather on her face and chest.

Fred looked at her, his face neutral. This information did not seem to surprise him. Joann looked away, her eyes beginning to tear up.

"So, I'm here because I want to understand my husband, why he lied to me, and if there's anything else I need to know to help me decide if I want to stay married to him. I'm hoping you can help me."

She didn't say *and help me figure out if he wants me dead.*

Fred scratched his belly and spoke after a moment. "First thing we can tell you is that we haven't seen or heard from Ryan in years. We didn't know he was married, but that's no surprise. He's always had an odd way of, let's say, putting his own twist on the truth."

"What do you mean?"

Fred looked at Joann, who nodded.

"If Ryan didn't like the truth, he made things up. He started doing that when he was a kid. If someone asked him what I did for a living, he didn't want to tell 'em I worked in a machine shop, so he told the kids his dad was a banker, or an engineer, or whatever he thought sounded important.

"He went off to college—got a scholarship—and when he came home on break, he never brought any friends around. Once, his phone rang, and I answered. A girl asked for him, I said he was in the shower, and she started to talk really friendly to me. She thanked me for offering her a summer internship *at my law firm.*"

He scoffed. "That's just one of many examples. Ryan can't deal with the truth, so he makes things up."

"He had a lot to deal with," Joann said, looking pained.

"Yeah, so do lots of people, but most people don't go around making up everything about themselves—they *deal* with it," said Fred, like it was a closed book.

"What is it Ryan had to deal with?" Hannah Lee asked.

Fred looked at Joann, who nodded again, but this time she spoke.

"We adopted Ryan when he was almost three. He was the son of my cousins' daughter, who had him when she was barely sixteen. The father never wanted anything to do with her or him after he found out she was pregnant.

"They tried to raise their grandson, but Julie—my cousin—and her husband had health issues. She had a bad heart, and he had severe back pain. They thought their daughter would catch on to mothering, but she never did. As Ryan got older, she went out more at night with friends, leaving the baby with her mother.

"One day, my cousin Janet had a heart attack. They rushed her to a trauma center, but she only lived a few more hours before the second attack took her. The baby was home with her husband, who could barely get around because of his back issues.

"After that, he got his daughter to agree to adoption, and we raised our hands. We couldn't have children ourselves, and we wanted to raise Ryan. But he was two and a half by then, and he'd already been through a lot."

Joann teared up, and Fred reached over to pat her hand. She pulled a couple of tissues from her sleeve and blew her nose.

"We did our best, but he was never quite right. When he got old enough, we told him he was adopted and who his real mother was, but he didn't seem surprised. He was so bright, so smart, I'm sure he'd found all the papers by then. He was always digging into things, curious about everything. His only question that day was about his real father."

"And who was that?" Hannah Lee asked, not sure if she should.

"He was a student at the university in town. At least, that's what Ryan's mother told us. But who knows? He could have been anyone. She didn't put him on the birth certificate, and no one ever showed up claiming to be Ryan's father. I mean, he had sex with an underage girl."

Joann sniffled, and Fred stared at the silent television screen.

Hannah Lee sat quietly. "Thank you for talking with me, telling me these things. I'm sorry if this was difficult for you," she said gently to Joann, who nodded while blowing her nose again.

"You know the worst thing?" she said, tears running down her face.

"No," said Hannah Lee.

"He's ashamed of us. We know it. Look at what he did—*he told you we were dead*." Her voice broke, and Fred's face darkened.

"That's it—she's been through enough," he said, standing up, the clear signal for Hannah Lee to leave.

She did, after thanking them again. Fred followed her out.

"Wait. If you can, would you tell Ryan we'd like to see him? His mother, Joann, wants to see him." He said it the way someone begs for water in the desert, with no belief that it will actually happen. But compelled to ask.

"Of course."

As she made her way down the sidewalk to the street, blinded by tears, she felt rather than saw Matteo. He pulled up in front of the mobile home, parked, and ran to Hannah Lee. He put his arms around her, and almost carried her to the car.

Hannah Lee sobbed as they drove away, feeling her entire body shake with withdrawal—from opiates, and from the man she thought she'd married. Tears fell, also, for the little boy who didn't know who he was, who didn't want to acknowledge his own family—the people who had rescued him and given him a home. The people who clearly still loved him.

Even so, how could he have lied to her so freely? The stories about his military dad, the tragic story of sitting in the hospital after their 'accident,' waiting for them to die. With her, pretending to be traumatized by their deaths.

Who was Ryan?

Even scarier—who was she? Was she really the woman who'd married a complete stranger, with no hesitation?

And what really happened to her that day on the mountain? Was it an accident? Or was it something else? And if so, *who wanted her dead?*

Terrified and broken-hearted, she believed she knew.

CHAPTER FORTY

BEFORE THE ACCIDENT

Kari poured another glass of wine, handed it to Ryan. He sipped, watching her, basking in her beauty. Things felt calm between them, settled. Maybe they could get back to the way things were, to their old routine. Then he wouldn't have to decide. At least, not right now.

After placing two salads on her small dining room table, Kari sat down and sipped her wine. Ryan began eating.

"I want to meet her," she said.

He stopped with a forkful of salad halfway to his mouth. He set it down and looked up at her. She looked totally, unbelievably serious. *"What?"*

"I think you heard me. I want to meet her—Hannah Lee. I want to know who she is. I think then I might understand what it is—her hold on you."

Ryan's stomach dropped. Appetite gone, he pushed back from the table, and took a large gulp of wine. Then another.

"Stop," she said, taking the wine glass from his hand. "Look, I'm not some bunny-cooking nut job," she said, sighing. "I'm not going to do anything or say anything to blow your cover. I just want to meet her, that's all."

"I know that," he said, but he wasn't sure he did. His stomach churned.

She was quiet, and he couldn't think of anything to say.

"You know, if I wanted to, I could figure out how to meet her without your involvement."

His head snapped up.

"But I'm not going to do that," she said quickly. "I want your involvement—in fact, I want you there. And, I think it has to happen in some way that appears natural. Not some weird, contrived moment at the grocery store or something like that."

She sat for a moment, tapping a fingernail against her wine glass. "How about paragliding?"

"*What?* That's crazy—she's not athletic, not the outdoor-loving type. She wouldn't go." He couldn't think of a more unnatural thing to happen—his wife and girlfriend meeting. He felt a sense of panic, a sense of the edges of his life fraying.

"Where is this coming from?" he asked, stalling, feeling out of control.

"I've been thinking about it a lot," she said. "I feel helpless—your hidden lover, waiting for some sign that this could go somewhere, that we might actually be together someday, out in the open, like a real couple."

"We will be together, I promise you," he said swiftly.

"Really?" she said deadpan.

"We will, but...things are complicated with me and Hannah Lee. I just need more time. I need to get my head around the issues."

"What issues?" she asked.

"The issue that all the money is hers and none of it is mine," he said, looking at her. "But you sort of know that already," he said. "I told you my background. I don't come from money."

"What about your business?"

"I do okay, but nothing that would match what I have with Hannah Lee."

"What about divorce?" she persisted. "California is a community property state, isn't it? Doesn't that mean you get half?"

"Not in our case. The money was all hers when we married. I knew I wasn't going to get any of it, except by enjoying the lifestyle." He felt guilty. How could he explain his feelings for Hannah Lee to Kari? He didn't want to say that it was more than the money; that would just set her off.

"That sounds awful," he said. "It sounds like the only reason I married Hannah Lee was for her money. I will admit, when I realized how much it was...yes, it was too tempting. But she's a good person, and I really do care for her."

Kari's face grew pink. She threw down her fork, stood, and took their plates to the kitchen. He flinched when she threw them into the sink. There was something about Kari that sometimes gave him a chill, and not in a good way.

After a couple of minutes, she came back to the table, her face composed. That was almost worse than the small signs of anger—the rapidly shifting moods that he saw more frequently as their relationship progressed.

She sat, chewed her lip, and looked thoughtful. "How much?" she asked.

"How much what?" he said, puzzled.

"How much money are we talking?" She asked in the same neutral way someone might ask about the weather.

Most people would rather chew off an arm than discuss money— their own or anyone else's. It was a greater conversational taboo than the subject of sex. But Kari didn't hesitate to ask the biggest question of all, the one Ryan would never have wanted to answer. It was private—it was Hannah Lee's business.

He sat quietly, then stood up, walked into the kitchen, and got a glass of water, stalling.

"Oh, I see. You don't have any problem knowing everything about me, every tiny, terrible detail. But it's not okay that I'm asking questions about you."

217

"That's not about me; it's about Hannah Lee. It's personal to her."

"It is about you—you said it's the reason things are so complicated that you can't just leave." Her eyes welled up with tears. "I just want to know what the issues are, so we can figure them out together."

What was it about Kari? He couldn't stand to see her cry, couldn't bear thinking that he might hurt her. Mostly, though, he couldn't bear the thought of losing her.

He told her the number, watched her eyes grow wide, and instantly regretted telling her. But he couldn't put the toothpaste back in the tube. Later, they talked about how she might meet Hannah Lee.

Ryan knew he'd entered a bizarre world—a strange reality in which he agreed to things he'd never have imagined doing. He'd told Kari about the money, and now, he was actually planning a way for his wife and lover to meet. But he felt pulled forward, dragged into a destiny that he'd never planned. He felt jumpy inside, locked in some kind of emotional no-man's-land between stark fear and wild excitement.

He couldn't stop the forward trajectory. He wanted out. He didn't want out. He felt the adrenaline and knew he couldn't stop.

THE DAY OF THE ACCIDENT

Ryan drove silently, not talking, watching the highway. Hannah Lee sat silently in the passenger seat. He cut his eyes over, caught her watching him. "Are you excited about flying today?" he asked.

"Sure," she said. "I'm excited because we're finally doing something together."

She hesitated when he gave her a questioning look. "I, well, I've been a little worried about us. We don't seem...as close as we were. I think paragliding together has helped, a little, but—"

"We're fine," he said quickly, the subject closed.

"No, Ryan. We need to talk, really," she said, her voice stronger this time.

"What is there to talk about? We're fine, I told you," he said.

"No, we're not," she said softly. "You know we're not fine. You're gone all the time, out all hours, traveling to supposedly do work, but you turn off your phone. I can't reach you. Most of the time, I don't even know where you are."

She sounded a little desperate, not at all like Hannah Lee, the perpetually strong woman who never needed anything. Or anyone. Especially him.

"We're not doing this now," he told her, trying to close the conversation.

"Then, when? When are we going to talk? You're always gone, and when you are home, you're not really there," she said.

"Not now. Let's just enjoy the day," he said. "I promise everything will be okay." He touched her hand as he drove, smiled at her. She visibly relaxed, smiled back.

It was embarrassing how quickly and easily he could get her to trust him—just a word or two, a touch of the hand, a smile.

He never had to work hard to win Hannah Lee's affection and love. She was open-hearted and trusting. She wasn't the challenge that Kari was.

But he couldn't help it. He was drawn to Kari in a way he'd never felt with Hannah Lee.

The day had finally arrived. Now, he was bringing the two of them together.

He'd talked Hannah Lee into paragliding lessons, almost hoping she'd put her foot down and refuse, but she acquiesced. He felt guilty he'd persuaded her so easily.

Surprisingly, she took to it, at least enough to continue with a handful of additional lessons. After that, his guilt eased, and he enjoyed going with her, seeing her wide-open smile after landing, the glow on her face.

For a while, Ryan imagined continuing his life with Hannah Lee. When he thought about that, he felt peaceful inside, whole. He felt good about himself again, the way he felt after they married and settled into their life together. After he put aside thoughts about the money.

But she clearly sensed something. Knowing she was suspicious, he felt the wholeness of their life together slipping away.

What had he done?

His hands gripped the steering wheel, his knuckles turning white.

CHAPTER FORTY-ONE

Hannah Lee felt indescribably free, the wind holding her aloft, the deep blue sea gleaming as it stretched to the horizon, the mountains hugging the shoreline. She had a sense of déjà vu as she sailed high in the sky, filled with the thrill of the beauty of the California coastline, from a vantage point that couldn't be found any other way.

The breeze tugged at her unruly hair, but she didn't care. She closed her eyes briefly, blissful. Then, she opened them, and everything changed.

She felt a tug, something not right. Then, she felt herself in the worst possible scenario—a free fall—nothing between her body and the rapidly approaching ground below, nothing to offer a safe landing.

Then, a jerk, a hard pull, as her back-up parachute unfolded, but she was too close to the ground. She anticipated the crash, heart pounding, breath caught in her throat, realizing she'd never land safely.

She screamed, and the sound of her own voice woke her.

❧

Someone pounded on the door connecting to the room next to hers. It was Matteo, calling out, "Hannah Lee! Let me in—are you okay?"

She tumbled off the bed, still dressed in sweats, and made her way, limping slowly. She opened the door, but only a small crack.

"I'm okay. Go back to sleep. I'm so sorry I woke you," she told him.

Concern laced his expression. "Let me in," he said.

She hesitated. The last thing she needed right now was another person feeling sorry for her, comforting her in her pitiful state of emotional collapse. But she needed to talk to him. "You might as well," she said, opening the door wide. "I remembered some things."

They sat on the sofa, Hannah Lee on one end, Matteo on the other, facing each other. She poured water and gulped it for a moment, feeling a sheen of sweat on her forehead and chest.

"I had another dream," she said, breathing a bit fast. "But after I woke up, I realized it wasn't just a dream. It was memories, I'm sure of it now."

⤝✦⤞

In the weeks leading up to her accident, Ryan went out more often, on weekends in particular, but also in the evenings. She thought nothing of it. She was independent as well.

Often, she met Danielle for dinner and wine, staying out late talking and laughing. She'd text Ryan and get back a thumbs up. She liked that they weren't joined at the hip, that they had a high level of trust and separate interests.

She knew Ryan often met with clients in the evenings and often worked on the weekends. She was comfortable with all of it, never concerned. One particular day was different.

Ryan came in that evening looking flushed, almost euphoric.

"Hi," she greeted him.

"Hi," he said, not looking at her directly. He went to the kitchen and got a beer, popped the top.

"How was your day?" she asked, genuinely curious.

"Great. How was yours?" Spoken like an afterthought, not like he really wanted to know. She stood, walked to him, put her arms around him, and tilted her head up for a kiss. He pecked her lips. He seemed wooden, his arms by his side rather than wrapped around her. She dropped her arms.

"I have some work to do," he said, turning away.

"Okay," she whispered to his back. She couldn't put her finger on it, but she knew something had shifted. She felt as though something had happened that affected her, without her knowledge, like a subtle sea change.

That became a pattern. It wasn't that he was gone more than normal. It was something else, a leaning away from her emotionally, less eye contact, and perfunctory kisses instead of the warmth they'd shared in the past. They made love far less frequently than their norm, and when they did, it was mechanical, unfeeling.

Then they stopped making love altogether, and he began offering excuses. She tried once or twice to entice him, but when her efforts were rebuffed, she stopped. She wasn't particularly assertive about sex to begin with, so a little rejection was enough to crush her desire.

After that first, odd evening, distance grew between them like a stream fed by mountain snow runoff in the spring, growing gradually wider and more dangerous, flooded by rushing water. Hannah Lee was afraid to wade across the emotional divide, to ask, to question, to risk being swept away.

She became afraid to challenge and uncharacteristically allowed herself to live in hope—hope that this was a temporary anomaly and would clear up on its own, with no help from her.

She'd learned in business that she had to be careful not to let herself be deluded by what was sometimes jokingly referred to as 'hope-ium,' the balm of people who flounder, whether in business or in life.

But the thought of confronting Ryan, of asking him to explain, made her shake inside. Then one day, he approached her with an astonishing request.

That day, Ryan told her, "I have a new hobby. I haven't told you because I wasn't sure I'd like it or that I'd stick with it, but I have." He told her about paragliding, that he'd been taking lessons, how amazing it was. His eyes glowed as he talked, and her heart lifted.

"I want you to try it," he told her.

Her first instinct was a solid 'no,' but she covered it up by asking lots of questions. *How safe is it? Where do you do it? How do you learn how to do it? How many accidents happen? How does that happen?* The kinds of questions she asked in business: who, what, where, how.

Hannah Lee wasn't athletic. She walked briskly every day outside because she loved it but hadn't seen the inside of a gym in years.

She didn't yearn for adventure. She had an active mind, one that found reflection, reading, and learning stimulating enough. She enjoyed travel, but not that often, preferring the quiet of home.

But with his request hanging between them, she knew she couldn't say no. This was the only opportunity in recent weeks to connect.

They made plans for her lessons.

❧

Hannah Lee stopped talking. She felt exhausted, strained from trying to remember all the details. Now her mind fogged again, leaving her frustrated. She couldn't remember the flying event on the coast with the new person. She had small flashes—someone standing close to Ryan.

She fell back against the pillows, let her eyelids close for a moment. "I can't remember things clearly after that," she said to Matteo. "I just have these glimpses of someone, and I can almost see her, the instructor that day."

"What can you see? It doesn't matter if it's clear or not. Just your impressions," Matteo asked, studying her intently.

"I can kind of see someone with blond hair, rather tall, with an intense look about her." She closed her eyes, trying hard to visualize. She opened her eyes and slumped.

"That's it, I'm afraid," she declared. "I don't remember what happened that day, or any of it until I woke up in intensive care." She felt mentally and physically drained. "I think I need some sleep."

"Of course," said Matteo.

"Wait—I do remember the guy who taught me how to paraglide," Hannah Lee told Matteo. "Just not his name."

Her instructor was a guy who took her tandem flying and taught her the basics. He introduced her to the sport with reassurance. *Paragliding is as safe as any other outdoor activity such as skiing, mountain biking, or climbing. It requires learning and practicing the right steps to ensure safety.*

She learned that accidents were rare, almost always caused by carelessness on the part of beginners who failed to follow simple guidelines for pre-flight checks and other precautions or who took unnecessary risks.

She took a handful of lessons, enough to qualify as a novice pilot. She qualified to fly solo, but she didn't feel ready, preferring tandem with Ryan. The comforting feel of his body behind hers, his strong arms guiding their flight, gave her the feelings of love and care she'd missed.

She felt safe with him.

Then one day, Ryan suggested they drive up the coast to an area that wasn't frequented by other paragliders. He told her, "It's a great site, and you can fly solo—you're ready for that."

She felt a bit unsure about it, but Ryan insisted. He said they'd meet someone there, someone who worked part-time as an instructor, who was highly experienced.

CHAPTER FORTY-TWO

RYAN, THE DAY OF THE ACCIDENT

They pulled into a parking area at the top of a cliff overlooking the beach and got out of Ryan's truck. It was a dirt lot, in a remote part of the coast, with only one other vehicle—Kari's.

She leaned against the driver's side door, waiting. As Ryan and Hannah Lee approached, his heart thudded viciously, threatening to jump out of his rib cage and expose everything.

He suddenly, desperately wanted to avert the oncoming train wreck. He grabbed Hannah Lee's elbow, stopping her. "I'm not sure this is such a good idea. You've only had a few lessons," he said. Over her shoulder, he could see Kari frowning.

"It's okay," said Hannah Lee, smiling up at him. "I know you're nervous about my first solo flight, but I'm really okay with it. I feel ready."

He let go of her elbow.

Kari pushed off of the car, walked up to Hannah Lee, and introduced herself. Her smile was friendly and warm. She said something about paragliding that made Hannah Lee smile. That somehow broke the ice, and after that, they talked freely.

To Ryan's astonishment, they seemed to actually connect in that baffling way women have—as if they'd always known one another.

Kari went about the job of getting their equipment ready, checking and testing lines. She chatted with Hannah Lee as she worked, in a natural and friendly way, occasionally flashing a knowing smile. Hannah Lee seemed relaxed, excited about the day's flight.

Miraculously, Kari seemed calm, okay with all of it. He tried to catch her eye and give her an encouraging smile, but she averted her eyes.

Ryan allowed himself to believe that everything was okay, that it was perfectly fine for these two women to meet. That it wasn't so odd, not so strange, really. They were both important to him, so maybe Kari was right. Maybe it was good for them to meet.

Maybe after today, he'd gain some clarity about what to do with his life, how to handle loving two women, or perhaps how to choose between them.

Yes, this would be a turning point for him, a day of gliding peacefully in the air toward a coastline destination, and also toward understanding—finally—the right course to take in his life.

✂

Kari gave final instructions for their flight, reminding them of their target landing spot on the beach far below and further down the coast. When Kari gave the signal that the wind was high enough and from the right direction, Hannah Lee turned, tugged her sail, which began to slowly rise, and loped downhill.

Her sail filled with wind, and she let out a little 'whoop' as it lifted her off the ground. Ryan waited until she was far enough away and launched.

She glided ahead of him and slightly below, having already sailed to a lower altitude. He couldn't see much—she was a small figure in his field of vision.

He took the opportunity to allow his mind to drift, to think of nothing—not Hannah Lee, not Kari, not his mounting life issues and the inevitable decision ahead.

228

It was a perfect California day. Normally, the dense marine layer hid this stretch of coast, but today, the sun had miraculously burned it away in time for their flight. The Pacific Ocean stretched away with a deep blue shimmer.

The beginnings of sunset tinted the cotton ball clouds with deep crimson and purple along the edges. The Santa Lucia mountain range pushed up dramatically from the shoreline, where they'd launched and over which they sailed. The mountains were covered in forest—Douglas fir, coast redwoods, and ponderosa pine.

The beach below—tan sand stretching for miles in both directions, blue/white surf rolling in—was unoccupied. It was easy to imagine that this was some remote place on the planet, far from humanity.

His spirit soaked up the beauty, the peace, and the glide. He closed his eyes for a moment, tuned into the sounds of the wind.

When he opened his eyes a few seconds later, it took a moment for things to register. He scanned around but didn't see Hannah Lee in the air. It was far too soon for their landing destination. Had she somehow managed to sail behind him?

He couldn't make a sharp turn, so he made a slow one, scanning in the other direction. Nothing.

He swung back the other way, searched the air. Nothing. His heart thudded.

He searched the beach and saw nothing, but then...there! In the forest, far below him, something bright blue, perhaps a strewn parasail or maybe the backup parachute. The trees impeded his view, and he couldn't be sure, but it could be Hannah Lee, crashed, on the mountain.

Ryan tried in vain to get closer, but he was already on his descent. If he tried to land on the mountain, he'd likely crash as he came in contact with the trees. There was no clearing to aim for, and even if there were, the wind could be unpredictable.

Panic-stricken, he continued the flight until he landed on the beach. It seemed to take forever, but at last, he felt his feet on the ground. He pulled out his cell phone, but there was no signal. *Of course, there wasn't.* This was a remote stretch of Big Sur—no nearby towns, no reason for cell towers.

He looked up and down the beach but couldn't see any sign of Hannah Lee, Kari, or anyone else. He couldn't remember the agreed-upon landing spot in his state of panic.

He started walking, leaving the parasail and gear on the beach. It was almost two hours later when he reached their launch site. Finally, there was one bar on his phone, and he frantically called 9-1-1, doing his best to describe where he thought Hannah Lee had crashed. Kari stood nearby, silent, eyes wide.

CHAPTER FORTY-THREE

"Don't worry, Mr. Winn, we'll find her. We're going to get her off of that mountain as soon as possible." The first responders did their best to reassure Ryan, but he knew that every passing hour meant diminished chances of survival. He thought about Hannah Lee—was she unconscious, lying on a mountaintop? Was she in pain? Did she know they were looking for her?

Kari was gone. As soon as he made contact, they agreed it was best for her to leave. Periodically, he received a text message.

What's going on? Have they found her? Is she okay? I feel terrible.

Did she? He felt a surge of anger. Kari had put Hannah Lee's equipment together. Did she do something to make it fail? Would Kari really feel bad if her lover's wife—*his incredibly wealthy wife*—didn't make it back from this adventure?

He felt numb, paralyzed by fear that Hannah Lee might not survive, or that she'd be disabled in some terrible way. And it would be entirely his fault. He'd created all of this, set everything in motion. *If she died, he was a murderer.*

❧

Ryan's eyes felt like they had sand in them. It had been hours of searching, well into the night, and still, no Hannah Lee. Suddenly, someone picked up a radio of some kind. Ryan heard a lot of static, but apparently, it made sense to the guy holding the radio. He turned around, and a bunch of people sprang into action.

Later, the helicopter landed at the hospital, and first responders rushed to put Hannah Lee on a stretcher and wheel her inside. Ryan tried to follow at her side, but they pushed him away—"Move aside! We've got to get her to the trauma team!"

He stood back while they rushed her inside. He felt light-headed, nauseated. He stood for a moment with his hands on his knees, head hanging down, gulping air.

Hours passed before he knew that Hannah Lee had survived but was in critical condition following emergency surgery. They told him she'd be out for quite some time and that her prognosis was guarded. But due to her age and overall health, he had reason to be optimistic.

Much later, he sat in ICU by Hannah Lee's bed, watching the machines beep and display various lines and numbers, none of which made sense. He touched her hand and called her name softly, but she didn't respond.

He'd turned off his cell phone long ago, not wanting to see or respond to Kari's text messages.

What would Hannah Lee say when she woke up? Would she be angry with him for taking her paragliding? Would she connect the accident to Kari and blame her? Would she blame him?

❧

Hours later, Hannah Lee woke up for the first time but immediately panicked when she discovered the breathing tube down her throat.

Later, she woke again, and they briefly spoke. But she was distressed, didn't remember what had happened, or how she'd been injured. She panicked at one point, needing sedation, and finally drifted off.

Ryan spoke with the doctor after that, who explained that it wasn't unusual for someone who'd experienced this kind of trauma to have problems with memory.

Memory problems. Maybe he had a reprieve.

He was exhausted and hadn't slept in over 48 hours. After getting reassurance from the nurses in ICU, he slumped in an easy chair in the family waiting room and fell into a deep sleep.

❦

His cell phone woke him—another text message from Kari. He'd turned the phone back on last night, sent her a message with an update on Hannah Lee's condition, and forgotten about it. *Ryan, call me immediately. It's important.*

He couldn't put off contacting her much longer. Now that he knew Hannah Lee was on her way to recovery—the doctor said she'd be moved to a private room the next morning—he felt relief. But he wasn't ready yet to talk to Kari, so he turned off the phone and tucked it in a pocket.

He made his way back to ICU, gazed down at Hannah Lee and tucked a strand of hair behind her ear. He drew up a chair, slumped uncomfortably, and went back to sleep.

❦

Ryan woke suddenly, feeling like something was off. His eyes flew open, and there stood Kari. She gazed crookedly at Hannah Lee. He stood up quickly, went to stand between her and Hannah Lee, for reasons he wouldn't be able to explain.

"You shouldn't be here! What were you thinking? Are you crazy?" whispered Ryan urgently.

"Why not? It's not like I had anything to do with it," said Kari, her eyes widening in shock.

"I find that hard to believe," whispered Ryan. "It was your equipment."

"I didn't do anything! How can you even *think* I would do something like that? You know what? You're being a jerk!"

233

She turned to go, her back stiff and her face flushed.

"Wait! Don't leave," said Ryan. "Let's step outside—we have to talk, figure this out. I'll go first, so it doesn't look so weird."

He stepped out and walked down the corridor, waited. After a moment, so did Kari. He took her arm, guided her through the hospital and out the door. He didn't let go of her arm until they got to her car. She pulled her arm away, angrily.

"How dare you?" she spat.

His anger drained away. "I'm sorry. It's just...it's been difficult the past couple of days."

She glared at him, crossed her arms, then turned away.

He stood next to her, both of them gazing into the distance, not looking at each other. He sensed, rather than saw, her softly crying.

"What was that text about? What was so important?" he asked, still not looking directly at her.

"Nothing. It's not that important," she said. Out of the corner of his eye, he saw her swipe away tears. He sighed, turned to her.

"No, really, tell me." He ran his hand down her arm, and she flinched.

"I have to go," she said, turning to get into her car, but he blocked her with his body. "Kari," he said.

She looked up at him with those impossibly beautiful eyes, deep blue-green pools that reflected the light. Her mouth trembled, and another tear slid slowly down her cheek.

"I'm sorry," he whispered, gathering her into his arms, not knowing why he'd just apologized. She sobbed for a moment, sniffled, and heaved out a sigh.

"I can't stand the thought of losing you," she whispered, "and I feel like I am."

He stroked her hair, said nothing.

"Ryan," she said, looking up at him again, imploringly. "Am I losing you?"

"I don't know," he said honestly, but that put another look of shock on her face. "I have to take care of Hannah Lee—you have to know that.

She has a long road of recovery ahead. What kind of guy bails on his wife while she's in intensive care?"

He thought but didn't say—*and what about after that?*

She was quiet.

"Tell me what happened, why you sent that text."

"It's Eric again. This time, he threatened to come here, to do something. He didn't come right out and say what, but I know it's going to be bad if he shows up."

Anger coursed through Ryan. But defeat followed as his stomach tightened. *What could he do?* And how could he possibly handle Kari's situation with Eric while helping his wife through a long and difficult recovery?

He said nothing, looking down. Finally, Kari spoke.

"I've decided to leave town, Ryan. It's the only way. I think I can do a better job of hiding this time, but now that he knows I live here, it's not going to work out for me to stay."

He was quiet. Though he felt a stab of pain at the idea of never seeing Kari again, he also felt relief. It would solve his problems. It would free him to focus on Hannah Lee, to make up to her for...cheating.

It would also be a chance to make it up to her for everything else.

For one brief, shining moment, Ryan felt freedom. He'd make it up to Hannah Lee; he'd be a good husband. They could have a life, a good life, here in this beautiful little oasis near the ocean. He'd feel clean and purposeful.

Kari pulled back a little, eyes searching his face. He looked at her, took in the pain.

He leaned down and kissed her, telling himself it was a good-bye kiss.

She kissed him back, deeply. He felt that pull, that frisson of energy. Before he knew it, he told her to meet him at her apartment. He raced there, deliberately ignoring everything but the anticipation of being with her one last time.

Breathless, they tore off their clothes as they kissed passionately, leaving a trail from the door to the bedroom. They made love the way doomed lovers do, who want to drink every drop of passion before draining the cup dry.

Afterward, she cried softly while he held her, knowing he'd just turned another corner.

He couldn't leave her—he knew that now. He couldn't stay with her, but he couldn't leave. He didn't know if he could leave Hannah Lee, either.

When he thought about his wife the next morning, he felt dirty again. Undeserving. As he shaved, he gazed at himself in the mirror in Kari's bathroom. He saw a guy with dead eyes, a guy with no hope. There would be no redemption.

∞

After that night, he and Kari resumed their old routine. When Hannah Lee came home from the hospital, he hired Ella to look after her, and spent more and more time with Kari. He reasoned that if he gave Kari most of his time and attention, she'd drop the subject of him leaving Hannah Lee, at least while she finished recovering.

Maybe later he'd figure out what he wanted. Maybe later he'd think enough of himself to put his life back on course.

It worked for a while, for a few weeks. Hannah Lee slowly improved, regained her health, rebuilt her strength. As she did, he pulled further away from her, as if he needed to see that she would be okay without him.

It was for the best. He didn't deserve Hannah Lee.

Ryan barely registered it, but Kari didn't bring up Eric again. He didn't question it.

CHAPTER FORTY-FOUR

Matteo sat deep in thought on the plane, chin in hand, elbow propped on the armrest. They'd booked an earlier flight, skipped breakfast at the hotel, and during the trip home talked little. It tore at his chest to see her eyes so heavy with sadness.

He had more bad news and didn't look forward to sharing it. But Hannah Lee had a right to know. Matteo turned to her. He told her something, a connection he'd discovered.

"We can't be sure until we look closer," he said.

She agreed, then sat back, looking stunned. "I can't believe Ryan is that evil," she said sadly.

❧

Hours later, at the coffee house, Matteo pulled up another website. He turned the screen to Hannah Lee, and she gazed at photos of paragliders on the California coast. Matteo clicked on a link and up popped a photo of an instructor named Bruce.

She recognized him immediately, and along with that recognition came other memories. But she had to be sure.

Matteo called the number, spoke to Bruce briefly, then hung up.

"He says that yes, he knows someone named Kari who teaches paragliding, but he doesn't know her that well. He remembers taking a group photo on an outing with other pilots, and she's in it, so he's texting it to me now."

His phone pinged at that moment, and he opened the text. He turned the phone so Hannah Lee could see the screen. He enlarged the photo with his fingers to focus on the blonde in the back row.

"That's her!" he said.

"I know her!" she said, at the same moment. They turned to face each other.

"She's the girl you saw at lunch," said Hannah Lee, and Matteo nodded.

"How do you know her?" he asked.

"I think I know her through Ryan. Let's go see Bruce," she said. "I need to ask him some questions, and I need to see his face while he answers."

Matteo texted Bruce and arranged a time.

⚜

"Sure, I remember you," said Bruce, smiling widely. He was tall, muscular, and rangy, with a scraggly beard. He wore a muscle shirt and cargo pants and was deeply tanned. "I haven't seen you in a while," he added, looking speculatively at Hannah Lee.

"I was...injured, and I'm still recovering," she said, not wanting to tell him it was a paragliding accident.

"Oh, God. You're the girl who got hurt paragliding," he said, eyes opening wide, face paling. "I saw the story on TV a few weeks ago." He looked hesitant.

"Yes, but don't worry. It had nothing to do with you or the quality of instruction. You taught me well—it was an equipment malfunction."

Bruce looked relieved. "So, when are we getting back to your lessons?" he asked brightly, then looked immediately embarrassed. "That is if you want to fly again, and I *totally* understand if you don't," he rushed to say.

"Again, no worries. I'll let you know about lessons later. Now, though, we wondered if you could tell us a little about this woman."

Matteo pulled up the photo, zoomed in on Kari, and showed it to Bruce.

He nodded. "Yeah, that's Kari, like I told you on the phone. She's new around here, but a really experienced paragliding instructor who teaches privately. Um, is your husband Ryan?"

Hannah Lee nodded, steeling herself.

"Yeah, I thought so. Well, they're apparently friends because she talked about him a lot. She said they went on flights together."

His face dropped, and he looked chagrined. "Uh, sorry if I'm speaking out of turn. My mom says I don't have a filter, that I'm always saying stuff people don't really want to hear," he said, looking down.

"It's okay," said Hannah Lee. "What else do you know about her?"

"Only with paragliding, that she sometimes teaches part-time on weekends. She's good at it—people like her, feel comfortable with her. We tried to bring her in full-time with our little group of instructors, but she said it was mostly a hobby for her, not a job."

They asked him a couple more questions, but he couldn't add much else, so they thanked him and left. In the car, they talked.

"I'm remembering more and more," said Hannah Lee. "I can almost see Kari on the hills, at the beach that day, but I don't really have full memories yet. It's just flashes, but I'm pretty sure she was there."

❧

While Matteo drove, Hannah Lee told Matteo about Ryan's visit to her attorney, that he knew about the money, and that he also knew about the trust Hannah Lee had set up for him. It was a revocable trust, designed to pass to Ryan only upon her death, or revert back to her main estate if they divorced.

She'd set up the trust shortly after they married. His general anxiety about money, increasing resentment about the difficulties of owning a small business, and pointed comments about her lack of financial worry had prompted her to act.

"I wanted him to be taken care of in case something happened to me," she said to Matteo, her eyes stinging. "More than ever, I see how important the money is to him, especially after the way he grew up. Obviously, Fred and Joann didn't have much. I can't imagine being ashamed of my parents, how that must feel. There's nothing wrong with them—they seem like nice people, so I don't really understand it," she said, shaking her head.

"Hannah Lee, do you realize what this means?" Matteo interrupted. "That trust goes away if you and Ryan divorce. He's seeing someone else, has been for a while, and apparently, it's serious. That means he's headed for divorce, but he doesn't get anything if that happens." He let those words sit.

"I understand," she said sadly.

"Do you?" He challenged. "There's more about Ryan," he said reluctantly. "We haven't had time to cover it in-depth, but remember what we talked about before? About Ryan's money issues?"

"Apparently, he opened a retail store for athletic wear in the Bay Area. That failed, and he had to file for bankruptcy. He was involved in several multi-level marketing schemes—nothing illegal, though. His credit score is low, which usually means someone who is either not managing money well, or who is chronically underemployed."

Hannah Lee turned her face to the window as the tears dripped. She silently wiped them away.

"Hannah Lee, you know what all of this means, don't you?" Matteo said softly.

"I understand completely," she said. "It means I'm worth more dead than alive to Ryan."

Matteo drove her home. At this point, she didn't care if Ryan saw her with Matteo, but his truck was, as usual, absent. After pulling into her front drive, they sat and talked. It was a heated conversation, their first ever.

Matteo protested vehemently about leaving her there and tried to get her to pack a bag and leave immediately. "How much more do you need to know? He's cheating on you, he married you for your money—" and at that point, he stopped.

Hannah Lee drew back in shock.

"Look, I'm sorry for being so blunt, but I'm worried about you. He might be dangerous. We don't know what happened that day with the paragliding—was it really an accident? Or did he do something to cause it? I don't see the point in staying any longer, taking any more risk. *Let me get you out of here.*"

But his urging only pushed her away further, solidifying her resolve. She still wasn't sure, couldn't quite believe her husband wanted her dead. That meant a level of evil machinations she couldn't grasp, couldn't see in Ryan's character.

Matteo drove off reluctantly as she hobbled to the door. Ella rushed to help her, settled her on the sofa, and went back to doing laundry.

Something nagged at her, a piece of the puzzle that didn't quite fit. How had Ryan found out about the money from the transaction?

She was certain he hadn't seen anything on her laptop—she kept it firmly locked with facial recognition software. She'd given all of her passwords and other access information only to her bank's trust officer, along with instructions for what to do if something happened to her.

Certainly, it didn't take much for him to know she was wealthy, even more so than she'd indicated prior to marriage. The house, the furnishings and décor, the flow of cash for their every need, everything upscale, no skimping, ever.

She wasn't extravagant—she didn't buy expensive jewelry, her car was a three-year-old luxury car but not the costliest, and they rarely traveled. Still, she clearly didn't need to work, and since they lived in one of the most expensive counties in the country, her wealth must be significant to sustain their lifestyle.

But Ryan somehow knew the *exact dollar amount*, the sum total of the money she'd pocketed from the sale of her business. *How had he discovered that?* Hannah Lee had never told anyone the number—not Danielle, not her own parents, not Ryan, *no one*.

CHAPTER FORTY-FIVE

On closing day, she already knew the sale price because it was negotiated in advance, but still, when she reviewed the closing documents and saw the number in black and white with her signature line at the bottom of the page, it became real.

Later, when she received her money, the after-tax amount was staggering. *Forty-eight million, three hundred six thousand, five hundred and eight dollars, and twenty-five cents.*

She stared at the banking app on her smartphone off and on, unable to believe it was true. She was so shaken up that she had to stop looking at it, put it into a mental box and close the lid.

Most people think a large amount of money will make them happier, that it will solve all their problems, and give them total peace of mind. Only the *suddenly,* truly wealthy know the truth: it is one of the scariest things that can happen.

As soon as your brain registers the unbelievable sum of real wealth, if it can register it, the next thoughts are the next set of worries in Maslow's hierarchy: *Now what? What will I do with my life now that I have more than I can ever spend?*

What about my relationships, my family, my friends? How will the people in my life react? Will they be envious? Jealous and resentful? Entitled, waiting for me to give them chunks of the money? Angry if I don't?

Will I lose them because of the money?

And what about losing the money? What if I screw things up and lose the wealth I've gained?

She hired investment advisors, but after hours of conversations, she chose to leave most of it in cash. Investing had a purpose—to increase your wealth in exchange for putting it at risk. But how much more did she need? None, she decided, but she felt she had to do some investing.

She bought some investment grade bonds and put a portion in high grade, dividend-yielding stocks. Her conservative portfolio provided a steady income of around $1.5 million dollars annually. She left the rest alone. After taxes, most of the interest income remained in her portfolio.

She essentially lived on a portion of it, about two hundred thousand dollars per year after taxes. Even that level of income was greater than her paycheck over the years she built and ran her business.

She felt embarrassed by the transaction dollar amount, but even more so about the fact that the principle continued growing because she couldn't even spend the interest income.

Lately, she'd begun wondering how to responsibly give away most of her wealth.

The other hidden truth about extensive wealth: if you don't have highbrow taste, if you are content with a moderate lifestyle, and if shopping isn't all that fascinating for you, then it can be a burden.

It can be something that occupies your thoughts, makes you doubt other people's intentions, and hinders ordinary love, connection, and trust.

But no one would ever, *ever* feel compassion for that. Who wants to hear about the troubles of the wealthy? Who cares if it's a burden?

Give it to me, most people would say, *and I'll show you what to do with it!*

Hannah Lee wasn't boastful. She knew she wasn't more intelligent or talented than others, more brilliant at business. Her fortune was simply the result of being in the right place at the right time and consistently doing what it took to run and grow the business. And luck.

She was lucky enough to sell the business to the right buyer at the right time.

She'd worked hard to make good decisions, mainly because of a sense of responsibility to all the good people working alongside her.

Over the years, she thought she'd like to retire one day, that the business might be worth enough to give her a nice nest egg. She figured that nest egg might be three or four million dollars, enough to create an annual cash flow of a couple hundred thousand, and enough to pay off her mortgage.

Nowhere in her dreams did she imagine a check for $48,306,508.25. And when it happened, she quickly realized it wasn't something she could talk about with other people.

Then Ryan came into her life. She wanted him to marry her for love, not money. So, she lied to him, by omission, never disclosed the truth of her wealth. If he didn't know about the money, maybe she'd feel secure with him, lovable for who she was, wealthy or not.

But by not telling him, by not revealing her insecurities, she remained hidden. Emotional intimacy wasn't part of their relationship. They'd explored each other's bodies for a time, but not their minds or hearts.

He lied to her as well, for his own reasons. She might never discover all of them, but she had to try to find out.

She flashed again to closing day. And out of the misty fog of memory came a person, a face she couldn't see clearly—actually, two people.

There were two assistants—a man and a woman—who mainly worked outside of the conference room but occasionally came in to process the paperwork.

Could that have been...? She picked up her phone, scrolled through her contacts, and called her attorney. He picked up on the second ring.

"Joe, I'm sorry to bother you."

"No problem. What can I do for you?"

"I was sitting here trying to remember details about the closing to sell the business. Do you remember the people who helped that day?"

"Let's see. We did it at the office of the investment bank, and we know all those people. Do you want their names again?"

"No, I know who they were—I'm wondering about the two assistants."

"I wouldn't know who they were, but I can find out," he said. A few minutes later, he called back with the names of the man and woman, his voice mirroring the shock she felt.

Her worst fears were confirmed.

Later, she lay in bed, hoping to escape the truth, but like a stack of cards slowly shuffled, the memories cascaded, and she remembered.

She remembered all of it.

CHAPTER FORTY-SIX

HANNAH LEE, THE DAY OF THE ACCIDENT

It was another beautiful California day. They meandered down Pacific Coast Highway, headed for their launch site near Big Sur. Hannah Lee drank in the stunning views, far below the winding ribbon of highway. It was one of the most beautiful drives in the world, with the coastline, redwoods, ocean, and plunging cliffs.

It pained her to mar the beauty of their drive, but Hannah Lee wanted to bring up the subject of their near estrangement—how distant they seemed, and how lost she felt. She struggled to work up the courage to ask.

"Ryan? I'm glad we're doing something together today. I...I miss you, miss having fun together. It seems like we've been distant lately. Are we, that is, are you...?"

"We're fine. Stop worrying," he said. He smiled and touched her hand. For a moment, she relaxed and felt reassured.

But then she wondered. *Did he mean it? Did he feel the way she did?*

He never wanted to open up, and that stirred her fears—that he didn't want to because it was bad, that whatever truly sat in his heart and mind was a closed book. A book of terrible secrets.

Maybe later, she'd have the courage to bring it up again. Tomorrow, perhaps, or the next day. Maybe then she'd ask more questions, get him to open up about whatever was troubling him, whatever was keeping him so distant.

She focused instead on the day ahead. Her first solo flight! Thinking of the fun ahead filled her with joyful anticipation.

She had no way of knowing that the opportunity to learn the truth of their relationship would be lost forever.

❧

They pulled in at the launch site and parked the car. Standing by another vehicle was a tall blonde woman. She was stunning. She strolled to their car and waited until they climbed out.

"Hi," I'm Kari," she said, shaking Hannah Lee's hand, her light grip lingering for a moment. Her eyes seemed to search Hannah Lee's, leaving a slight feeling of discomfort. Then she smiled broadly, and the feeling went away.

Kari carefully spread the equipment on the side of the hill sloping toward the ocean. The cobalt blue sail was a long, narrow strip of strong material, 2-sided with baffling that created cones along the entire front edge. The lines were stretched downhill from the sail. Finally, there was the harness, to which the lines were secured with metal carabiners.

The harness was essentially a cushy seat for the paraglider, with straps for the chest and legs. The lines attached to the harness had risers and brakes that the pilot gripped to control the direction, speed, and overall drift of the paraglider.

Kari carefully checked the entire sail—every line, every carabiner, and every attachment throughout the equipment, for both Hannah Lee's and Ryan's paragliders. As she did, she talked them through the pre-flight checklist. They talked about wind speed and direction, and Kari reminded them of the proper way to launch.

They would put on the harness, then wait for the wind. As the wind began to rise, they would turn around to their sails, grip the lines, and tug. This would lift the sail, allowing the wind to fill the tubes, pulling the sail into the air. They had to be ready at that point because with the sail's lift, they'd have to turn around, take a few running steps down the hill, and quickly be airborne.

Landforms push air up, so the mountainous Big Sur coastline made paragliding both possible and fun. There were long stretches of mountains and coast, ensuring stunning views and persistent wind to keep them aloft for at least an hour, maybe two if they were lucky.

As Ryan and Hannah Lee sat on the hillside waiting for the right wind direction and speed, Hannah Lee stole a glance at Kari, who stood near Ryan talking in a low voice. Ryan shook his head and looked away. As Hannah Lee watched, Kari looked up and caught her staring. She smiled, and Hannah Lee flushed.

She came over and stood by Hannah Lee.

"You're not nervous, are you?" she asked. "There's nothing to be afraid of. You've flown quite a bit, according to Ryan. You're ready for a solo flight."

Hannah Lee was nervous, a bit scared. She looked into Kari's sea-green eyes and found the steadiness she needed. She nodded and swallowed, then smiled crookedly. "Thanks. I guess I needed that."

"Great. It won't be long," Kari said. She checked her handheld wind meter again. "It's time!" said Kari. "You go first, Hannah Lee."

Hannah Lee lifted her sail, then turned around and loped downhill. She let out a small 'Whoop' as she went airborne. She felt the magic again as her feet lifted off the ground, which quickly dropped away beneath her dangling legs.

Soon, she soared easily, gently pulling the risers to guide her direction. She didn't want to wind up far over the ocean, so she maintained a course over the coast but near the mountains.

She breathed in and out and grinned. Joy filled her heart as she drank in the view.

Suddenly, she felt a strong tug beneath her. It felt like the harness. Something didn't feel right, and anxiety tightened her chest. Instinctively, she steered toward the mountains and down, fearing a problem with her sail.

She felt the tug again, and this time, she felt the harness rip. The main support now gone, her body began to fall, held aloft only by her grip on the risers. Panicked and horrified, she steered as close to the mountains as she could, feeling her grip loosen by the second.

She remembered the back-up parachute and fumbled for the pull, which she yanked as hard as she could.

The parachute ejected, but she noted with increasing horror that it didn't inflate as it should. Now rapidly approaching the mountain, she steered her failing paraglider into a small clearing, but she knew her rate of descent meant a definite crash.

She lost her grip on the risers and fell to the ground. She didn't remember actually hitting the ground, thankfully. But she remembered lying there, broken, and scared.

CHAPTER FORTY-SEVEN

PRESENT DAY

Matteo knocked on the door. He felt a presence on the other side, no doubt looking through the peephole. He gave her a little wave and a smile.

"What do you want?" The voice was muffled as it passed through the door.

"Hi there. Me again. I know you recognize me from the restaurant. Please, can we just talk? If you could come outside, maybe?"

There was a long wait, then the door opened. Kari stood there, and he had to admit, she was breathtaking. "Come in."

He did, and they sat in her living room across from one another, both stiff.

"Why were you spying on us?" she asked.

"I wasn't spying. Okay, maybe I was, but I was trying to help out a friend."

"A friend."

"Yes, and I'm sure you can figure out who that might be."

"Hannah Lee," she said softly.

"Yes."

She was quiet, her eyes fixed on his.

"Hannah Lee is one of my best friends. We worked together years ago, and she called me to help her figure out what her husband was up to." He let that bomb sit there, hoping for a reaction, but all she did was continue to gaze at him.

A smile slowly formed on her full lips. But it wasn't warm, didn't quite reach her eyes. Aside from her astonishing beauty, she had a calculating look about her. "I understand now," she said.

As she smiled, he felt an unpleasant trill of energy, as though something vile had just peeked into his soul. A small chill ran down his spine and the tiny hairs on the back of his neck lifted.

Maybe coming here to confront this woman was a bad idea.

"What do you want?" she asked, now smirking.

"How about you leave Ryan alone? How about getting out of here, out of both of their lives? She loves him, and, I think, deep down, he loves her. I mean, after all, he married *her*." He sat back and waited to see if the hook might set.

Anger flashed across her lovely face. "*You have no idea* how Ryan feels. Who do you think you are, coming to my home and telling me to get out of town? This isn't some game, and it's none of your business."

She stopped abruptly, gazing at Matteo in a probing way, and he felt her crawl inside his head. "But that doesn't matter, does it? Because you've got something going on with Hannah Lee, don't you? I can see it all over you, *smell* it on you. You're in love with her."

A knowing look passed across her features, and his stomach tightened.

"But I wonder, does she know, or does she care if she does?" Her voice had fallen to a seductive whisper. "She's way too good for you, isn't she?" She sat back, observed the impact of her words.

Matteo felt his stomach clench, his face flush. He felt deeply embarrassed, ashamed of loving Hannah Lee so much, realizing she didn't share his feelings.

"That's right—the *great and amazing* Hannah Lee doesn't give you the time of day, other than to get you to do things for her, like spying. I'll bet you worked for her, one of her minions in her business, probably worked all hours of the day and night to please her. *Matteo, fetch this, do that*," she mimicked Hannah Lee, sounding nothing like her.

But the words penetrated. They hit painfully home.

His face flushed deeper. Somehow, this woman made him feel dirty, as though his feelings for Hannah Lee were misplaced, wrong. And as though her friendship with him had been nothing more than her getting what she wanted from him.

How had she gotten to him so fast?

She looked confident, almost gloating. But there was something else behind the bravado—a tiny twist of fear in her eyes.

He looked for the vulnerability, found it, and honed in.

"Uh-huh," he said. "I see what you're doing. And I know what you're after. You know about the money, don't you? Hannah Lee's money. You had something to do with her accident."

"That is crazy. Get out," she said, standing up, walking to the door, yanking it open, and gesturing for him to leave.

"You and Ryan are two of a kind, aren't you?" he said, twisting the knife. "You know, we went to Texas and met his parents. They live in a trailer park and haven't heard from their son in years. The story they told was really interesting—all about Ryan's secrets and lies."

"*Get out!*" Her face twisted in anger, no longer lovely.

He rose slowly, walked to the door, and stopped. He turned and dropped the final bomb. "I guess you're wondering how long it will take before Ryan gets bored with you, moves on to his next little sex pal, or makes up with Hannah Lee. She loves him so much, she'll probably forgive him. And you'll be out in the cold again."

She slammed the door behind him. He chuckled to himself as he walked away. The hook was set.

❦

Kari stood behind the closed door, fists clenched, breathing deeply. She pulled her cell phone out of her back pocket and tapped a message.

Come over here, now. You have a BIG problem.

RYAN

Ryan sat on Kari's sofa in shock. Hannah Lee—his sweet, innocent wife—brought a former employee to town to *spy on him*. Even more shocking—they traveled to Texas *together* and met his parents.

Hannah Lee had met his parents and undoubtedly knew all about him by now.

She stayed overnight in Texas, maybe with this guy—Matteo?—in a hotel room. The same room, no doubt, since he was acting like her prince coming to the rescue.

His face burned.

"I hope you can see now what you're really dealing with, who she really is," said Kari.

"What did he look like?" he asked her, ignoring the comment.

"*What?*"

"I said, what did he look like—old guy, young, ugly, good looking, *what?*"

His voice was steel.

"Are you *kidding* me?" She rolled her eyes, but at Ryan's look, answered. "He was great looking, okay? He looked like that guy that's married to the gal on morning television. Same name, in fact."

Ryan felt a rush of crazy emotions—anger, jealousy, embarrassment, and others he didn't understand.

Kari looked daggers at him. "What, are you *jealous*? Of this guy and Hannah Lee? I don't be*lieve* this," she said, standing up, her fists clenched. He felt her glaring at him, and he didn't care.

What was happening? This unknown guy, Matteo, was all up in his business, and he felt things he'd never felt before. He couldn't sort it fast enough in his mind.

Matteo, whoever he was, was with his wife in some kind of way. Were they involved? It was unfathomable that she would cheat on him.

Or was it so far-fetched? He'd neglected her emotionally, not to mention in the bedroom, for months. He replayed the scenes. Hannah Lee asking him where he'd been. He—lying to her. She—asking him if something was wrong; were they okay. He—lying again.

But that was nothing new. He always lied. It was how he dealt with conflict, how he managed the anxiety that ran through him every day of his life. It was how he pushed down the darkness, the awareness that he was unloved, unwanted, and didn't even know his true self, his origins.

Now those same insecurities coursed through his body, threatening to roar, irrepressible at last. He vibrated and stood, pacing, blinded to Kari.

It was all going to come out now. Hannah Lee knew about his background, who he truly was and was not. Sure, he'd told Kari, another lost soul. But for Hannah Lee to know was unbearable. Until now, she'd loved him, or at least, she loved who she thought he was. She thought he was a stand-up guy, someone worthy of her love. She'd never again feel the same way about him.

Then his mind switched to another topic. Had she found out about the closing? Had she put those pieces of the puzzle together?

Did she realize, now, that he'd romanced his way into her life, to reap the benefit of her wealth? Did she think that he'd never loved her?

"Ryan!" said Kari, and he realized she'd said it more than once. He refocused on her, but everything was different, now. "I have to get to work. It's a mandatory employee meeting." She grabbed her bag and strode to the door.

He stood there, frozen.

"What are you going to do?" she asked, pausing.

"Nothing. I'm not going to do anything," he lied, still.

She nodded slowly. "Of course, you aren't."

He looked at her in confusion, but she turned to leave. "We'll talk later, okay?" she said over her shoulder.

He nodded. She left. He felt empty. "Wait, you forgot your—" he said, as he picked up her cell phone from the coffee table. But she was gone.

CHAPTER FORTY-EIGHT

As Ryan held Kari's phone, a text message came in. Without thinking, he read the message.

> *Hey, Kari. It's been a long time, and we never got a chance to talk about what happened. I hope you're doing well. When can we get together to talk? I'm only in town for a couple of days. If you can't meet, we can always talk later. I don't want to cause you any problems, I just want to see you for a few minutes. Thanks in advance.*

The message was from someone Kari knew because his name and pic resided in her contacts. *Eric.*

His brain couldn't process it. Wait. Was this *the* Eric? Stalker ex-boyfriend Eric? This was definitely not coming from a burner phone. And he didn't sound like a stalker. But that didn't mean anything.

He pressed the number.

"Kari! I'm so glad you called. Um, how are you? I hope everything is working out for you, but hey...I'm sorry things went down the way they did. I've been thinking about you a lot, and I wanted to just get a little, you know, closure?" He paused.

Ryan sat frozen, breathing heavily.

"Kari? This is you, right?"

"Actually, it's not. This is Ryan, Kari's...boyfriend."

"*Dude*. Why are you answering Kari's phone? Is she hurt or something?"

"No, she's fine. She left her phone here, and I saw your text and, I shouldn't have done it, but—" Anger flared, but it was mixed with suspicion that Eric might not be how Kari had portrayed him. "Why are you calling Kari?" Ryan asked harshly.

"Uh, well, I haven't talked to her in a long time, and we have some unfinished business."

"I'll bet you do."

"Hey, listen, I'm sorry to intrude. Would you just tell her I called?"

The more Ryan listened to Eric, the less convinced he felt about the ex-boyfriend, stalker story. Eric sounded so...normal. "Wait. Don't go yet. Can I ask you something?"

"Uh, I guess."

"Kari told me she had an ex-boyfriend named Eric who...abused her."

"*What?*" The guy on the line paused, then sighed. "Actually, that's not a total shock."

"So, you did abuse her, and now you're stalking her?" Ryan's anger rose again.

"No! No, man, listen to me. Uh, I don't know how to say this. Kari has...emotional problems. She didn't have a good experience growing up—in fact, it was pretty awful. And she...she didn't come out of it entirely okay. Look, I feel terrible saying all this stuff." He stopped.

"Go on," Ryan said, still skeptical.

"Okay. We dated for a few months, but I broke up with her because, well, she was jealous of things that weren't even happening. Look, I work as a schoolteacher, and I do parent-teacher conferences all the time, but she started getting this idea that I was having *personal* conferences with some of the single moms. Know what I mean?

"I thought I could handle it, but things got a lot worse when she made threatening calls to a couple of the moms. When things didn't go her way, she would, like, make things up, try to manipulate me. Really bad things. I finally had to break it off, and quite suddenly. I probably should have left well enough alone. But I'm getting married soon, and I wanted to reach out to Kari to see if she ever got help. I thought maybe we could mend those fences. Stupid idea, I guess," he said.

Ryan didn't want to believe it. But he sounded so reasonable, his story so plausible. He sounded, to his surprise, like a nice guy. Nothing like the sociopathic stalker guy Kari had described.

"Look, I don't want to cause her any problems," Eric said. "I only called because, I guess, I felt bad about breaking up so suddenly. I felt like our relationship had gotten so...toxic...that it was best to cut all the ties. But that probably hurt her a lot, and I never meant to do that. I wanted to, I don't know, talk it over, make sure she's okay. You know?"

Ryan was silent.

"Hey, are you still there?" said Eric.

"Yeah, I'm still here. Look, I'm sure you'll hear back from Kari. I'll tell her you called. I've got to go, but thanks for what you told me." He hung up before Eric could say anything more.

⚬

Ryan's head spun. Kari had made up the whole thing—the entire story of her relationship with Eric. She'd woven a fantastic tale, one that had sucked him into her life in a swift, passionate, deep way.

The last pieces of how he saw her quickly collapsed, like one of those building implosion demolitions. He'd seen it on television—explosions like rapid gunfire, the building suddenly enveloped in a huge, billowing cloud of dust, reduced to a pile of rubble in a matter of seconds.

Like his relationship with Kari. Nothing but rubble in a matter of minutes.

He was left with a hollowed-out feeling. *Who was she? What was she doing in his life?*

Ryan's mind raced as he flashed over the past few months. It was like watching one of those old-fashioned slide shows, with the carousel spinning out of control, each slide a piece of his life popping up, then disintegrating.

He felt almost disembodied, noticing that he still stood there, frozen, unmoving. His mind couldn't decide what to do, so he did nothing. Just like Kari said. *Of course not.* It had always been hard to make a significant move at the critical junctures of his life.

When one of his businesses began failing, instead of getting into gear, solving problems, and making decisions, he slumped into a mild depression and withdrew. He escaped by going to bars and picking up women.

He'd sat there, emboldened by alcohol, and bragged as if he were a business tycoon of some kind. It always worked.

He went home with them, had sex, and when he left the next morning, he promised to call later, but he never did. Why would he want to see someone again who had no clue about him and only cared about his wild fantasies?

It was pitiful, and he followed the pattern for most of his adult life. That is, until he met Hannah Lee. He approached her differently. Instead of building himself up in her eyes, he focused on her, on listening to her, understanding her.

With Hannah Lee, he'd wanted, needed, to build a relationship. Though he'd sought her out because of her money, as he got to know her, he found he wanted something more from her.

When she looked at him, there was something in her eyes, something he'd never experienced before. Pure love, admiration, and respect. She saw something in him, something worthy of love.

Hannah Lee's love was a priceless gift. And that love was slipping away, perhaps gone forever.

His mom and dad. What must they think now that they'd met his unheard-of *wife*? How did they feel after years of distance, finding he was too embarrassed to introduce them to Hannah Lee?

Hannah Lee. What was she feeling now that his real life, who he really was, was exposed?

Even worse, what was she doing about it?

His mind suddenly stopped whirling. Something clicked into place, and it chilled him.

Kari—*emotionally disturbed, lying Kari*—had met his wife and knew her.

He flashed back to the day of the accident, and prior to that day, when Kari talked him into meeting Hannah Lee. When he quickly gave in and agreed.

He did it—brought Kari into his life without thinking of the consequences to Hannah Lee. He brought Kari into *their* lives, and Hannah Lee had been severely injured. Hannah Lee could have died that day on the mountain.

He felt sick. It was all his fault, and now he was almost certain that it wasn't an accident.

The cold finger of dread touched his heart. He sprang up and ran out of Kari's apartment, her cell phone still in his hand.

✁

Matteo watched Kari drive away after seeing Ryan arrive earlier. Oddly, Ryan didn't come out of her apartment right away, but when he did, he ran to his truck and roared out of the parking lot.

Matteo waited a moment, then followed, but slammed on his brakes just before turning onto the busy street, narrowly missing another vehicle. As soon as he could, he pulled out more carefully, but he'd lost Ryan's truck.

He pulled over, opened the tracker app, and saw that Ryan appeared to be headed toward their home. He threw the phone on the seat and headed out, driving despite not knowing where to go. Should he go to Hannah Lee's? Or wait to hear from her?

And where did Kari go? He had a strong sense that something was going down, but what, and where?

CHAPTER FORTY-NINE

KARI

Kari slammed the car door, started the engine, and sped off. Her vision clouded by tears, she swerved in time to avoid an oncoming vehicle as she pulled out of the parking lot.

She slammed her palms on the steering wheel and let out an unearthly howl of rage. That felt better. There was nothing worse than tears of helplessness. She wasn't helpless.

She knew what to do, but it would require a careful approach. It was time to put the next plan in motion, a plan that would secure every dream and give her the life she'd only envied until now.

No one would see it coming, see her coming. She laughed bitterly to herself. No one ever expected her to do the things she did. She'd always been underestimated.

❦

Kari learned the value of planning ahead at an early age. It was how she avoided being noticed in ways that were threatening and dangerous. That was before she learned how to use the attention she attracted to her advantage.

As a little girl, she danced around the house, singing songs to herself, twirling about innocently, trying to get her mother to notice her. It was fun, if frustrating, because her mother always seemed distracted and rarely played with her.

She drew pictures, put love notes on them, and showed them to her mother, who tiredly pushed her away. She followed her around the house, peppering her with questions until her mother sent her to her room.

She did everything she could to get her mother's attention. Until the wrong person noticed her.

One day, she sensed the eyes, felt the odd discomfort, as if unseen hands explored her small body. The first to do it was her stepfather, the man her mother had married when she was six.

He watched her, drinking beer, pretending to watch television with her mother, but with his hand draped on his lap in a funny way. He rubbed himself between the legs, cutting his eyes over at her, and Kari ran away and hid.

He opened the door to her room one night and stood there making strange noises while she pretended to sleep. Her heart thumped wildly as she tried to figure out how to escape. But he left that night without saying a word.

Still, she knew something bad was headed her way.

She discovered at an early age that beauty brought unwanted attention. Later, she found it could also shield her from being really seen.

People tended to not focus past her looks, assuming there wasn't much more to see. They thought her outside beauty meant that the insides of her were some improbable mixture of centerfold and sweet housewife. No one saw her for who she was.

She found it easy to hide her true thoughts, the ones that led her to dark places, that enabled her to get things done her way when others wouldn't.

If you didn't want to be seen, you could do things to change the situation. So, at age eight, she pretended she was still that innocent girl, but she no longer twirled around the house.

Days after the unwanted intrusion into her bedroom, she woke to the sound of a stumble, a hard thump, and swearing. She'd strewn tiny, sharp Legos around her bed. Her stepfather sat on the floor, pulling them out of the soles of his feet, cursing her.

Her mother opened the door and found him there, Kari lying wide-eyed in bed. Her mother's eyes slowly swept the scene, and her face hardened.

The next day, her stepfather was gone. Kari felt an extraordinary sense of power that day.

But it didn't last.

Her mother chose the next guy haphazardly, and the next, and the next. While none of them came into Kari's bedroom, they also failed miserably at providing whatever it was her mother craved from men.

One by one, her mother invited men into their lives and kicked them out. Over the years, Kari and her mother's residences shrank in size and quality of neighborhood.

With each chaotic upheaval, Kari's anxiety grew.

Later, struggling to earn enough money to live in California, Kari realized she didn't yet have all the pieces to life's success puzzle. Men were drawn to her, and at first, that meant she held the cards, the majority of the power.

But then, inevitably, they would pull away, fueling her growing sense of losing control, and the fear and panic would rise.

With panic, her behavior changed, sometimes without any awareness. It was almost as if someone else became the actor, not her. And that actor did things she later regretted. But couldn't undo.

⚯

As she drove, she thought of Eric and was flooded again with rage. Eric had proven all too easy to seduce, and for a while, she thought he was the one. But the inheritance from his grandparents turned out to be a

265

pittance, and his salary as a schoolteacher didn't amount to much. Still, he loved her.

Then, she noticed there were any number of desperate, besotted moms at his school, trying to take him away from her. She saw their eyes watching him when they ran into them at restaurants. She smiled but fumed as they openly flirted with Eric.

Then she realized he *liked* their attention and was *attracted* to them. She wondered what they did during their 'parent-teacher conferences.' She obsessed about it and called Eric repeatedly while he was at work. The fear and the darkness reared up, and she lost control.

She tried to fight it, to change things back to the way they were before, but it proved to be too much.

How dare he break up with her? As if there was something wrong with *her?* She burned inside again at the shameful memory of Eric saying in an apologetic voice that he needed to move on.

It was okay, she told herself now, because Eric would have never given her the life she truly deserved.

Now, she had Ryan, and he was everything she wanted. With Ryan, and with the money, she could, at last, take a deep breath. She knew exactly what they would do with their lives together.

It would be just the way Ryan had promised, and the way she envisioned. A beautiful home, a vineyard, and no more worries about money.

No one else to worry about, to steal him away. He would be hers.

There'd be no need to move again, find someone new, and go through the whole seduction routine. Again. She was tired of it all. Exhausted, really. But Ryan needed a little help to free himself from the burden of a wife he didn't love.

⚮

It wasn't easy, but she figured out a way to sabotage Hannah Lee's paraglider. The lines and the carabiners at the attachment points were all highly visible. There was no way to go through pre-flight checks without Ryan and Hannah Lee catching something because they'd quickly notice any frayed lines or damaged carabiners.

No, the place to do damage and hide it was the harness. The webbing, which was the strong support part of the harness, was covered in cushy materials to make the ride comfortable for the pilot. She found a way to pull up a flap or two and cut the webbing, then cover it up.

In the air, Hannah Lee's weight would cause the webbing to pull apart, and without that support, the rest of the material would rip, causing her to fall. She even sabotaged the backup parachute just in case.

She wasn't certain it would work, but it did. Beautifully, except for one thing.

Hannah Lee crashed on the mountain, but she was too close to the ground for the crash to kill her.

⚬◦⚬

Now, there was only one remaining problem, and it wasn't insurmountable.

Ryan was hesitant. He didn't lean toward decisive action. He was like water flowing downhill, taking the path of least resistance.

That was okay because she could act, she could decide. She could make things happen. She'd done it before, and she could do it again.

She waffled between clarity and confusion and back again. There were obstacles, and it was time to remove them. While stopped at a light, she opened the glove box, removed her handgun, and placed it on the passenger seat.

MATTEO

Matteo drove aimlessly, thinking. Something was going down. He could feel it. He thought about Ryan, staying behind at Kari's, then tearing out like he was on fire, and now seemingly headed home. Or was he?

He pulled to the side of the road, took out his phone, and opened the tracker app again. It took a few minutes, but soon, he saw the dot on the map showing Ryan's location for the past fifteen minutes or so. He apparently left Kari's apartment and drove to Carmel Valley Rd., where he proceeded to an area filled with local restaurants.

There, he parked and stayed for a few minutes. Then he left again, and now, he appeared to be headed home. *Home.* Where Hannah Lee waited.

She didn't want Matteo to stay with her, and she didn't heed his warning to leave before something bad happened. He didn't know what the something bad was, but danger trickled up and down his spine, and he didn't think he was being overly suspicious. Matteo didn't lean toward paranoia.

What would Hannah Lee think if he showed up unannounced? Especially if her husband was sitting there and everything was normal?

If only he knew where Kari had gone. But he hadn't thought of putting a tracker on her vehicle, only Ryan's, and since it didn't look like they were together, he had no idea where to find her.

Wait. Maybe he could find out if there was anything to worry about. He turned around and headed for the restaurant where Ryan had stopped. There was a cluster of restaurants in the area, and since the tracker app wasn't that precise, he wasn't sure which one was Ryan's destination.

He chose one, a steak house. He pulled into the parking lot and went in. At the host stand, he declined a seat. "Actually, I'm looking for someone who I think works here. She's tall, blonde, maybe mid-30s?"

The woman at the host stand, who gave him a bland smile, shook her head. "Sorry, I don't know her. You just described half the girls in California. Plus, we work in shifts, so I have no idea if anyone like that works here. On my shift, there's no one."

He thanked her and left. The next restaurant was a tapas place. This time, before going in, he opened the group paragliding photo with Kari in it, cropped it to her face, and saved it.

Inside, he asked for the manager, and when a harried-looking guy appeared, wiping his hands on a napkin, Matteo showed him the photo of Kari. "I'm trying to find this woman, a family emergency. Does she work here?"

The manager peered at the photo, then nodded. "Yeah, I think I recognize her. Are you looking for Kari?"

Matteo nodded.

"She worked here for a while but quit a couple of days ago. A good thing because we were getting ready to fire her."

"Fire her?"

"Can't really talk about it, but let's just say she's not easy to get along with. In this business, you have to roll with stuff. Customers won't come back if you..." He stopped and shrugged.

Matteo thanked the manager and left.

Back in his car, he considered what he knew so far. Ryan followed Kari here, apparently, because he thought she was working tonight. But she no longer had a job at this restaurant, and that was something she'd failed to tell Ryan.

Ryan clearly left after that. But where did he go? And where was Kari?

Matteo looked at the tracker app again and quickly spotted Ryan. Yes, he was headed home. In fact, he was almost there. Matteo put his car in gear and sped out of the parking lot.

Two blocks later, he stopped suddenly, and before he could back up to find another route, a truck pulled up behind him, blocking his exit. Ahead, he watched the slow crawl of a train.

He grabbed his cell and punched Hannah Lee's number. It went straight to voice mail.

CHAPTER FIFTY

RYAN

What the hell? He drove frantically, not sure where to go next.

Apparently, Kari quit her job a couple of days ago and hadn't told him. She lied about having an employee meeting.

His thoughts skated through the events of the past few weeks.

Kari—the perfect lover, the woman whom he thought was his soul mate. Her vulnerability, which hit a raw nerve in him, had awakened a buried desire to be the hero, to have someone who needed him.

And something else.

There was a magnetism between them, the recognition that at their depths, they were painfully alike. Ryan had never before met his equal on the strata of deep-down damage that had never been addressed. Damage that had lain dormant for decades, now awakened.

They pinged off of one another in ways that set off emotional fireworks, sexual ecstasy.

Hannah Lee—even after being almost killed—was still so strong, so capable. She dedicated herself to physical therapy and recovery, asking so little of him. But she had always been that way with him.

From the moment he saw that astounding number at the closing, he attached its significance to Hannah Lee and saw her in one way, as the woman who'd earned and amassed a fortune.

He found her, pursued her subtlety, and later, found her more attractive than he'd anticipated.

But he didn't bother to look deeper into who she was. She didn't need him, not really. Yes, they had a good life together, but he longed for something else, an intensity, a touching of the raw places in his soul that needed contact.

And he found that in Kari—a woman who was sick, emotionally disturbed, and dangerous. Because he knew now that Kari had tried to kill Hannah Lee, that she found some way to sabotage the parasail so that it failed, sending her plummeting to the earth.

He chose Kari over Hannah Lee, sickness over health. The more he thought about it, the further his stomach dropped, and he fell with it. The sickness washed over him in waves.

Hannah Lee gave him a pathway to wholeness for the first time in his life. With her, he might have had a great life, one with the possibility of real love. They could have had children, built a family together.

But that was impossible now. He'd built his relationship with Hannah Lee on a lie, and that lie was crumbling. His life was in free fall. He flashed back to their second meeting, months after the closing.

∞

Ryan pushed his way into the coffee shop, looked around slowly, then stopped when he saw Hannah Lee. He paused, knowing he was about to embark on a journey of deception and greed. But it wasn't difficult to push aside those thoughts, that hesitation.

Forty-eight million dollars sat in front of him, and he wasn't going to stop. He made his way over, spoke to her, and soon found his way into her life.

On their first date, he opened the door for her to tell him the truth about her circumstances, but she chose to lie by omission. At that moment, he felt his heart harden just a bit as he stepped into the justification.

After all, if she could lie to him and cover up her true wealth, how were his actions so different?

He woke one morning with Hannah Lee curled by his side. He touched her curly, tumbled hair, slid his hand along her side. And realized that he did care for her, that being with her had opened his eyes to her, opened his heart. She was nothing less than amazing.

He admired her intelligence, the way she solved problems swiftly and easily, and her persistence at doing so. He enjoyed watching her read, her intensity as she absorbed a story, or the financial news, or whatever her focus at that moment. She enjoyed feeding her mind, and he benefitted from the tidbits she dropped into their conversations.

She was a giver. She found ways to extend care to others. She was shy and socially inhibited, which he initially thought was odd but later found endearing.

Did he love her? He pushed down that question. Not everyone marries for some kind of fairy tale love, he told himself. After all, he cared enough, and maybe it would deepen with time.

He rolled her over as she opened her eyes and smiled at him, stretching.

"Let's get married," he said, actually feeling good about it, no longer the predator. Now, he was the good guy, the boyfriend taking the next step.

"What?"

He touched her lips, kissed her gently, flooded with something new, something other than passion.

"Ummm," she said, reaching for him, eyes half-closed.

"Uh-uh," he said, shaking a finger gently. "I need an answer, missy."

Her eyes flew open, her eyebrows ascended. She pulled herself up into a sitting position.

"You're serious," she said, gazing at him.

"I am." He let those words sit.

"Okay," she said. He smiled, she smiled.

✁

Yes, they happily married, but no, it was never clean, never whole.

He'd tried to curate the perfect life, with the right person, the money, and the circumstances. But it was impossible.

Trying to make it perfect imbeds the cracks that become the fissures that lead to the terrible earthquakes that render people and lives asunder.

Ryan shook his head, feeling tears in his eyes as the earthquake ripped away what remained. He stomped on the brakes, swerved into his driveway.

Kari's vehicle. *She was here.*

HANNAH LEE

Hannah Lee sat in her great room. She fingered the top of her cane. It was time to figure out what to do with her life. Her husband had a lover, had apparently been cheating for a long time—for weeks, maybe months.

Was he in love with her? Did he want a life with his...girlfriend?

He'd also apparently married Hannah Lee for her money. Now she knew the trail of breadcrumbs that he'd followed into her life.

Ryan was one of the assistants at the closing.

THE CLOSING

He was in the shadows to her because her vision was tunneled that day.

Selling her beloved business was overwhelming. She stilled the emotions by focusing narrowly, reading each page carefully, blocking out the conference room full of expectant people. The assistants, coming and going, were a blur.

How could she actually sign away her business—the place where she experienced the closest thing to family since her parents—to strangers? How could she walk away from her one source of day-to-day fulfillment?

FREE FALL

In the end, she chose to sell because of her shareholder employees—other people who could only draw salaries, who had this once-in-a-lifetime opportunity to secure their nest eggs.

She wanted to help them realize a level of wealth they'd never have obtained on their own. She sold the business because of them.

With each document placed in front of her, she stopped, focused, and called up the faces of her employees, one by one. With their images in her mind, she was able to continue.

Finally, she placed the last document into the stack and carefully laid down the pen. She was exhausted.

"I believe that's all, gentlemen," she said, raising her eyes to the people around the table, the faces she'd largely ignored.

She made her way home that night and celebrated by going to bed early with a good book.

The next day, she went to the office.

CHAPTER FIFTY-ONE

HANNAH LEE

Her heart sank at the thought of the events that had unfolded following the sale of her business. Ryan followed her to California, with the intention of seducing her. He made it his goal to win her heart and her money.

And she made it easy for him, with her social awkwardness, her long-buried need for someone to love her. And her recently acquired need to be loved apart from her wealth.

She fell for every move—the serendipitous arrival at the bookstore, bumping into one another at the Chamber of Commerce event, sex on the first date.

Sex—the raw passion, how enchanted he seemed. She'd never had a real lover before Ryan, someone with whom to explore the most private and intimate moments, someone who filled the emptiness that had never been filled before. Her senses had awakened with him—her femininity, her sexuality, the pleasure.

She mistook that for love, believed that because he took her to the heights of physical pleasure, it meant he loved her. Lying in his arms after making love, she *felt* loved, and therefore, she believed that he loved her.

Did she love him? If someone had asked that question weeks earlier, she'd have shaken her head at the obtuseness of it. Of course, she loved him! Wasn't it obvious, clear to everyone?

Now, it wasn't so clear. How can you know you love someone if you don't truly know that person? How could she be sure of her love for him when she was no longer sure of anything about him?

What difference did it make if she still loved him, anyway? Clearly, he did not love her.

Did he love Kari?

That thought stung deeply. Hannah Lee felt overwhelmed, at a loss.

She was the woman who could solve any business problem, but it had been at a price. She put all of her life eggs into the basket of building a business, none in the basket of relationships.

She didn't know how to do relationships. She had one close friend—Danielle—a best girlfriend. But she'd barely stayed in touch with Danielle after college, had only recently reforged a relationship when she moved to California.

And she had one former employee who somehow was a friend— Matteo, about whom she had mixed feelings.

Most women her age, she thought, had lives that were much more developed than hers. They had husbands who loved them and children who depended on them. Sometimes, on top of all that, they also had satisfying careers.

After selling the business, she told herself it was okay to enjoy her solitude, the absence of a job to go to every day, and she did. Most of the time.

Of course, she'd always told herself that she was content without a man, that she didn't need a romantic relationship or a husband.

She rarely thought about having children. She didn't feel driven enough to take any of the steps so many single women did these days— IVF with a sperm donor, surrogacy, adoption.

But then, she met Ryan, and all of the unfulfilled needs surged. The void in her life demanded filling, and he answered that demand.

For a while, she thought she'd miraculously arrived at a place in life with deeper rewards, the ones that had nothing to do with money. She'd even begun thinking about having a baby. But that was long before the accident.

Now, she felt emptier than she'd ever felt before.

KARI

She knew the path because she'd traveled it so many times.

She followed Ryan the first time—it was easy because, as she figured, he never noticed the vehicle behind him, the one driven by the woman whose bed he'd just left.

Once she knew the way, it was even easier. Sometimes she drove there, parked a half-mile away so her car wouldn't be spotted, and walked. She wore something dark, after sunset, late at night. She liked moving around on foot, unobserved and undetected by the unsuspecting homeowners.

California nights are beautiful—cool, dry air carried the night sounds far, especially in the quiet hills. She listened to night birds calling and trilling. She heard other vehicles pull slowly up the hill, traverse the narrow road, and park in front of their homes.

She listened to their low voices, their laughter, as they exited vehicles, slammed doors, and walked into their beautiful Carmel Valley homes.

She walked slowly through the neighborhood, sometimes sneaking around the sides of homes so she could observe people on their decks, talking, laughing, and clinking wine glasses.

Then, later, when most of them were in bed, the hour still not late—then, she crept up to Ryan and Hannah Lee's house.

If she got close enough, she could see through the glass panes of the front door, all the way through their living room. She saw Hannah Lee sitting on the sofa, reading, Ryan nearby on his laptop.

She watched them, and dreamed about being the woman on the sofa, Ryan by her side, safety and security enveloping her. The feelings were so strong she lost time.

MATTEO

Finally. Matteo inched forward over the train tracks, impatiently waiting for the traffic ahead to move faster. Why did people linger so long after the passing of a train? He was tempted to speed around the vehicle in front of him, and then the next one, but it was too dangerous. The road was impossibly narrow.

He called Hannah Lee again. It went straight to voice mail, and this time, he left an urgent message telling her to call back.

Why did he let her talk him into leaving her alone at the house? He knew it wasn't safe, that things were now moving rapidly. This was no longer a case of a guy who'd gone astray, cheated on his wife, and whom she would now quietly divorce and then move on.

Kari was the wild card in Hannah Lee and Ryan's life drama. The vision of Hannah Lee sitting in her home, still hobbled from her injuries, alone and unsuspecting, terrified him. She was far too trusting, too willing to assume the best.

She'd always been that way. Rarely had they needed to fire employees because of character issues or behavior that threatened the business. But Hannah Lee had always given them the benefit of the doubt—counseling, HR, and multiple chances to change.

Hannah Lee was a sitting duck, and he knew it.

KARI

She parked, walked to the door, and rang the doorbell of the house she'd wanted to enter for so long. Hannah Lee opened the door and gazed at Kari, surprise registering, perhaps more because of the gun in Kari's hand than her actual presence.

Hannah Lee leaned slightly on a cane. "I know who you are," she said.

"Great. That saves me from wasting time explaining it to you. Now move," said Kari, waving the gun at Hannah Lee, who stepped back.

They sat improbably in the great room, Hannah Lee on the sofa and Kari perched on the edge of an overstuffed chair. Kari gazed around the room, openly admiring. *What would it be like to live in a home like this?* She'd soon find out.

Her thoughts twisted like a snake in heavy brush. She felt confused but also resolute.

She focused on Hannah Lee, tried to make sense of things. First, she was nice looking but by no means beautiful. What did Ryan see in her? Besides the money, that is.

Hannah Lee's eyes flashed with quiet intelligence, and Kari felt envious. What did this woman have that she did not?

Hannah Lee said nothing to Kari, tension reflected in her eyes and stiff posture.

But Kari didn't want Hannah Lee to feel afraid. It was far easier to get what you wanted in other ways.

She looked down at her own hand, holding the Beretta Tomcat 3032 automatic. She purchased it long ago for personal protection, or so she'd told herself.

She tucked it in her purse but left the top open for easy access. She smiled at Hannah Lee.

"What a beautiful home," Kari said. She cocked her head and narrowed her eyes a bit. "You, though, I don't understand. Why are you still here?"

CHAPTER FIFTY-TWO

HANNAH LEE

Her pulse raced, and she tried to think clearly. *Where was Ryan?* Oh, wait, it might not matter since his girlfriend was sitting here, with a gun, the silent threat protruding slightly from the top of her bag.

Kari was stunning. Her physical beauty was astonishing, but Hannah Lee also saw and felt the deterioration, the descent into some form of madness, the absence of warmth, the lack of humanity.

The presence of cunning.

Kari's eyes explored Hannah Lee's home, and then she felt those brilliant sea-green eyes slowly scanning her. A chill ran down her spine. This was not a once-over, but an assessing look. She felt like a specimen, peered at through a microscope. No one had ever looked at her that way.

Hannah Lee met countless people in the business world over the years, and they sat on the spectrum of humanity: from the stoic, analytical types who almost faked their emotions, or didn't bother to, all the way to the most sensitive and caring types, who typically sat in H.R. roles.

But never had Hannah Lee met anyone like Kari, whose cold, inhumane perusal felt threatening on a visceral level. This was someone capable of violence. She knew that, in a way she couldn't have explained.

Something told her to engage Kari in conversation and keep it non-confrontational. She picked up on the comment about the beauty of her home.

"Thank you."

"Did Ryan do this? Did he build this house?"

"No, it was done before we met."

"Of course, it was," Kari almost sneered. Then, bizarrely, she asked, "How about a tour?"

Her voice was odd, disconnected from the surreal scene in which the two women sat. This could have been cocktail party chatter. Showing off your home was a normal thing to do with a guest who'd never been there before. But now, she was going to show her home, *their* home, to Ryan's lover.

She rose awkwardly, using her cane, and turned toward the kitchen. Kari followed, carrying her bag. *If only she'd left the bag with the gun behind.*

There were knives in the kitchen. She thought quickly about which ones might be easiest to reach. Her eyes scanned the countertop and found the wooden knife block. She thought about the serrated vegetable knife with the sharp point on the end. No, it should be the much larger chopping knife. That was sturdier.

She shivered. *Could she actually use a knife on another human being?* If she could get to the knife block, and if she could draw one out quickly enough, could she actually *stab* Kari?

She knew she couldn't if it meant she had to take the first step without provocation. Despite her treacherous situation, she couldn't imagine plunging a knife into Kari's chest, blood pouring out of the wound, and maybe having to do it again, and again, until she dropped the gun.

She shuddered at the thought. No, that was impossible.

What if Kari threatened her with the gun? If she did, there wouldn't

284

be enough time to use a knife in self-defense. The old saying, *never bring a knife to a gunfight,* flashed in her mind.

But it was better than having no way of defending herself. She moved carefully toward the knife block.

"Wait," said Kari. "Stop right there. You think I'm stupid, don't you?"

She pulled the gun out and gestured. "The kitchen. Knives. Nice try! Get over here," she snarled, waving the gun at the living room sofa.

Hannah Lee made her way back and sat carefully, keeping her eyes on Kari and on the gun. Back and forth. Kari. Gun. Kari.

There was no point trying to be subtle anymore.

KARI

"What do you want?" asked Hannah Lee.

Kari smiled, feeling her eyes burn.

"It's not just what I want. It's what *we* want. Ryan and I."

"You and Ryan."

"Yes. He loves me—we love each other—and we want to be together, so you have to let him go."

"He's free to go anytime, Kari."

Once again, she was being underestimated. Anger rose.

"I don't think so," she told Ryan's wife-who-should-be-dead-already. She should get it over with; kill her now. The urge almost overpowered her. She was justified, after all. This woman had tried to grab a knife, was planning to attack her. Was going to kill *her*.

Her finger tightened on the trigger.

But now was not the time. The plan had to be in place first.

She couldn't afford to let the darkness overtake her and ruin the plan. She willed herself to stay calm, to stay in control.

HANNAH LEE

She dared not breathe for fear of setting her off. She focused her eyes on Kari's, while her mind focused on the gun she held.

Kari clutched the small bag and her eyes burned with intensity.

She's losing touch with reality.

"What did you say?" she asked Hannah Lee, confusion playing across her lovely features again.

"I said, he's free to go any time. Perhaps you're right. Maybe you and Ryan belong together," said Hannah Lee carefully, feeling the gall.

"No, he's not free!" Kari exploded, then seemed to pull herself back. She rubbed one hand over her eyes as if to scrub away something obscuring her vision. "He's not free," she whispered. "You know he's not. It's the money," she said, louder, more confidently.

"His background—growing up in poverty, his parents. He'll never leave and risk going back to that. He won't leave as long as he can have *this*," she said, waving her hands wildly at the great room, swinging around the gun.

Hannah Lee said nothing, watching Kari while keeping her secondary focus on the gun. If Kari pointed the gun at her, she'd have to do something. But what could she do?

She could dive for the floor and hope to dodge the shot. She'd read somewhere that most people are terrible shots and greatly overestimate their ability to hit even an up-close target such as another person across the room.

Or she could dive toward Kari's legs, tackle her, and hope that the shot went toward the ceiling. But Hannah Lee knew she couldn't dive anywhere. She lacked the range of motion and couldn't imagine her body moving swiftly in any direction. It simply hurt too much.

She wasn't the star of an action movie, ready to spring into impossible action at just the right moment. Not on her best day, and certainly not while she needed a cane.

"If we get a divorce, he will get half the money," Hannah Lee lied to Kari, speaking slowly and calmly, drawing out the conversation. "It's a community property state. That's plenty of money."

"No! That's a lie," said Kari, eyes boring into Hannah Lee. "It's in a trust, and he doesn't get it unless you die," she whispered harshly.

Hannah Lee's breath caught. *How did she know?*

Ryan. Of course, he'd told Kari all about the money, about the trust.

Ryan told his lover about Hannah Lee's money, including the part about how she'd have to die for him to get it.

CHAPTER FIFTY-THREE

HANNAH LEE

The totality of Ryan's betrayal punched another hole in her heart, threatening to level her. Dread settled in her stomach. This woman—*Ryan's lover*—was going to kill her. Perhaps she had already tried.

"Was it you?" she asked. "I heard someone while I was in ICU, someone who said something about why I didn't die on the mountain."

"You heard that? That was a slip. I didn't think you were awake, but of course, you were faking. What else did you fake to make Ryan feel sorry for you? To get him to stay with you?"

Hannah Lee's cheeks burned. She could almost hear the conversations that he must have had with Kari about her while she lay alone in the hospital, and later, alone in this house, struggling with her physical therapy and recovery.

Yeah, she's really a lot better, just pretending it's worse than it is. Sad, really, how pathetically she's holding on, trying to keep me there. But it won't work.

"What about the paraglider? What did you do to make it fail? You were there that day. You rigged everything for the flight."

"Paraglider?" Kari pretended to think, to be puzzled. "Yeah, it's too bad it failed that day, but it certainly wasn't my fault."

But her words didn't ring true. She didn't even bother trying to cover it up.

Heartache and devastation threatened to overcome Hannah Lee. But something else drove her more. *What about Ryan?* She had to know.

"Did Ryan help you do it? Did he rig the paraglider with you? Did he know you were going to do it? Tell me, Kari. You might as well since it doesn't matter anymore."

And Kari, in that inexplicable way people often feel compelled to reveal their misdeeds, told her. "Of course not. Don't you know your own husband? Do you think he can act, change things when needed? No, he can't. He's too passive. I can't stand passivity," she said venomously.

Hannah Lee searched for a way to penetrate the rage, the lack of control. "Listen to me, Kari. If you hurt me, you won't get away with it. You'll go to prison for murder, and then you can't be with Ryan."

Kari smirked. "Not really. I know how to cover up evidence. Did you know there are videos out there that show you how to commit the perfect crime?"

Hannah Lee felt a deeper chill go down her spine.

Kari's fake smile dropped. "Besides, I'm not going to murder anyone. *You* are going to fix this, and Ryan and I will get on with our lives."

Hannah Lee felt a hum in her body.

The old brain senses what the new brain tries to deny. It is too primitive for the language of reason, sensing the proximity of a predator before the rational brain registers danger.

There was an aura of violence about Kari that belied her words, an energy that was growing minute by minute. Hannah Lee knew she couldn't trust what Kari said. Kari held the gun and all the power. Hannah Lee was still crippled from her accident, and she stood in the way of everything Kari wanted.

"Okay, I'll fix it," she told her. "I'll see my attorney first thing tomorrow and change the terms of the trust. Ryan will get half of it when we divorce." She held her breath, praying silently.

Kari stared at her. Rubbed her eyes with one hand again and looked up with intensity. "No, no, no, no, *NO!*" she said, shaking her head, her voice rising with each no. "That's not going to work—you're lying! You'll never do that. No, there's only one way."

She stood, pulled the gun out of her purse again, and pointed it at Hannah Lee, whose heart leaped into her throat. She froze.

"Come on," said Kari, gesturing to Hannah Lee. "It's time to go."

Hannah Lee's focus narrowed, and she searched her mind for potential solutions to this problem.

She sat still, thinking.

"Move!" Kari said, gesturing with the gun.

She moved, but as slowly as she possibly could, leaning more heavily on the cane than needed, her mind working on the problem. She groaned a bit, hoping to stall and gain more time, but Kari wasn't having any of it. She yanked Hannah Lee's free arm, almost causing her to fall.

They moved toward the front door. Hannah Lee knew the worst thing she could do was leave and go anywhere with Kari, but she had no choice.

Hannah Lee heard a vehicle pull up outside. *Oh no*, she thought. *Ella!* She tried to call out to tell her to run, but the front door flew open.

MATTEO

Matteo sped up the hill to Hannah Lee's house, hoping he was wrong, that Kari would never go there, never actually do anything violent. But she'd shown the depth of her rage, and he helped trigger it, knowingly lit the fuse.

He provoked and manipulated her, hoping for a confession, or a breakdown, and then, Ryan's exit from Hannah Lee's life. It was a fantasy— Ryan away with his girlfriend, the road clear to Hannah Lee's heart.

He felt ashamed that his own desires had led him to his actions.

He'd completely underestimated the degree of Kari's pathology, poked a hornet's nest, and now the stingers were aimed at Hannah Lee.

If anything happened to Hannah Lee, *it was his fault*. He prayed as he stepped on the gas.

CHAPTER FIFTY-FOUR

RYAN

Ryan threw open the door and bolted out of his truck. His legs seemed to move in slow motion, like those dreams in which you are pursued by something terrible and can't get away.

He knew what to do now. He'd hurt Hannah Lee beyond repair. Their marriage was in shambles. He cheated on her and lied about it for months. That was one thing. But putting her in danger was another. He could do something about that.

He felt resolute, strong in his intention. It wasn't too late. It *couldn't* be too late.

He could stop this, stop whatever Kari had in mind. He could protect Hannah Lee. His heart sang with the purity of it, with the certainty and realization that at last, he could do something good.

Maybe, if he were truly lucky, eventually, Hannah Lee would forgive him. If she forgave him, he could go on. His feet moved faster as the scenes flashed in his mind. Hannah Lee forgiving him. He flooded with hope, with the shining vision of a clear heart, a clean life.

He threw open the front door. Kari stood there, waving a gun, her eyes wild, her hand gripping Hannah Lee, who was deathly pale.

KARI

Kari faced Ryan and smiled at him through tears that began cascading down her cheeks. Something was terribly wrong. He wasn't supposed to be here. *Why was she crying?*

"What are you doing, Kari?" he asked, freezing in place.

Certainty set in, and Kari casually waved the gun in Ryan's direction. It was good that he was here, good that he could see how much she loved him, that she was willing to do anything for him.

He wouldn't take care of their problem, but she would. She could take care of all of it. If only he would just back off.

No one expects the beautiful girl to have the ability to fix things, to figure out the winding pathway to a solution. Everyone had such low expectations of her. They didn't see her coming, had no idea of the extent of her capabilities, how far she would go to make everything okay.

"Hi, honey," she said brightly. "We were just talking about things."

"What are you *doing*, Kari?" Ryan stepped toward her, but she pulled back and aimed the gun at Hannah Lee. He stopped and put his hands up.

"I'm taking care of things like I always do," she said in a sing-song voice, the damaged little girl overtaking the woman. Now Ryan would see how much she loved him, would see that she was the right woman for him.

He'd be done with Hannah Lee because she would be gone, *forever*. Kari wouldn't have to compete for love ever again.

She felt a slight sheen of sweat on her upper lip. She drifted momentarily as her mind replayed scenes from the past. *What was he saying?* Something about Eric, that jerk.

"I talked to Eric," Ryan said. "He told me about you and your relationship. *I know,* Kari."

She waved away that comment with the gun, irritated. "He's a lying scumbag, like I told you, honey. You can't believe a word he says. Anyway, what does that matter?"

"Kari, put down the gun. Let's talk about this," Ryan said, taking another step toward her, holding out his hand.

Kari aimed the gun at him, not sure why. What was he doing? Was he trying to protect Hannah Lee? Was he putting *her* before Kari? *Unbelievable.*

Rage rose and began to burn her insides. Her vision tunneled. Her hand shook, and she gripped the gun tighter. "Shut up, Ryan. Like I said, I'm taking care of things. Now, why don't you just turn around and leave?"

≈≈

Matteo slammed on the brakes just before hitting the back of Ryan's truck. He threw open the door, and ran to Hannah Lee's front door, which stood open. He slowed down, listening intently.

He heard voices inside, but more importantly, he heard something that sent a chill down his spine. The voice that spoke now was low, feminine, but menacing. He peered inside and saw a terrifying scene that galvanized him into action.

Kari held a gun, pointed at Ryan, but with Hannah Lee standing nearby, her arm gripped by Kari's other hand. Suddenly, she swung the gun toward Hannah Lee.

"No!" Matteo yelled as he ran, swiftly, yet so slowly. Too slowly for the flash of the gun.

CHAPTER FIFTY-FIVE

HANNAH LEE

What happened next did so in slow motion, at least it seemed that way later when she recalled the events of the evening for the police. This time, her memory was painfully intact—she had no problem remembering every horrific detail.

After telling Ryan to leave, Kari swung the gun, pointed it at Hannah Lee, and fired.

But Ryan was already in motion. He reached out to Hannah Lee and pushed her. She fell in slow motion, her arms windmilling for something to grab, finding only air. She crashed into the hardwood floor, her already broken body screaming from the pain. She both heard and felt her pelvis fracture again.

Ryan lay still, downed by the bullet meant for Hannah Lee.

Kari's wild eyes took in Ryan's body on the floor. "Noooo!" She ran to Ryan, kneeled by him, and put her hands on his chest.

"No!" she screamed again and raised her now bloody hands, one of them still gripping the gun.

She stood and turned to Hannah Lee, face twisted with rage.

"No!" cried Matteo. Kari's eyes darted to Matteo, who had suddenly appeared on the scene.

"This is your fault!" she screamed, swinging the gun toward Matteo.

Matteo tackled Kari as the gun fired for the second time. There was a loud thud, and Kari let out a whump, followed by quiet.

Hannah Lee pulled herself up, using the cane, her movements agonizingly slow. The pain was intense. She quickly surveyed the room. There was blood everywhere, and three bodies lay on the floor.

Instinctively, she went to Matteo, knelt painfully, and felt for a pulse. It was there, but weak. She couldn't tell where the bullet had hit him, but a small lake of blood slowly grew under his body.

She turned to Ryan, horrified by what she saw. His chest was a mass of blood, and he lay with glazed eyes. She had to get help fast.

A small figure walked in the open front door and froze in shock.

"Ella," said Hannah Lee in a firm voice. "*Get out*—it's not safe here. Call the police from outside."

But Ella stood frozen, scanning the scene. Kari, on the floor reeling from hitting her head on the wooden arm of the sofa, moaned softly. She reached out to retrieve the gun that lay a few inches away.

Kari stretched her fingers, and Hannah Lee knew she'd never have time to get to the gun first.

She focused intently. "Ella," said Hannah Lee, voice low but commanding. "Ella, *the gun*. Kick it away."

Ella's head swung toward Hannah Lee, eyes wide and panicked. Hanna Lee pointed at the gun.

Kari's hand stretched to the gun, fingertips touching it, grasping.

"*Now*, Ella," Hannah Lee said loudly.

Ella ran over and kicked the gun away from Kari, who screamed, enraged. She pulled herself up and stood, wobbly, and lunged toward the gun again.

Ella stood dazed, her body slack.

Hannah Lee, almost passing out from pain, hobbled with the help of the cane to Kari, grabbed her by the shoulder, spun her around, and hit her in the jaw as hard as she could. It hurt like hell, but Kari dropped like a sack and lay still.

Ella ran over, put her arms around Hannah Lee, and they stood there hugging, sobbing with a mix of relief and fear.

Sirens sounded in the distance, summoned no doubt by neighbors who'd heard the unlikely sound of gunshots in their quiet neighborhood.

～✀～

Hannah Lee knelt on the floor beside Ryan, holding his hand. First responders rushed around doing their jobs. Paramedics were focusing on Matteo. She prayed he would be okay. After taking Kari away, the police were questioning Ella, who'd calmed down enough to talk.

"Hannah Lee," whispered Ryan, blood bubbling from his mouth.

"Shh, don't talk," she said. "Help is coming."

"No, I have to tell you," he said, his voice raspy. "I'm so sorry. You're amazing and beautiful. Don't ever think it was all about the money. It was, but then it wasn't, and I never meant—the accident—it wasn't me, but I put you in danger when I brought her into our lives."

He coughed, and more blood bubbled.

"Ryan, I know it wasn't you. You didn't have anything to do with the accident."

"It's all my fault," he gasped before his eyes rolled up into his head, and he lay still.

"Ryan," she said, "Ryan! You have to hang in there."

Paramedics rushed to Ryan, pushing Hannah Lee aside. She groaned, and one of them helped her to the sofa and into a reclining position.

She couldn't stay there. She lunged up, using the cane, almost screaming from the pain, and hobbled out of the house behind the paramedics, who quickly loaded Ryan into the emergency vehicle.

"Wait! Please, I'm his wife. You have to take me with him."

One of the paramedics helped her in and pointed to a place to sit. He asked her a few questions and quickly determined that most of her injuries predated tonight's mayhem. "Still, you need to be checked out when we get to the hospital," he told her, then turned his attention to Ryan.

As they rendered first aid, Ryan's eyelids fluttered, and he focused on Hannah Lee. "Hey," he rasped.

"Hey," she said. "You're going to be fine. You have to hold on for just a few minutes. These people are taking great care of you, and when we get to the hospital, you will get the best of care."

"Just remember what I said," he gurgled. "I meant it. You don't deserve what I did to you."

"Stop talking, Ryan. Everything's going to be okay," she said, a sense of urgency threading into her voice.

He smiled sadly and whispered one last time, "I'm so sorry, Hannah Lee. Please forgive me." His eyes closed.

The rescue vehicle raced down the hill, siren bleating. Hannah Lee leaned back and tried to rest.

Suddenly, Ryan's eyes flew open wide. "Hannah Lee! Please, tell my mom and dad—tell them I love them."

"You can tell them, Ryan," she said. "You're going to be okay," she finished with her last bit of energy.

She closed her eyes, the pain too much, and darkness descended.

CHAPTER FIFTY-SIX

The next few days dragged like a slow-moving bad dream for Hannah Lee. It began with waking up from surgery for the injuries from her fall on the night of the shooting. The first thing she noticed was that her room was too quiet. Too empty. But that didn't last.

It wasn't long before she received a visit from a detective who queried her extensively about the shootings. It was exhausting but she knew she had to tell the story, keeping it short and as factual as possible.

Nurses came and went. She could hear them whispering outside her room, but no one would tell her anything about Ryan. Finally, Danielle rushed in, sat by her side, and told her.

Ryan never made it out of surgery. His injuries were too severe. Thankfully, she refrained from expressing her contempt for Ryan. Instead, she was the real friend she'd always been, holding Hannah Lee's hand tightly while she sobbed.

After that, she focused on recovery while others were present. But alone, the tears slipped silently down her cheeks and soaked her pillow. She couldn't let go of the notion that Ryan had died alone, that she hadn't been there in his last moments.

Matteo's condition was touch-and-go for a couple of days, but finally, she was told he'd been moved into a private room next to hers. She immediately demanded a wheelchair and now sat in his room.

MATTEO

He woke up enough to register her presence, smiled, then started to sit up, concerned. "Hannah Lee, what are you doing in a wheelchair? Are you—?"

"It's okay. I'm fine. I had to have surgery again for the fracture, but they say I'm actually doing great. You are the one we were all worried about."

He lay back again, tiredly, eyes half-closed. But they popped open. "What about—?"

"Ryan didn't make it," she said, gazing down.

"I'm sorry," Matteo said, meaning it. The dude was corrupt to the core, but he didn't deserve to die like that. "And...?"

"Unfortunately, Kari's still around. She's been charged with one count of murder and two counts of attempted murder. She has a celebrity lawyer, and she's pleading not guilty by reason of insanity." Hannah Lee looked disgusted.

"Her lawyer says she's been diagnosed with Borderline Personality disorder, which means her attorney can claim she had a psychotic break. If the jury believes her, she could walk away."

"That is messed up," said Matteo.

"Even more messed up is the media exposure she's getting."

Matteo could see that. The media loves a beautiful criminal, almost as much as a beautiful victim.

But he was grateful, flooded with gratitude. Hannah Lee was okay. They were both alive and would be well again, and that was nothing short of miraculous.

HANNAH LEE

After discharge from the hospital, Hannah Lee went back to her house, which Ella and Danielle had purged of all signs of violence. As an extra step, Danielle hired an energy cleansing 'shaman,' who used an herbal smudge stick to rid the house of 'negative energy.' *That is so California*, thought Hannah Lee.

She insisted on Hannah Lee's presence and led her through a ritual with the smudge stick. Hannah Lee went along with it but secretly thought it was frivolous.

Still, she never had a dark moment in the house after returning home. It wasn't that she couldn't remember what had happened that night. She remembered all of it. But the memories were, thankfully, mostly tucked away.

Hannah Lee contacted Ryan's parents to inform them of his death. She left out most of the details, sparing them the horror of hearing about their son's dark descent. Of course, she knew they would eventually find out during the trial.

Ryan's memorial service was unspeakably sad. Hannah Lee wrangled a private nurse and wheelchair so she could attend. She insisted on flying his parents to California and putting them up in a local bed and breakfast. Her reasoning was that Ryan's life was here in Carmel Valley, so it was the right place.

A sprinkling of Ryan's construction friends attended respectfully, along with Danielle, who stood stoically throughout, and Joe.

Hannah Lee would never forget his parent's shattered faces, his mother's anguish. He'd hurt so many people, broken so many hearts. How would they ever recover? Still, she refused to accept that the hurt and pain was the entire legacy of Ryan's abbreviated life.

After the service, Joe sat down with Ryan's parents and gave them the news that they'd inherited some money from their son. It wasn't a fortune, but it would make them more comfortable.

Only Joe and Hannah Lee knew the true origin of the money. She knew it wouldn't heal their broken hearts, but she also knew they would feel more secure financially. She knew that Ryan—the Ryan who'd begged her to tell his parents he loved them with his last breath—would have wanted that.

That day, she finally, truly grieved. She grieved for Ryan and his parents, for a life cut unbearably short. She grieved for the person she'd glimpsed at the end of his life, the man who, had he lived, might have become a real partner to her.

She grieved for her mistakes, for the life she thought she had, and for the life she wished it could have become.

She silently prayed for God's forgiveness for Ryan.

She'd already forgiven him.

The person she struggled to forgive was herself.

⤚⦿⦿⤙

A few days after the memorial service, she returned to the hospital to help Matteo check out. It was his last day in the hospital, and he told her he planned to stay in a local inn before going home.

"You can have the spare bedroom," said Hannah Lee.

"There's no need for that," he said, not meaning it.

"I know. But I want you there for a while. It's a little too quiet," she said, wondering if it was more than that.

"Are you sure?" he asked.

"Of course," she said firmly.

When Hannah Lee made up her mind, there was no arguing the point. And this was one argument he didn't want to win.

CHAPTER FIFTY-SEVEN

Days turned into weeks as Hannah Lee and Matteo recovered. Between her physical therapist and his, plus Ella, they rarely had time alone together.

Having him there eased her days. They read quietly while music played, napped on the deck in the afternoons, played cards, and sipped hot tea while gazing into the fireplace in the evenings.

One evening, she turned to him and sighed. "Matteo?"

He looked up from his book and smiled.

"We need to talk," she said hesitantly.

❧

Uh oh. He carefully closed the book and waited.

"I'm sorry, so sorry that I dragged you into my messed-up life and put you in danger."

Her eyes welled up, and he moved over to sit by her, slightly alarmed.

"No, it's okay," she said, sniffling. "I'm fine. But what I did to you is not. I should never have called you. I should have handled my own problems with Ryan."

She shook her head, mournfully. "When I think about what might have happened to you, I—well, there are no words. I'm so terribly sorry. Can you ever forgive me?"

Forgive her?

He pulled her into his arms and held her close. "There's nothing to forgive," he whispered into her hair. "I am so glad I was there to help. I'm so glad the bullet hit me instead of you."

She pulled away and looked at him in shock.

He couldn't help it. He took in her tousled hair, her full lips, partly open as she struggled for something to say. He leaned in, his eyes beginning to close. But she'd already turned away. She went to her desk, pulled something out, and handed it to him.

"What is this?"

"It's your hospital bill. I paid your deductible, and I'm covering all the home health care costs that aren't covered by insurance."

"What?" he said. "You know I can afford to pay my own bills. Why are you doing this?"

"Because I—I need to."

He threw the papers down. "No."

He burned silently. Here he was, warming up to a romantic moment, and instead of sharing the vibe, she was all about paying him back for some imaginary debt.

Great.

He stood to go to the guest bedroom. *Guest* bedroom.

He'd felt his feelings growing for weeks, felt his heart opening up with her even more than in the past. What a fool. She'd never seen him as anything but a friend. That wasn't going to change.

"Matteo, wait," she said.

"It's okay," he said, stopping for a moment to look back at her. "I'll be out tomorrow."

"Matteo," she whispered. He turned away, suddenly cold.

What just happened?

Hannah Lee sat in her room, her mind tracing back over the past few weeks. When had Matteo's warm feelings for her changed? They were doing so well. Sharing her home, sharing so much time together. It could have been awkward—after all, so much time had passed since he worked for her.

Instead, it had been near perfection. She'd never felt so comfortable around a man before. With Ryan, there'd always been an underlying thread of tension. But not since their honeymoon had she really felt carefree with Ryan. She sometimes wondered if those early, wondrous feelings had ever been real.

Ryan brought passion into her life, but along with it, darkness. She'd denied it, told herself it was stress from his work. But there was something that she felt prevented him from being fully with her, something that had hung around the edges of his personality. Something oppressive.

Now, she knew her husband had always had a secret agenda. She remembered everything, all of the confusion and heartache leading up to the day of the accident. And knew why Ryan had pulled away even more.

The only comfort she had was knowing he hadn't tried to kill her; Kari had.

Once again, she sagged with the pain of it. How had she married someone who hadn't really loved her? Someone who plotted to marry her for money, and then cheated on her?

But recovery was possible, and she'd experienced it. Her heart felt lighter and freer each day.

Being with Matteo the past few weeks had been so good, so comfortable. She'd start to tell him something, and he'd finish her thought. She caught him gazing at her at times, a warm smile playing over his lips.

There was something so incredibly light and warm about Matteo's presence. When he walked into the room and greeted her, her spirits lifted. When he playfully threw down the cards and swore that she cheated, it made her laugh out loud.

At night, before going to their separate rooms, they hugged warmly. And there, in Matteo's embrace, she felt truly safe. And, perhaps, something more.

She'd taken a risk, asking Matteo to recover in her home, and she'd never once regretted it. Now, she wondered. Had she misread him? That wouldn't be surprising. She'd always had trouble reading between the lines with men.

CHAPTER FIFTY-EIGHT

Flight booked, bags packed, Mateo sat alone in the living room waiting for his ride. She begged him to stay longer, citing the fact that he hadn't fully recovered. He politely declined. She begged him to let her take him to the airport, but he refused.

"You've done enough for me," he said coldly. "I'm grateful for having a place to stay, but I'm fine now."

He didn't bother to look up as Hannah Lee made her way over to him. She sat gingerly nearby.

"Matteo," she said softly. "Please, talk to me. Don't leave like this."

"Just leave, right?" he said softly but bitterly.

"No! That's not what I meant."

"What did you mean?" he asked, looking at her, searching her face, her eyes. Hoping once more for an indication of something more.

"I...I meant to say, I'm so...grateful," she finished lamely, looking down at her hands in her lap.

"Grateful. Yes, I know. You don't have to be," he said, closed off again.

"Yes, I do! You literally saved my life. How do I ever thank you? If you could stay a little longer, maybe..." she stumbled to a halt.

❧

What *did* she mean? *What was she really trying to say?*

Hannah Lee's breath was shallow as she sat, frozen. She felt his eyes on her, his breath held, as he waited. Finally, he sighed and stood up.

Still, she sat mutely.

He grabbed his backpack and bag, opened the door, and electricity coursed through her body.

"Wait!" she cried out, looking up in panic.

But the door was closed.

Her body refused to move. *How could she go after him, no matter how much she might want to?*

She had no right to say anything to Matteo other than *thank you.* He'd already given enough, been through enough, for her. He didn't need one more minute in her messed-up life.

Her mind blank, she rose slowly, walked to the door, pulled it open.

Outside, she saw Matteo standing at the curb. He climbed into the rideshare he'd called. The car began pulling away.

She stopped thinking. She ran, grabbed the car door handle, pulled it open, and stood there, shaking, and breathless.

The driver slammed on the brakes and stared at her. "What the—?" he exclaimed.

"Hannah Lee," said Matteo. "What are you doing?"

"It's just that—I don't know myself anymore. How can I tell you how I really feel when I'm so screwed up? I thought I had it all figured out, Matteo. You know? I had this great little life here, more money than I could ever spend… How did this happen?"

The driver's eyes flew open wide.

"Then, Ryan came along, and I thought I knew him. I married him! And I had no clue who he was, not really. I loved him, or at least, I loved who I thought he was," she said, tears welling up in her eyes.

"Hannah Lee," said Matteo.

"No. Let me say this. Now, I don't know what's real and what isn't. I don't trust…I don't trust…"

"Anyone," said Matteo, resigned.

"No! *I don't trust me*," she said raggedly. "And I don't know how to do that, how to get through my life not knowing if what I see, or what I feel, has any merit."

She wiped away tears.

"After everything that's happened, I know I have no right to ask for anything from you. No right at all. Your Mamá would tell you to run away fast and far, and she would be right. But—" Sobs wracked her now.

"Stay," she finally croaked, gasping. "Please, Matteo, stay."

He did.

They stayed up late into the night, talking.

―――

Hannah Lee was exhausted, spent. She'd never unburdened herself so much, never opened up, and shared all of her pain with anyone like this. Even Danielle. Through it all, Matteo listened, nodding, getting up to bring hot tea. He never once interrupted, never once tried to stop her from talking. Nor did he try to fix it. He just let her talk.

Amazing.

She drew a breath and looked into Matteo's eyes, dreading what she might see. He smiled a tiny bit.

"It's okay. You don't have to have any answers right now. I'm just glad you felt like you could tell me."

"Right," she said, sighing.

"You know, I do know how you feel," he said, gazing into the distance. "I married someone for all the wrong reasons. The worst part is I thought I knew what I was doing."

Again, Hannah Lee felt acute embarrassment about the choices she'd made. In the beginning of her relationship with Ryan, a voice she hadn't wanted to hear had issued a faint warning. But she'd tamped it down, choosing, instead, a life that wasn't hers.

Now she knew the high cost of ignoring that voice and, in so doing, betraying herself. Now, she had the work of rebuilding her own trust in herself and in her life choices.

She checked her gut, listening intently for any faint warnings about Matteo, any little voice telling her he was yet another bad choice.

She breathed out slowly, testing herself. Peace washed over her in waves.

They sat quietly. Then, surprising herself, she leaned over and softly planted her lips on his.

❧

That night, they shared the same bedroom. And every night after that.

CHAPTER FIFTY-NINE

FOURTEEN MONTHS LATER

"I'm telling you, it doesn't matter anymore. Who gets married these days? Twenty-somethings who dream of big weddings and white princess gowns. That's not me. Let's see," said Hannah Lee, stabbing her salad with a fork.

She chewed thoughtfully while Matteo stared at her, smirking.

"Oh. And people whose religious beliefs dictate marriage before, or shortly after, sex. *Definitely* before babies. Or, shortly afterward."

"Yeah. After babies. Or maybe, one baby?" he asked playfully.

"Again, that's not us. We're secure. I'm secure. Are you?" she challenged him swiftly.

"Totally. *Te amo, mi amor.*" He blew her a kiss.

She caught it in the air and planted it on her lips, smiling.

"But what about Bella?" he asked innocently.

"Bella is totally secure. She has two parents who love her to the moon and back," she said, playfully defiant. "She will grow up knowing that her parents adore each other and are totally committed. Right?"

"Right," he said, smiling.

"Even your Mamá is okay. She's come to terms with our...family life."

"My Mamá adores you and Bella," he confirmed.

"Speaking of," she said, rising to the sound of a little one's cries of distress. Ella walked into the room carrying their three-month-old baby girl. Hannah Lee took her in her arms, lifted her blouse, and began nursing.

"You know I'm not going to give up," he said, carrying plates into the kitchen. "My dream is to marry you. I don't care about your dress or the size of the event. I want to stand there, with you, in front of the people who matter, and declare my commitment to you."

"Well, you're going to have to surprise me, then," Hannah Lee said. "Because if I think about it too much, it won't happen. You know why."

"Yes, I do, but no, I don't. What happened before has nothing to do with us. It wasn't marriage that hurt you, Hannah Lee. It was your broken picker—"

"My broken *what?*"

"Your broken *picker*. You *picked* the wrong guy. Uh, guys."

"Right," she said, rolling her eyes.

"Right. You just hadn't met the right guy yet. Or hadn't noticed he was right in front of you the entire time." Matteo smiled, and she smiled.

"After I put Bella down for her nap, let's go over the floor plans," she said, cleverly changing the subject.

He knew it for what it was. He'd treaded again on the territory that remained sensitive. He sighed. "Of course."

Later, they reviewed plans for the small business they intended to open. It was somewhat frivolous, their idea, but it was something that excited them both. They worked so well together, enjoyed collaborating, again.

Hannah Lee insisted on setting up a foundation with the goal of identifying philanthropic opportunities to make a difference. She poured most of her wealth into the foundation, joyfully and with no hesitation.

For the first time since the closing, she felt comfortable about money. It was no longer a weight she carried. She felt free.

She kept the perfect amount for her "nest egg," as she'd always intended.

Matteo insisted that they legally partition their assets when they found out she was pregnant. She pushed back, but he made his point. Neither of them ever wanted money to be a dividing issue between them.

A FEW WEEKS LATER

"What else do we need to do?" Hanna Lee mentally checked items off her list, still trying to put together the rest. "The caterer has everything else handled. Oh—I almost forgot. There was one more paycheck to sign at the store. The bookkeeper forgot to include our newest employee."

"Let's swing by there on our way to get the wine," said Matteo.

As she headed to the door, he grabbed her playfully and pulled her in for a quick kiss. She smiled as they pulled apart. Tonight's party promised to be fun, and she was determined to minimize the stress so she could actually have a good time.

Her cell phone rang, and her heart dropped when she recognized the number. She answered, listened, nodded, and punched off. "That was Joe. I need to go see him now."

❧

"I thought you might want to hear the update," Joe told her as they sat in his office. "The trial date has been set by the judge. It's next month, I'm afraid."

"Will I have to testify?" But she knew the answer. "Of course, I will. I am not looking forward to that," she said quietly.

Joe reviewed a few more details about the trial and what to expect, but there wasn't much more.

Hannah Lee and Joe reflected again on the bizarre chain of events that had led her to this point. The closing—Ryan, the assistant she hadn't remembered due to the stress of the day. Ryan—following her to California and romancing his way into her life and her money. Then, Ryan meeting Kari, and bringing her into their lives. And Kari—two failed attempts on Hannah Lee's life. Tightness gripped her chest as she flashed again on Ryan that terrible night—losing his life. To save hers.

There was little she didn't know, now, about Kari, about the upcoming trial, and about the sordid tale of Ryan's relationship with the defendant. All of which was already public, but which would now be exposed in excruciating detail—endless fodder for the media, available for repeated loops on the morning and evening news.

Mistress Kills Rich Girl's Husband

It was a story that she'd be re-living for months and possibly years.

THAT NIGHT

"Hannah Lee!" called Danielle. Hannah Lee turned to greet her best friend, smiling. Then she did a double take.

Right behind Danielle stood Matt, the guy she'd been dating for the past few months. He looked happy and was the first guy she'd ever seen Danielle try to please.

Something is up with those two, for sure, she thought. They were grinning like Cheshire cats.

The deck was beautifully lit with tea lights and strings of white lights. The tables were set, and flowers brightened the area outside and in, where the party flowed. The quiet buzz of conversation was punctuated by laughter, and soft jazz played in the background.

Hannah Lee sighed and felt like pinching herself. *How had she found this life so full of love and joy?* She'd never aimed for it, never dreamed it was possible.

Other people had lives like this, she'd once thought. Not her.

Clink, clink, clink. Someone tapped the side of a wine glass with a spoon.

Matteo. Getting ready to make a fun toast, no doubt. The buzz died mostly down, and the rest of it stopped when he began speaking.

"Thank you, everyone, for coming to our home and spending time with us. We appreciate each of you for the love and friendship you bring into our lives. So, cheers to friendship!"

He smiled as someone called out, "Cheers to that!" Everyone clinked glasses, and the buzz soared again.

Matteo made his way to Hannah Lee's side, put his arm around her waist, and drew her in for a kiss. A couple of people standing nearby said, "Awww!" and laughed. Matteo dipped Hannah Lee, and when she came up, breathless and smiling, he kissed her deeply, prompting calls of "Get a room!"

He took her hand and pulled her into the house, into their bedroom. She protested, but he tugged playfully.

CHAPTER SIXTY

She yielded to his private kiss, then pushed back to look at him quizzically. "What is this all about?" she asked, smiling. Matteo didn't normally go for public displays of affection, although he couldn't seem to keep his hands off of her privately.

"Do you remember when you said, surprise me? About getting married," he said.

"What?"

"You said, and I quote, '*Well, you're going to have to surprise me because if I think about it too much, it won't happen.*' Remember?"

"I remember something like that, but what are you saying?" she asked, her heart beginning to flutter.

"What I'm saying is, Hannah Lee, you are the love of my life. I can't imagine a single day without you. Please marry me," he finished, then dug into his pocket and pulled out a small velvet box. He popped it open.

Hannah Lee gasped. The ring was perfect. It was completely non-traditional, with colored gemstones and scattered diamonds. He'd paid attention when they browsed jewelry stores.

She looked up into his adoring eyes, so warm, so full of love, and sighed. Her mind was totally blank, her heart bursting.

"Yes, of course, I will."

He slipped the ring on her finger and pulled her into his arms.

He blew out a huge breath after kissing her thoroughly. "I wasn't sure if you'd actually say yes," he said, relieved.

She pulled him in for another kiss. After all, it was just an engagement. She could deal with the whole marriage thing later.

But Matteo still looked distracted. She pulled back again and searched his face.

"There's something else going on, isn't there?" she asked, concerned.

"Well, yes, there is."

"What?" she said, frowning.

"Um, maybe you should look in your closet," he said.

"Look in my closet? Whatever for? Are you saying you don't like what I'm wearing?"

This was totally unlike Matteo. He was the kind of guy who declared her the most beautiful girl in the room no matter how she dressed, what she did to her hair, or how many extra pounds she carried.

He took her hand and led her to their closet, opened the door, and stood back. There, on display, was a gown.

She stood in shock. It was exactly her style—again, non-traditional. Lace bodice, scoop neck and short sleeves, with a slim skirt to the ground, also lace. Deep champagne in color, her favorite.

Matteo came up behind her and softly asked, "So, what do you think?"

"It's beautiful," she breathed.

"Why don't you try it on?"

"Now? No, we have guests waiting. We've spent enough time in here."

"Right. We have guests waiting," he said.

His tone.

He couldn't possibly mean...

"Wait. What? Are you suggesting—?"

"Not suggesting. Insisting," he said, smiling.

"You...you planned this, didn't you?" she said, astonished.

"Yes, I did. Guilty as charged."

"But...but...," she said.

But her protests grew weaker. The reservations, the fear, the doubts, all drained away like water after a Spring rainstorm.

And in their place rose the most amazing bubble of pure joy.

"So?" he asked.

"So, let's get married," she beamed.

THE END

Other Titles by Nina Atwood

Unlikely Return, Nina's previous full-length novel, is available on Amazon and through these retailers: Nook, Apple Books, and Kobo.

Nina's next full-length novel, *What About Roxanne?* is scheduled for release in mid-2021. (See excerpt next.)

Get Nina's FREE Novella, *Unlikely Beginning*, when you join her **VIP Reader Club**:

www.ninaatwoodauthor.com/freenovella

Acknowledgments

One of the best things about writing is getting the opportunity to pick the brains of knowledgeable people who can help fill in the technical blanks. The risk to those people is that writers may take their brilliance and exercise creative license, thereby altering details to fit the story or whatever else strikes the author's fancy. I have done so here and I'm sure I will do it again. *Any technical errors in this book are entirely mine.*

Caveats aside, I wish to acknowledge the following people for their much-appreciated expertise.

For legal information, thank you to Harry Barth (barthattorneys.com), guru of all things pertaining to estate planning and asset protection.

For hang gliding expertise, I wish to thank the participants on the Paragliding Forum (paraglidingforum.com). They generously shared from their experiences and were a bit anxious that *Free Fall* might put some people off of the sport. I encourage readers to visit the forum and check out paragliding from those who love it and vouch for its overall safety.

Additionally, I want to thank Cynthia Curry, owner of Raven Wolf Skysports (ravenwolfskysports.com), for the generous gift of her time and expertise. I understand you can book paragliding lessons with her in various parts of the western U.S.

If you enjoyed *Free Fall*, please give it a review on Amazon. Reviews help authors continue doing what we love—writing—so you have more to read. I thank you in advance for taking the time for a review!

Please keep reading for a preview of my next book.

WHAT

ABOUT

ROXANNE?

(Working Title)

PREVIEW

NINA ATWOOD

PROLOGUE

Two women drove down the two-lane road in two separate vehicles.

The first, exhausted after a long day at work, reached over to her cell, held upright by the brace in the cup holder, and pushed the button to ring her husband's cell. She quickly returned her eyes to the road, swerving slightly to get back in her lane.

"Hey," he answered.

"Hey. It's me."

"Hey, me. Are you on your way?"

"Yep. Just passing the freeway, so I'll be home in about five minutes. How did it go with your dad today?"

"Okay, I guess. I mean, he knew me when I got there, and we actually talked for a while. But then he didn't remember who I was. I tried to tell him, hey, I'm your son, remember? But he got all upset and I had to leave after that." He sighed over the phone.

"I'm sorry, honey."

"Yeah, I know. Hey, did you get the chow? The game is tonight, and I thought—"

She glanced in the backseat at the two large pizza boxes, smelling the aroma. She smiled. "Chow?" Just the right note of puzzlement in her voice.

"*Really?* Did you forget? I sent, like, five text messages today."

He went silent and she giggled. "Did you honestly think I'd forget your favorite pizza? *After all this?*"

It was one of their little jokes. Do you still love me, *after all this?*

Followed by, *Still, after all this?* And then the affirmations, the kissing, the laughter.

The vehicle in front of her slammed on the brakes, so she slammed hers as well. She halted a few feet from the back of the SUV. She couldn't see any kind of a traffic jam ahead.

Really? Some people just didn't know how to drive, always pumping the brakes for no reason. The SUV moved forward and increased speed, so she did as well.

"What was that?"

"Oh, nothing. Somebody slammed on the brakes. But traffic seems to be moving."

She glanced at the backseat again, and that's when she saw the pizza boxes, still stacked, but now teetering on the front edge of the seat, about to fall onto the floorboards. She glanced at the road. The SUV was far ahead.

She reached back, glancing back and forth between the road ahead and the pizza boxes in the back seat, straining to reach them. Her fingers stretched, she pushed, and, finally, made contact. She gave it one more push, lifting up a little in the driver's seat, and the boxes slid back.

When she looked up, bright headlights were headed directly for her. She slammed on the brakes as hard as she could, but it was no use. The next second, she heard and felt a sickening, grinding slam. Her vehicle swirled and rolled in impossible ways, and when it was over, she lay there, her body mangled.

She whispered her husband's name, and then, "I love you."

FREE FALL

Then darkness.

The other woman strained to make sense of the road ahead. It was just a bit out of focus. Wait, was she in her lane or in the other lane? She swerved to compensate, but suddenly found herself on the side of the road, tall weeds slapping the underside of her car. She swerved the other way.

She couldn't remember why she was driving. She always took an Uber or Lyft car after she'd been out...doing what she loved to do. But tonight was different, for some odd reason. Oh, right. Her husband needed the car early tomorrow, to take it in for servicing.

No problem. She'd only had a couple of drinks. She could drive safely.

She hummed to herself and reached over to turn up the music. When she looked up again at the road, two bright headlights were headed right for her.

She didn't feel anything. Didn't hear anything.

When EMTs arrived on the scene, they found two women in critical condition. Both were rushed to the nearest hospital. One was dead on arrival.

CHAPTER ONE

Roxanne opened the front door of her home. She heard Henry and the girls talking in the distance. She paused for a moment. *What an incredible day.* She sighed.

Henry stood cutting up vegetables while six-year-old Rose, sitting on the massive marble-topped island near her dad, talked animatedly. Rose's legs swung and she painted pictures of her day in the air with her small hands. Her deep blue eyes were wide, and her dark curls flew around her head.

"Um, and then what happened?" Henry asked, taking a moment to tuck Rose's hair behind one ear.

"And Miss Taylor told her to sit down," said Rose. "She was in trouble."

"I don't think Katie did anything wrong," observed Annie, her older sister, sitting on a stool at the island with an open book. "She was just trying to pick up the papers from the floor. It was James's homework, and he was crying. That wasn't very nice of Miss Taylor, was it, Dad?"

"But if the teacher says—" began Rose.

"Just because the teacher says it doesn't mean it's right,"

interrupted Annie, glaring at her sister. Her unruly, burnished gold hair loosened from clips as she shook her head.

Rose's eyes began to well with tears. Henry put down the knife and swooped her up for a hug. She wrapped her arms around his neck and tightened them, hiccupping a bit.

Annie rolled her eyes and went back to reading.

Henry looked so good. He was tall, lean, and well-built from daily workouts. He wore a long-sleeved tee shirt with the sleeves pushed up, exposing toned forearms. His muscled shoulders and upper body tapered to his slim, hard waistline. He wore cotton slacks tied at the waist. He was clean-shaven, including his head, and his gray eyes caught the light over his daughter's head as he held her close.

Roxanne's stomach relaxed for a moment. She couldn't remember the last time she'd really looked closely at her husband, noticed him, registered the tender way he cared for their daughters.

After giving Rose a few gentle rubs on her back, Henry set her down, then resumed the vegetable chopping.

Annie looked up again, stared at her father. "So, Dad, what are we going to do about Mom?"

Henry's shoulders dropped a bit as looked at his daughter.

"There's nothing to do about your mom, Annie."

What?

Roxanne couldn't believe her ears. She was here, right in the room with them, and they were talking about her like she wasn't there. She opened her mouth to speak, but before she could get the words out, Henry spoke again.

"Mom's going to be fine," Henry said quietly.

"No, she's not," said Annie, dragging out the words slowly, as if she were the adult speaking to a child having difficulty tracking the conversation. "You know she's got a big problem. She's here, but she's really not here, Dad. You know it. She works all the time, and now she's—"

"Don't bring that up," said Henry sternly but gently.

"Dad, you can't ignore it forever. It seems to me that if you keep ignoring it, she's going to get worse and worse. That's if she makes it home."

With that final statement, Annie's eyes took on a sad look and tears gathered in the corners of her eyes. Henry paused, then spoke gently to her. "That's not your concern, Annie. There are some things that the adults have to take care of, and this is one of them. You are only ten."

"So, because I'm ten, I'm not supposed to notice things that are right in front of my nose?" challenged Annie, roughly swiping away her tears, anger replacing the sadness. "I'm ten, not *stupid*." She glared at her dad.

"Mommy!" Rose began crying again. "I want Mommy," she wailed.

"I'm here, baby," said Roxanne. "I'm here. Shhh, everything's okay."

Rose continued to cry. Biscuit, their Golden Retriever, padded into the room, went to Rose, and nuzzled her.

"Now you've upset your sister," said Henry, looking at Annie and shaking his head.

"Rose, stop being a baby. We're just talking," said Annie. "Come here. Let's play checkers." She got up, went into the living room, and came back with an iPad. She set it up on the countertop and Rose climbed on the stool next to her sister, the beginnings of a smile playing across her lips.

"Amazing," said Roxanne softly. "How does Annie always know what to do to help her sister feel better?"

"Thanks, Annie," said Henry, giving his daughter a grateful smile. He went back to chopping vegetables.

"Roxanne," he breathed. "I know there are…issues, but really, you just need to get better." He gazed in her direction, his face softening.

"What do you mean, get better?" she asked, feeling suddenly frightened.

"I hope you come home soon," he said sadly, shaking his head slowly, looking away.

Annie looked up at her father but didn't say anything. Rose happily moved her piece on the screen.

"Henry, *I'm here*. Why are you talking to me that way?" she said.

Biscuit looked up sharply in Roxanne's direction. She whined and padded over to Roxanne, who reached out to pet her. Her hand touched their dog's head, but she felt nothing. Biscuit continued to whine, looking directly into her eyes. A cold shiver trailed down Roxanne's spine.

Roxanne thought about pouring a drink. But oddly she didn't feel the usual longing for ice-cold gin slipping down her throat. Instead, she felt a sense of separation from everyone else.

She tried to feel her arms, crossing them, and hugging herself, but everything felt so far away. Her own body felt distant, disconnected. She looked down but couldn't really see her feet.

"Henry?" she asked in a small voice.

Henry slowly shook his head as he transferred the chopped vegetables into a large skillet on the stovetop.

"Henry, I don't feel so good," she said, feeling a watery sensation flood her body and brain. "*Please*," she said.

Biscuit barked once, and then again. Henry shushed her.

The scene in front of Roxanne began to slowly recede. Her family moved away from her and darkness crept into the edges of her vision.

"Henry! No!" she cried as they slipped away.

Then there was darkness.

Other Titles by Nina Atwood

Unlikely Return, Nina's previous full-length novel, is available on Amazon and through these retailers: Nook, Apple Books, and Kobo.

Nina's next full-length novel, ***What About Roxanne?*** is scheduled for release in mid-2021.

Get Nina's FREE Novella, ***Unlikely Beginning***, when you join her **VIP Reader Club**:

www.ninaatwoodauthor.com/freenovella

About the Author

Nina Atwood is a licensed psychotherapist and award-winning executive coach. A published self-help author for the past 24 years, Nina recently turned her pen to fiction. *Unlikely Return* is her first novel, *Free Fall* her second, with more on the way. She lives in Dallas, Texas, with her husband and two adorable fur babies.

Made in the USA
Middletown, DE
05 March 2021